D0277058

the library
IN EAST AYRSHIRE

East Ayrshire
COUNCIL

Please return item by last date shown,
or contact library to renew

− 1 NOV 2012

1 5 MAR 2012

1 NOV 2012

2012

2 2 MAR 2013

2 4 APR

2 2 MAY 2014

DARK PARTIES

DARK PARTIES

SARA GRANT

EAST AYRSHIRE LIBRARIES	
475951	
Bertrams	13/02/2012
	£16.99

Indigo

First published in Great Britain in 2011
by Indigo
a division of the Orion Publishing Group Ltd
Orion House
5 Upper St Martin's Lane
London WC2H 9EA

An Hachette UK Company

1 3 5 7 9 10 8 6 4 2

Copyright © Sara Grant 2011

The right of Sara Grant to be identified as the author
of this work has been asserted.

All rights reserved. No part of this publication may be reproduced,
stored in a retrieval system, or transmitted, in any form or by any
means, electronic, mechanical, photocopying, recording or otherwise,
without the prior permission of the Orion Publishing Group.

A catalogue record for this book
is available from the British Library.

Library hardback ISBN 978 1 7806 2019 0
Trade paperback ISBN 978 1 7806 2010 7

Typeset by Input Data Services Ltd,
Bridgwater, Somerset

Printed and bound by
CPI Group (UK) Ltd, Croydon, CR0 4YY

www.orionbooks.co.uk

To my parents for teaching me the sky's the limit and
to my husband, Paul, for giving me wings.

CHAPTER ONE

I'm standing in the dark, not the gentle grey of dusk or the soft black of a moonlit night but pitch black. My heart batters my ribs like a bird beating its wings against a glass cage. I wave my hand in front of my face. I can't see it. I never knew it could be so dark. My edges are merging with the inky blackness around me. My dad would finally be proud of me. I've blended in.

Someone touches my elbow. I jump.

'I'm right here, Neva.' It's Ethan. By my side, like always. He's here but not here. I grope for his arm, his shoulder, his neck, and touch his face. He guides my fingers to his lips and kisses them. 'Follow me.' I feel his words on my thumb, his warm breath, the nudge of his lips as they form sounds. He pulls me to the floor. Every cell in my body ignites with the thrill of possibilities. In this nothingness, anything can happen. Maybe I can find what I've lost with Ethan. Tangle my body with his and only feel, not think, not see.

But we all agreed: no sex. Not just tonight. No sex until we're sure we won't create another generation like us.

I take a deep breath and exhale slowly. I clear my mind as we crawl toward the nest of pillows we piled in one of the corners earlier this afternoon. I try not to form pictures in my head. That would defeat the whole purpose. We are supposed to be escaping in the dark, but I am a hostage to my fear. Any time the lights go out panic grabs me by the throat. My skin sweats and stings like blisters forming after a burn.

I'm tired of being scared all the time.

I can do this.

I can.

I grit my teeth and try to ignore the rush of blood in my ears.

Just move.

I bump into a pair of feet. Pointy-toed boots. Braydon Bartlett. I see the red leather in my mind's eye. That's how I think of other people. I distill them into the defining features they have created for themselves. Braydon always wears those shoes, shiny with no creases or scuffs. All most of us have ever owned are hand-me-downs with other people's footprints. We shouldn't have invited him. Like me, he's got a last name with a direct genetic link to one of our founding fathers, but I can't hold that against him. There's just something about him that I don't trust.

My best friend begged me to let Braydon come. The girl with the jagged scar, a rosy S still healing on her cheek. She told her guardians that it was an accident. But I watched her sketch the letter before she carved it permanently with the knife. She shouldn't have done that. Anyone with an identity mark gets more hassle from the police. But that's Sanna.

I move forward and stumble over her bare feet. She rebels against any constraints, including shoes.

'Sorry,' I say. She steps around me and whispers something to Braydon. Then I hear soft squeaks as their lips meet. I'm glad it's dark and I don't have to watch.

I sweep my hand back and forth across the floor. 'This way,' I say to Ethan, whose hand is touching my ankle. We move together. The darkness gives us the illusion of solitude, but we're the opposite of alone; my friends have gathered for a little experiment before we go our separate ways.

We've been planning this for weeks: a Dark Party. One final

8

rebellion before we take our place as respected members of society. It was another of Sanna's brilliant ideas. We want to discover who we are without the burden of sight. It's easy to believe we are the same inside because we look so similar. Sanna says only in the dark can we know the truth, but I'm not sure. Darkness conceals.

Sanna persuaded me to host the party. A Dark Party at the Minister of Ancient History's house. That's how she talked everyone into it. The greater the risk, the greater the thrill. I've known most of these people all my life, but they're Sanna's friends. They don't trust me, never have. My dad's job in the government has always made me guilty by association.

Sanna convinced everyone to pitch in. Nicoline brought black plastic bags. Ethan found towels to tuck under the doors. Sanna's brother gave her three rolls of duct tape. We never ask how he gets the things we need.

It took us an hour to make my living room lightproof. We taped black bags to the windows. We switched off the lights. After a few seconds, our eyes adjusted, but we could see each other in shades of grey. Not good enough. We attacked every point of light and doubled the bags on the windows.

We could still see outlines, silhouettes of ourselves. The small red light on the backup generator seemed to illuminate the entire room. We unplugged everything. When I switched off the light again, there was only pure, dark silence.

Now I hear the hum of hushed voices and the rough-and-smooth sounds that bodies make when coaxed together. Maybe we've made a mistake. We hoped we would find ourselves in the dark, but instead we are risking our celibacy.

Ethan and I finally find our pillows. We lie side by side, our elbows and ankles touching, yet he feels miles away. Darkness dips its icy fingers under my skin, but I refuse to give in to my fear.

I try to erase all thoughts and images. Don't think of the

colour of the pillowcases or the holes in their lace ruffles. One image – no matter how small – leads to an avalanche of pictures. First I see the living room with its worn leather sofa, the fireplace and its fake flames, the bookshelves crammed with dusty volumes of our approved history. But now, as if lifted by balloon, my vision expands to include my square brick house, which blends with the dozens of similar houses in my neighbourhood. As I float upwards, I see the green and concrete squares of the City, which is multiplied a thousand times to create a haze of grey that is Homeland. I let the image blur and fade to black.

I shiver.

'It's OK,' Ethan says, and slips his arms around me, which makes me colder somehow.

My eyes ache for shape and colour, but the blackness surrounding me seems to have substance. I roll up on one elbow to face him. Don't think of his name. His name conjures up the images I'm trying to escape: his skin the same colour as the milky tea we drink, his ears the same shape as my father's, his short brown hair a confusion of waves like everyone else's. I see myself around every corner – every minute – like living in a maze of mirrors.

My grandma told me once about a time when we were different, a long, long time ago. Stories, handed down through the generations in whispers, about life before the Protectosphere. I still see her every day, even though she's long gone.

'Once upon a time, my little snowflake,' she'd say, 'people were the most beautiful colours. Everyone was unique.' That word made me giggle. 'But it was too hard to be different and equal.' She told me fantastic tales of wars caused by differences – different religions, different cultures, different skin colours. 'We shut ourselves off. Now each generation grows more alike.' Grandma was breaking one of the

10

government's many unwritten rules. There's officially nothing before The Terror and the sealing of the Protectosphere, and nothing can survive outside it any more. But my grandma suspected that what's official is not always what's true. She made me promise not to repeat her stories.

'What can it hurt, telling me?' I'd snuggled in closer. She'd stroked my hair.

'You're different.' Her words tickled my ear; she always spoke them so close, as if they were a secret prophecy.

I'm the only one who remembers her. One day she was tucking me in and the next day every trace of her was gone. Not even her son, my dad, will speak her name.

'Neva,' Ethan whispers, and brings me back to the present. I lie my head on his chest and I hear the steady *thump thump* of his heart – a rhythm I know well. Sanna and I have begged him to create an identity mark, but he says he can't. My mark is still healing, red and raw from hundreds of pinpricks. Sanna helped me etch it into the valley between my stomach and hip: a small snowflake falling towards my pubic hair.

He gently rolls me on my back and lies on top of me. We kiss as if choreographed. I realize I am tensing the muscles in my arms and drawing him closer and closer. I urge my body to respond like it used to. We linger here in this timeless place. Ethan's hands race over my body. His breath comes in short, sharp pants. He fumbles and I pretend I still love him. In this void, I feel even more alone.

Someone clears their throat. It's Sanna. I know it is. A new panic flashes through me. She's really going through with it. We talked about it for weeks. This secret scheming is what's kept us sane, but I suddenly realize it's not like skipping school or dying our beige graduation robes pink. The government could erase us – like her dad and my grandma – for unpatriotic acts. I've got to stop her. I sit up, knocking heads with Ethan.

'Ouch,' he says, and then lowers his voice. 'What's going on?'

'Sorry, Ethan.' I need to find Sanna. We were wrong about finding ourselves in the dark. Maybe we are wrong to believe we can change anything. 'I'll be right back.' I stand and shuffle forward. I am lost. The darkness provides no orientation. Up could be down, left could be right. My chest tightens. The dark closes in. I struggle to breathe.

'Can I have your attention?' Sanna asks. I'm too late. My body pulses with the pounding of my heart. 'Sorry to interrupt whatever I'm interrupting.' Her voice is soft and apologetic as if she's trying to disguise it. 'I've got something to say.' We agreed she would be the one to talk. It's hard enough for me to be in the dark, and I am taking a big enough risk hosting the party. My dad would freak if he knew. He disapproves of anything that even hints that Homeland isn't perfect. Mum promised to keep Dad out late tonight. She thinks I'm simply having a party to celebrate our graduation. I haven't told her about our plans. I haven't told anyone.

'We're sixteen.' Sanna pauses and everyone cheers. The weight of what we are doing overwhelms me. 'They tell us we are adults now.' I concentrate on Sanna and try to calm down. I notice a slight tremor in her voice. 'It's time we make a stand.' We expected cheers at this point, but the room is deathly quiet. 'OK then,' she seems to say to herself. There's a long silence.

'The Protectosphere is killing us,' Sanna blurts.

Someone gasps. No one says things like that out loud. Her words hang in the air like crystals searching for sunshine. 'We all know it. The government is squashing our future. Fewer choices. Fewer resources. They keep us trapped with their lies. We deserve to know what's outside. There has to be more.'

My heart swells, I'm so proud of her. If only I was as brave.

Sanna continues, 'We have to do something. Stay, if you

12

want to join us and demand they open the Protectosphere. We deserve a future.'

My grandma believed there was still life outside the Protectosphere. Knowing there's something beyond our electrified dome is like my faith in life after death. I want desperately to believe it.

'If you don't want to join us, you should leave now,' Sanna says. 'Even if you don't want to join us – and it's totally legit if you can't or won't – I'm trusting that you'll keep your traps shut.'

We hoped the anonymity of the dark would be enough, but now I feel exposed. I hear someone moving. I wait for them to pass, but they don't. I wave my arms in front of me like a blind man without a cane. Our outstretched fingertips touch, and the person walks right into my arms. I think it might be Ethan, until fingers gently trace the line of my necklace and pause at the snowflake pendant that rests between my breasts. A hand cups my neck and tilts my head ever so slightly. I am being kissed, but it's not soft and sweet like Ethan's kisses. This kiss is insistent and passionate. He slips strong arms around me. Our bodies mould together. My body aches in a way I've never felt before. I try to pull away, but his kisses don't relent. He holds me tighter. I wrap my arms around this stranger. I kiss him until I'm breathless. I have never felt so alive. I should stop, but I kiss him again and again.

Bodies are bumping into us. People are leaving, but I don't care. For the first time in a long time, I feel as if my life could be different; *I* could be different. I hesitate before I release him. My knees are weak. I melt to the floor.

As he passes, his foot brushes my hand. I feel the unmistakable smooth leather and shape of Braydon's boots. Sanna's boyfriend.

I touch my lips. Braydon?

I can hear the tape being torn away, and the door opens

as many of our friends reject our call to action. The room materializes in fuzzy greys. Sanna waits until quiet returns and switches on the lights. I am blinded momentarily. The room is nearly empty; less than a dozen people squint nervously at one another.

Braydon is hugging Sanna. He glances at me. I look away. Why was he kissing a stranger in the dark? Does he know it was me?

I look for Ethan, but he is gone. I hoped he would stay. But it was too much to ask of this Ethan. The old Ethan would have stood by me, but this Ethan's given up, given in to our government-sanctioned future.

Sanna tells our ragtag group of revolutionaries where and when to meet tomorrow.

I feel as if the light has stripped me bare and everyone is staring at the betrayal etched on my skin. I've betrayed my dad, my best friend, and Ethan.

'You better go before my parents get home,' I say, and look anywhere but at Braydon.

A darkness is growing inside me now.

CHAPTER TWO

A crystal snowflake nightlight glows in the corner of my bedroom. It casts triangles of light on the ceiling. I can't sleep. Every thought circles back to earlier – the announcement and the kiss.

It's as if I've lit a fuse and I'm waiting for the explosion.

I remove the journal from under my pillow. The cover is faded shades of pink. Two long cracks, like jagged scars, expose the brown cardboard below. The plastic coating curls away from the cover and flakes like scaly, dry skin. Its spine crackles when I open it. I run my finger over my name printed on the inside cover. Grandma wrote it there, the last in a column of scribbled-out names. Several pages have been ripped unevenly from the front of the journal. Other people's secrets so easily erased. The paper is rough and its edges raw. She gave this to me the night before she disappeared.

'Thanks,' I'd said without understanding what it was. I was six and had never seen a book of blank pages before. I hugged Grandma and felt the scratchy knit of her polyester suit. 'I love it.'

'You're welcome, my little snowflake,' she whispered, even though we were alone in my bedroom. She kissed me on my forehead. 'Best to keep it hidden,' she said, and slipped the journal under my pillow.

I smiled. I liked secrets. I didn't have many of them back then. As I nodded in agreement, a lock of hair fell across my face. She tucked it behind my ear, tracing the curl over and over with her finger.

'I love you, Neva,' she said. 'Remember that. No matter what.'

She smelled like rose petals. She hugged me and wouldn't let go until I wriggled free when the warmth and the scent became suffocating.

The first journal page is still blank. Even at six I understood the importance of camouflage. If someone ever found my hiding place, they might think the book was empty. Every night I tuck it among the globs of matted cotton in my mattress. The hole was already there, as if I wasn't the first to use it. I'm never the first.

I flip to the next page, a page I read every night. There's my grandma's name and the date of the last time I saw her. I didn't write it down until months later, when I was sure she wasn't coming back. I wrote it down so I wouldn't forget. No one else seems to remember she was here. But she was real. I know it. My six-year-old self drew a picture – a circle with curlicues of hair, big round eyes and a broad smile. That's still her somehow.

I have listed things that I remember about her. She comes back to me in small fragments – a sound or smell will trigger something and I'll rush to capture it in my journal. I saw a grey-haired lady in a turquoise suit and recalled the way Grandma dressed. She loved bold colours. Colours were brighter back when we could buy new clothes, instead of recycling the life out of everything. She wore blue, purple, orange, and red suits with matching glittery brooches and big earrings that covered each lobe.

I read the list again. I added the last item a few weeks ago. I was applying some of Sanna's homemade lip gloss. I rubbed my lips together and made a smacking sound. That's when I remembered. Grandma used to make that sound when she applied her peach sparkle lipstick, sucking air through the corners of her pursed lips. I'd forgotten the sound and the way the lipstick collected in the wrinkles around her lips.

I've left the next few pages blank, hoping to fill in pieces of her and complete an ever-fading picture. I turn to my List of The Missing. The first entries are written in the erratic print of a child: Maud Riker, the lunch lady with the chipped tooth, Tommy Donovan, Lukas Freely, the man in the brown suit who used to visit my dad every weekend, Jemma Johnson. The list goes on for pages. I include the date I noticed each person had gone missing, even if I don't know their name.

When I asked about Maud Riker, my dad said she'd died. She was sixty years old, but I've searched the church's graveyard and I've never found her tombstone. Jemma Johnson was my age. I sat next to her in Mrs Powell's class. She never came back after the summer holiday. My mum expected me to believe that her family had moved up North. Maybe they had. All I know is I never saw Jemma again.

Sometimes I'm mistaken. A few weeks ago, I wrote: *The man at church who smells like cheese and always offers me peppermints.* I found out that he was visiting his daughter. So now I draw a long straight line through his entry and write *FOUND* in big bold letters, tracing the letters multiple times without tearing the paper.

I reread the last page: Megan, Abbey, Tamryn, Jill, Madeline, Vanessa, Kelley, Morgan, Victoria, Molly. All girls about my age. Megan and Victoria graduated a few years ahead of me. Sanna told me about Madeline and Kelley, although she said that they had both moved across town. Tamryn used to work at the coffee shop around the corner. Molly was the daughter of one of my mum's friends. I haven't seen her around in a while. I used to add someone once every few months, but now it's almost once a week. I press my palm on the page as if I can stop the trickle of names from becoming a flood.

Only Sanna knows about my list. Everyone she loves disappears, one way or another. Her mother died when she was eight. At least she knows what happened to her. When her dad went missing a few years later, Sanna and her brother had to live with guardians, Mr and Mrs Jones, good patriots whose ancestors died in The Terror. Sanna's brother went underground a few years ago. She begged him to take her with him, but he said it was too dangerous. He protects her with his silence, never telling her where he lives or how he survives. He's like this rebel angel who watches over her.

I caress my snowflake pendant between my fingers. I wear it to remind me of my grandma and all The Missing. When they were confiscating my film collection and anything else my grandma gave me, the police didn't take the necklace because I'd slipped it off and put it in my mouth. The entire time they were robbing me of my grandma, I was tracing the snowflake pendant with my tongue.

The next morning when Mum and Dad returned from wherever the police took them, they acted as if nothing had happened. I asked Mum about Grandma. She pretended she didn't know who I was talking about. I asked Dad, but he left the room. From that minute, she was erased from my life. Erased on the surface, but captured memory by memory in my journal.

I hear the rattle of keys and the click of the front door lock. My parents are home. I close the book and slide off the bed. If she thinks I'm still up, Mum will want details and what would I say? I kissed my best friend's boyfriend and broke the law? A guilty sludge oozes through my veins.

I remove several large clumps of cotton from my mattress, tuck my journal deep into the centre of my bed and dive under

18

the covers. Sometimes I think I can feel the journal's rounded corners beneath me. I guess in some ways I'm like my dad, recording history so I never forget. But it's not enough any more.

CHAPTER THREE

I'm up early the next morning to meet Sanna at her mum's grave. It's one of the places we meet when we want to make sure no one's watching or listening. I stroll down the hill in the church graveyard. Most people are superstitious about walking on graves. Not me. I imagine the people below whisper their wisdom to me as I pass. They want to be remembered. I read each tombstone. I note the date of birth and death. The numbers are getting closer together. The oldest dead person I find is sixty-two years old. There are also more small plots for children. I tiptoe across the tiny graves. Mum had four miscarriages before she accepted that I'd be an only child. Our graveyards are filling up too quickly, but no one talks about it. I heard the government is secretly cremating people to obscure the fact that our population is shrinking.

'Hi, Mrs Garcia.' I plop down on Sanna's mum's grave. She died during childbirth, but there's no marker for Sanna's dead sister. They don't bury anyone under a year old any more.

I lie down next to her grave and admire her view. The sun catches the Protectosphere, and it seems to twinkle like a sky full of cubic zirconia. The first time I saw, really saw, the Protectosphere was when we passed near the border on a family holiday when I was eight. Dad stopped the car, flashed his badge at the Border Patrol, and we walked the rest of the way. He wanted me to be proud of my heritage. We walked for about a mile before we saw the final warning signs. When you're that close you can see the edges of each triangular Protectosphere panel. Dad stood tall and rested his hands on his hips. He stared skyward as if enjoying a Protectosphere light show. I looked at the cracked, dusty ground, dotted with dead animal carcasses. Dad explained that animals don't always see the Protectosphere, just like birds don't always see windowpanes. If they run into it, they get electrocuted. Dad wanted me to see this shining example of technology and progress. All I saw was a clear cage and a line of rotting corpses.

The memory still gives me the creeps. It's when I first felt trapped. Back then, I thought the Protectosphere might collapse or explode, killing everyone instantly like those poor animals. Now it feels as if it's killing us slowly. Sanna's brother says it's genetics. We are too alike. He says *inbred*. We come from a limited gene pool, which makes us weak. But the government insists that the Protectosphere is a safe haven, not a prison.

'Oh! My! God!' Sanna calls from near the church. She doesn't bother with greetings. When I'm around her I feel like everything is for the first, last, or only time. She comes bounding down the hill, her huge patchwork handbag banging against the tombstones. 'Hey, Mum,' she says when she reaches her mother's grave. She sits next to the marker, one hand resting on her mum's name.

Act normal, I tell myself, but sweat is collecting on my cool skin. I see Sanna and think of Braydon and our kiss, and how alive it made me feel then and how guilty it makes me feel now. It was one kiss, spontaneous. I didn't know who I was kissing. I got carried away. It was the excitement of anonymity.

At least that's what I keep telling myself.

'I can't believe it.' Her face is red and blotchy and she's breathless. 'Braydon—'

'What?' I sit up, my heart suddenly racing. I can't tell if she's excited or upset.

'Braydon told me ...'

My eyes flare wider. She knows. But she can't know.

'... he wants us to be exclusive.' She laughs. 'How wild is that?' She touches the scar on her cheek, which is distorted by her wide smile. 'I'm his one and only,' she says in a singsong fashion, as if she's making fun of herself, but I can tell she's genuinely excited.

'Oh.' I exhale. She doesn't know about the kiss. I should be relieved, but her news heightens my guilt and makes my heart feel heavy. How can he kiss me one minute and tell her she's the only one the next?

'I love him, Nev,' she says, hugging her handbag to her chest as if it's Braydon. 'I mean the gooey, tingly, toe-curling kind of love.'

'Really?' I respond too quickly, almost angry that she's used the L word. 'You've been out, what, three times? And one of those was in the dark.'

'But it was so intense, wasn't it?' She swoons. 'Kissing in the dark. The kiss was the only thing. There was no Protectosphere. Or guardians. Or limits.'

She's right. The dark stripped everything else away. Braydon and I connected in a way we never would have in the light of day. If I'm honest with myself, maybe it was there all along, that spark between us.

'Nev! I'm telling you the most important thing ever and you've got your head in the Protectosphere.'

'Sorry. I'm happy for you, Sanna. I really am,' I say, but I can't muster up the appropriate best friend enthusiasm. Sanna's the type of girl who guys like but never date. She's got more personality and more curves than the rest of us and I think guys are intimidated.

'Nev!' She swats me with her handbag.

22

'Ouch!' I don't know what she's got in there, but it thuds on my arms and I focus on the pain and not the kiss.

'Me and Braydon. Can you believe it?'

My best friend finally has a real boyfriend, and he kisses me. What am I supposed to say? 'Just take it slow. I don't want you to get hurt.' We make eye contact briefly before I have to look away.

'Yeah, I know. It probably won't last,' she says, leaning against a nearby tombstone. 'I'm not in his genetic sphere.' Sanna is the human equivalent of a mutt. Neither of her parents were descendants of our founding fathers. No one in her family died in The Terror.

'You're too good for him.' And his cheating and lying ways. 'Him and his stupid red shoes.'

She removes two blueberry muffins from her handbag. 'Please try to like him.' Her mood has turned serious.

'Where did you get blueberries?' I ask, hoping to change the subject. I haven't tasted blueberries in years. 'And how did you get enough sugar for muffins?' She offers me one.

I record missing people, but I could fill volumes with missing things: chocolate; balloons; fizzy, flavoured drinks; electronic gadgets that blinked and buzzed and hummed. We used to have stores with brand-new shiny things. Now we have markets for trading and swapping what's already tired and grey.

'Braydon knows someone who knows someone.' She takes a huge bite of muffin. 'We went back to his last night. We made muffins together this morning. I mean isn't that a-maz-ing.' Tiny crumbs fly from her lips as she speaks.

I divide my muffin in half and then in half again. 'Did you ... you know ... have you and Braydon ...' I stop myself because I don't really want to know.

'I promised, didn't I?' she says after a long pause.

'That's not an answer.'

23

'Nev. Chill. We did stuff but not *that*.' She plops a plump blueberry in her mouth.

'If you're going to ... you know ... then take precautions. Be careful, OK?' I study the crumbs in my hand.

'Careful!' she practically cackles. 'They've made it impossible for us to be careful.'

'You could always use condoms.' My stomach lurches.

'Not anymore. My brother says they've pulled those off the shelves. Something about a product defect. More lies.'

'What?' Two months ago the supply of contraceptive pills dried up. Shortage of supplies, they said. That's how they do things. No big pronouncements. Our choices dwindle – clothes, careers, and now contraception. 'That makes our vow even more important.'

'I know. I know. Braydon and I are abstaining. We aren't stupid.' She gets a silly grin on her face. 'It's not easy.'

'But it's worth it,' I add. 'The government can't run every aspect of our lives.'

'Yeah. Yeah. If they want more babies, they can build a mummy factory. My body's not government property.'

I laugh, but it's not funny. That's all the government seems to want – more people. It doesn't matter that the citizens they have are miserable and dying. They don't want thinking, feeling people. They want bodies. More workers. They promise that more people mean more resources. Old factories back in production. Barren farmland flourishing again.

'There's got to be more to life than birth and death.' She pauses mid-rant and, in Sanna style, makes a hairpin turn in the conversation. 'Did you know he makes masks?'

'Who? What?'

'Braydon. He recycles paper and other stuff. He makes moulds of people's faces. He paints them with fantastic designs. It's proper art, Nev. It was like we were making out in front of an audience.'

24

'Weird.' He doesn't strike me as the artistic type.

'No,' Sanna replies. 'A-maz-ing.' Sanna stretches her legs and wiggles her toes in the grass.

'If you say so.' I take a bite of the muffin and savour the tartness of the blueberries. How can she love him? What does she know about him? He makes masks and wears red boots. He's a good kisser, I'll give her that. But he's quiet. It's not a shy quiet. It's an intense, eerie quiet — like the eye of the storm.

'Do you want to hear the best part?' She looks around conspiratorially. 'He's staying in this huge house outside of the City. He's, like, squatting or something.'

I nearly choke. 'What?' I cough to dislodge a muffin lump from my throat. 'He's a Bartlett. He doesn't need to camp out in some abandoned house.' I wipe my mouth on my sleeve.

She looks around again. 'His parents are missing in action. And this house is really bizarre. It's like whoever owned it before just walked out. It's fully furnished. There are even clothes in the closets.'

More Missing. 'I wonder what happened to them.' What happens to them all?

She pinches off a piece of her muffin and throws it at me. 'You are missing the point, friend o' mine. He's got no parental supervision. He asked me to spend the night with him and I thought, why not?' She takes a dramatic pause. 'So I did, and it was a-maz-ing.'

Braydon showed up a month ago with his new red boots and no explanations. He didn't need any. His last name was Bartlett. We all assumed he was relocated to the City like so many others. The government started consolidating and then closing towns up North and now people migrate in a steady trickle. Rumour is that they'll force migration from the East next and continue to sweep clockwise until we are all collected on one dot on the map. The government tells us it's more efficient to move people to population hubs. But I know, from things I've overheard and pieced together, that the government can no longer afford to supply basic necessities like electricity and water to smaller communities. Also, it's easier for the government to watch us if we are crammed in fewer places.

'What do we really know about this guy?' I ask. She should know what kind of guy he is, but I can't tell her. He's a jerk no matter what his heritage is, but to incriminate him is to incriminate myself. How can I possibly be attracted to someone like him? My stomach threatens to turn inside out.

'I know everything I need to know.' She punches me in the arm. 'Can't you be happy for me?'

'Ouch!' I rub my stinging arm, but I'm glad to be punished. 'I am happy for you.' And I am. Well, sort of. I'm glad that she's found someone who makes her happy. I only wish it was someone else.

'Are you ready for tonight?' she asks, lying down and staring up at the Protectosphere.

'As I'll ever be.' I stretch out next to her. We didn't want to give people time to chicken out, so we planned our first act of rebellion for tonight. 'Are we really going through with this?' I whisper.

Sanna nods. 'It will be exciting.'

'What if we get caught?' I look around, not keen to talk about it out in the open, even here.

'You worry too much.' She knocks my shoulder with hers. 'What are we hanging around here for?' She kisses her mum's name. 'Sorry, Mum. We gotta go. We've got to get the last of our supplies and get busy.' She's talking to her mum's tombstone. 'I'll make you proud.'

'You think it will make any difference? What can a few teenagers—'

'Adults,' she corrects.

'Adults.' I laugh. It's ludicrous. One day we're children. A

26

diploma and a stupid ceremony and now we're adults.

'We've got to do something. Or we're going to end up here sooner than we think.'

I try to imagine living without a synthetic ceiling between me and the sky, but I can't.

'That's what I love about you, Nev.' She's up and dusting herself off. 'I want to make a splash, and you want to make a difference.'

It's what my grandma would want.

Sanna helps me to my feet. 'We've got a lot to do.' She's chasing the wind up the hill. She makes me believe in the impossible. 'What are you waiting for?' she calls, waving wildly.

I push thoughts of Braydon out of my mind and race after her.

CHAPTER FOUR

There are moments, like photoflashes, when I think I'm destined for something greater. My grandma told me I could do whatever I set my heart and mind to. But that was before the government started assigning careers. My grandma planted this optimism like a tiny mustard seed. Right now I feel it's finally sprouted.

Sanna is hunched over her bathtub mixing the paint. She's stirring the gloopy mess in a bucket with her brother's cricket bat. She mashes the potion up and down. Then she stirs round and round, banging the metal bucket with the bat. Sweat beads on her forehead and drips from her chin.

I sit on the toilet and try out slogans. 'Bubble Buster,' I say, spitting out the Bs.

'Bubble Trouble,' she replies.

'Sounds like a witches' brew.'

'Exactly,' she says, switching from stirring to mashing.

'It needs to be short but say more.'

'Like innuendo?'

I nod. We've been trying to come up with a slogan for weeks, almost as long as we've been collecting our paint supplies. I bought chilli powder and paprika in small increments at the market whenever I could find them. Everyone knows my mum makes homemade salsa with our greenhouse tomatoes, so I didn't arouse much suspicion. Sanna's brother purloined a few of the more difficult

ingredients – something called builders lime and linseed oil –
no questions asked. Sanna and I both stole our families' weekly
rations of skimmed milk. I'll tell Mum I spilled ours. Sanna
won't make any excuses. The Joneses are used to Sanna's daily
sabotage of their happy home.

Sanna's clattering stops. 'We need something that will
initiate a thought explosion.'

'Thought explosion,' I repeat. Where does she come up
with these things?

'Something that says the Protectosphere is killing us and
we want out.'

I almost believe it's possible. 'OK,' I say. Think slogan.

'Open with Care.'

'Grand Reopening.'

We both laugh.

'Opening Time.'

'Open and Closed.'

I'm not sure that makes sense. 'Don't we need to make sure
people understand we are talking about the Protectosphere?'
I ask.

'Yeah, right.' She mashes and bangs a little more. She dips
her fingers in the bucket. Her hand is red and looks like it's
dripping congealed blood. Congealed blood with bits in it.
She rubs the red between her fingers. 'I think it's about done.'

'But we don't know what we're going to write.' I smoothe
a curl behind my ear and think of my grandma.

'We better figure it out. Once this stuff sets, we can't use
it.' She drops the bat in the tub. A spray of red splatters the
yellowing tiles. She grunts as she hefts the bucket out of the
tub. She closes the shower curtain and turns on the water.

'No Protect Us Fear,' I say as the slogan pops into my head.
No Protectosphere. No protect-us fear. We are tired of being
scared all the time. We don't want this artificial barrier any
more. It says all that.

She's leaning over the tub with her arms behind the curtain as if she's doing a magic trick. 'What good . . .'

'Four words,' I say. 'No . . . Protect . . . Us . . . Fear.' I pronounce each word clearly. She's rubbing her hands together. Her whole body is shimmying. Wait for it.

She stops and turns to face me, pink water dripping from her fingertips onto the cracked colourless linoleum. 'A-maz-ing!'

Even though the film hasn't begun, we face forward and focus on the big screen. We have time-and-date-stamped ticket stubs: it's the perfect alibi. We'll have one hour and forty-three minutes to complete our mission and then return unnoticed to the cinema. We lost a few people between yesterday and today. Now we're nine people strong. It's not an army, but it's a start.

Sanna picked a row near the back of the cinema. We took the two middle seats. Naturally, Braydon sat next to her. I'm trying to ignore him. It's the first time I've seen him since our kiss. I lean forward a hair and glance at him. He looks the same. My body tingles remembering the kiss. He catches me staring and smiles. The tingle multiplies and zaps through me. How can one look hijack my body? I don't understand this control he now seems to have over me. I press myself back into my seat and hide behind Sanna. I vow to never think of him again.

Delia is sitting next to me. She's been chewing the skin around her fingernails ever since we sat down. At this rate, she won't have any fingers left by the end of the film. The sound of her sucking at the tiny flecks of skin sets me on edge. I want to tell her to stop, but we don't want to draw any attention to ourselves.

'Ready?' Sanna asks me.

'I guess,' I say, but I'm not really ready. My palms start to sweat. Everyone is paired off. For the first time today, I think of Ethan. I wish he were here. Not because I miss him, but because it's the way it's always been. Neva-and-Ethan. I'm pen without paper. Soap without water. He called me earlier. He wanted to see me. I told him I was busy. He didn't ask any more questions and I didn't offer any more excuses. We pretend nothing has changed, even though I know he can feel the distance between us as much as I can. We agreed to meet tomorrow morning. Like always.

'Careful,' Sanna whispers, as she lifts plastic bags filled with homemade red paint from her handbag, and passes along one bag for each team of two. The bags are from my mum's collection. You can't buy these any more, not the heavy-duty kind that zip closed. I haven't decided how I will explain why four bags that have been in her family for generations have suddenly disappeared.

I survey the theatre. There are a dozen couples tilted into each other. Four loners are dotted around the cinema, slumped in their seats, trying not to be noticed. A group of kids, a few years younger than we are, is huddled near the front. We haven't done anything wrong yet, but I feel as if I'm being watched.

Sanna elbows me. 'Stop it.'

The theatre goes black. I hold my breath and try not to panic in the seconds it takes for the screen to illuminate. Music crackles from the old speakers and two young, scantily clad bodies wrap themselves around each other, sweating and kissing and groping. The government has created new 16+ rated films that are steamy tales of romance and lots and lots of sexy scenes spliced together from old movies. Sanna calls them 'joy of sex' films. The government can't just say 'procreate for Homeland' so they try to arouse us and hope we can't control ourselves. We squirm in our seats, laugh nervously, and try not to look at the film screen.

I check my watch and notice that almost everyone in my row is doing the same. The first two teams peel off and sneak out to the bathroom, then out of the window, and off to one of four quadrants of the City. Delia has agreed to stay in the cinema in case something happens we should know about. The films sometimes break. Or maybe the kids get thrown out during a big kiss scene. We tried to think of everything.

Sanna nudges me. It's time for me to move out. The film flashes in the whites of her eyes.

I turn to Nicoline, my partner in crime. She was one of the first in our class to create an identity mark. When she was seven she drew a red star with a permanent marker like a beauty mark on her cheek. Her star faded. Now she re-draws it every few days.

Once Nicoline and I have climbed out of the bathroom window, we pull up the hoods of our sweatshirts. The bag of paint is tucked in the front pocket of mine. We weave our way through the City to the embankment. I'm careful to use side streets, dimly lit by the glow from a window or a rare streetlight. I avoid dark alleys. Tonight my fear of the dark is equalled by my fear of getting caught. I race from one pool of light to the next, but the darkness seems to chase me.

'Now what?' Nicoline asks when we arrive at the riverside. She's looking around, not at me.

'You keep the lookout and I'll do the painting.' I take a slow turn. The promenade is empty. The moonlight glistens on the river and keeps the darkness at bay. I knead the bag and look around again. It's hard to believe I'm here and that we are really going to do this.

'I think we're OK,' Nicoline says and gives me a weak smile.

How can I be excited and terrified in the same moment? I bend over and hesitate before tearing the tiniest tip off one corner of the plastic bag. The blood-red paint beads like a pinpricked finger. I steady my hand and write 'No Protect Us Fear!' in capital letters on the greyish concrete. The letters almost sparkle. Adrenaline surges through me and something else: pride. It's not much, but I've made my mark. Neva was here.

Nicoline raises her hand and I meet it with mine. I can tell she's feeling it too. The water laps at the riverbanks, as if it's applauding. I run to a wooden bench and write the same thing on one of the slats. God, I feel a-maz-ing!

Nicoline and I crisscross paths as we find unsuspecting billboards for our message: the base of a streetlight, encircling a manhole cover. Nicoline races ahead and scouts out a spot. She wants to have a go. I hand her the bag of paint, then hop up on a bench and scan the landscape while she loops the slogan together in artistic cursive, not like the wobbly sticks of my printed slogan. I check the time as she darts off. We've got less than thirty minutes until the film ends and so does our alibi.

I catch up to Nicoline, who is squeezing out the last few drops of paint and writing each word of our slogan on ascending steps that lead to the street above. Her fingers are tipped with red. 'I think we need to get going.'

Nicoline twirls on her toes and shouts to the Protectosphere, 'This feels incredible.'

'Shhhh,' I hiss, but I completely agree.

'God, don't worry so much.' Nicoline pauses and looks around. 'We're almost home free.'

'Almost,' I repeat, and grab the gooey plastic bag from her. I rush to the river's edge and lean as far over the railing as I can. I catapult the bag into the water – a girlie throw, Ethan would say. The wind catches it and the bag floats in a zigzag pattern down to the murky water below. I watch it float, bobbing on the low waves, until it's pulled under and sinks out of sight. We start to walk back to the cinema.

Nicoline tugs on my sleeve. 'Listen.'

Over the sound of the river, I hear it – heavy, rhythmic footsteps. I know what we are both thinking: police. It could be anyone, I tell myself, but the panic I feel defies logic.

'W-we sh-should run.' Her voice quivers and each word gains extra syllables.

'No,' I say, and shove my hands in my pockets. 'Keep your hands out of sight.'

The sound gets louder. The footfalls seem to echo on the hard surfaces. We are a half block away from the last graffiti – Nicoline's message on the stairs. If the person walks along the embankment, they might miss it. Nicoline and I stand as still as statues.

The footsteps grow closer and closer. I want to look, but I can't.

'Evening,' a deep male voice says when the footsteps are practically upon us.

'Oh, hi,' I say, turning slightly and trying not to react when I see the jet-black of his police uniform. Homeland citizens live in pastels and shades of grey, but somehow the police still have uniforms that are bold.

'Nice night,' he says, and pauses right behind us.

'Uh-huh,' we both agree.

'What are two nice girls like you doing out on your own?' he asks, and takes a step closer. He means, why aren't we partnered off and having sex like good little girls?

'We were just leaving.' I somehow manage to speak. I think fast and add, 'Off to meet our boyfriends.' I bump into Nicoline. We both giggle nervously and sidestep away from him. 'Good night, officer.'

We walk. For what seems like forever, the only sounds we hear are our footsteps on the pavement. Is he watching us? At last I hear the click and tap of his shoes mixing with ours and getting fainter. I turn around. He's walking with his head held high. He's scanning the horizon, not looking for messages underfoot. In his dark uniform, he almost seems to disappear into the night.

Now we run and don't stop until we reach the cinema. I boost Nicoline up to the window and she pulls me through. We lie panting for a few seconds on the cool bathroom floor. We wash our hands with foamy pink soap and dry them on our jeans. We slowly, casually return to the theatre. Our row is full again except for our two empty seats. We edge between bent knees and chair backs until we are back where we started. Sanna looks at me with wide, questioning eyes.

'Don't ask,' I whisper to her as I pass.

White words on the black screen start to scroll by. I try to read the words – production assistant, Anthony Mitchell, key grip, caterer, Colin, Miranda. I think of my ever-growing List of The Missing. If we were caught, I could be adding all our names to my list. Are the credits scrolling by faster? The white words seem to bleed together. The theatre goes black. The darkness pulls me under. I gulp in air, but it seems to catch and snag and drift away before it can satisfy my aching lungs. My face is getting hot. Sanna leans in close and whispers, 'It's OK. Close your eyes and think of sunshine.'

She thinks it's my fear of the dark, and it is, but it's more than that. I almost got caught. If the officer had known what we were doing, Nicoline and I could have been arrested or worse.

'Nev, chill.' Sanna rubs my back. 'Don't give in to it.'

She's right, but my mind is as blank as the darkness around me. Then Braydon and our kiss pops into my mind. A flush of passion is followed quickly by the rush of guilt. It's worse than the darkness. I try to swallow down my fear of the dark, of the government, of being caught by the police or, worse, of my best friend finding out about the kiss.

The lights come up. I can feel everyone's eyes on me,

especially Braydon's, and I hate it. Sanna waves the others away. I fold in half and stutter in little gasps of air. It's enough. The vice grip around my chest loosens. I stare at Sanna's bare feet. She wiggles her toes at me.

'I'm OK.' I stand up and shake off my panic.

'We did it, Nev,' she whispers in my ear.

'We did it,' I say and sigh.

CHAPTER FIVE

I'm late. I'm doing a combination run-walk to get to the Mermaid Coffee Shop by ten to meet Ethan. I'm still buzzing from last night. Maybe things *can* change. It's an impossible thought, but this hope is now a balloon floating above me and I'm holding on to it with a very thin string.

I skid to a stop and look though the cracked window of the coffee shop. Ethan is sitting in our usual spot with his sketch pad open. Dark circles ring his deep-set eyes, making them appear disproportionately large for his face. His hand and pencil dance lightly across the page. I love to watch him draw. He always used to have a pencil and paper handy. He saw beauty everywhere, even in me. He'd sketch a dandelion trapped in a pavement crack. A shattered sliver of glass that glittered in the sun. He'd try to draw me but only manage my squinted eyes or lopsided smile. He's captured pieces of me on paper since I was ten.

I know that shell is Ethan, but he hasn't been the same since he was arrested. It was all because of a silly dare. Loads of people do it. I don't know what the police said or did to him. He won't talk about it. All I know is he isn't my Ethan any more.

It was a Saturday night six months ago. We were hanging out in his bedroom. He was drawing snowflakes on my stomach. That's where I got the idea for my tattoo. His eyes sparkled with mischief. We lunged for each other with a passion that would have melted my imaginary snowstorm. Kissing turned into the erratic dance of undressing. Suddenly he sprang away from me as if he'd been burned.

'We can't keep doing this,' he said, panting. 'It's too difficult to keep taking things so far and then stop. God, I want you, but we promised.'

Stunned by the sudden shift in temperature, I reached for him, ready to say, *Damn the stupid vow.* I could only think of one thing. I placed my hand on his thigh.

'Neva!' He batted my hand away. 'Cut it out.' He tugged on his jeans. 'We can't. We both agreed. Stop making this more difficult than it already is.'

I hugged my nearly naked body. He was right. One of us had always been strong enough to stop but our resolve was weakening. I willed myself to think of something, anything besides the way he looked and how his lips felt on my body. I was trying to think of the opposite of sex. 'Let's climb the Capitol Complex,' I suggested. Remembering thousands of people killed in The Terror would darken any mood.

He pulled on his shirt and tossed me my jeans and sweatshirt. 'Let's do it.'

The next thing I knew I was in the heart of the City staring up at the massive pile of rubble that was once the centre of power for our government. One dark day a group of terrorists levelled the Capitol Complex with one massive bomb, killing our governmental leaders and thousands of others. That's all we're told. The government thinks that's enough information. According to our history book, the one my dad puts together, Dr Benjamin L. Smith and the rest of our founding fathers established order from chaos. After The Terror they gave us a new beginning under a sparkling dome. Once the dead were extracted from the fallen Capitol Complex, not one pebble has been touched. Its twisted frame and crumbling stone are supposed to remind us of The

Terror and what happens when people abandon patriotism and uniformity.

That night Ethan climbed up the mountain of debris. I held my breath as he catapulted himself higher and higher. He made it look so easy. When he'd nearly reached the top, where the Homeland flag flies forever at half-mast, he waved down at me with a big stupid grin on his face. His beige shirt was smudged with black and his jeans were covered with a fine white dust. I was more in love with him at that moment than I had ever been in my life.

We'd talked about this since we were kids, but I'd never thought he'd do it. I started to scale the rubble. I wanted to feel what Ethan was feeling. I took a few tentative steps, testing the mass beneath my feet before I shifted my weight. I'd only managed to climb a few feet when I slipped and tumbled back down to the ground. I heard Ethan calling my name, but I was laughing so hard, I could only wave up at him to let him know that, other than a bruised ego, I was OK.

That's when I heard the siren. Ethan shouted for me to hide. I should have been standing next to him. But I did what he told me; I found a pocket created by crossed beams and I waited and watched. The police cuffed him and dragged him away.

They released him the next day, but Ethan is the new kind of missing. His body is still here, but there's a part of him that's vanished. A part the government stole. I've tried everything I can think of to bring him back, but any attempt to get him to talk about what happened seems to make him retreat further and further away from me.

'Susan?' A man touches my arm, and the memory slips away. I turn towards him and he scans my face.

'Sorry,' he says, hands up in apology. 'My mistake.'

I follow the man into the coffee shop and walk over to Ethan. 'Hi,' I say.

He jumps. Even though he's surrounded by people, he's very much in his own space. I kiss him on the cheek. Scattered in front of him are pages of sketches: a steaming, chipped mug of coffee; a perfectly drawn set of hands; a pair of lips; and an intricately sketched skirt, detailing every fold in the floral material.

'Hi,' he says, and shuffles his sketches together.

'These are great,' I say, taking the chair next to him and slipping a sheet from the pile. He has drawn an eye in minute detail. It stares, unblinking, from the page. From the wrinkles at the corner, the shading on the eyelid and the long lashes, I know it's a woman's eye. The tiny jagged lines in the white of the eye hint at sleepless nights. I can even sense sadness somehow. I survey the other patrons and quickly spot Ethan's model: a young woman hunched over her mug. Her eyes are welling with tears.

'You should pursue your art,' I say, and take a drink of his coffee. It's cold.

'I don't want to talk about this again.' Ethan's words have sharp edges. 'The art school closed, so what do you want me to do?'

'Look at these.' I pull page after page from the pile. 'You are so talented.'

'What about you? Do you really want to study nursing?' he asks, snatching the pages from me.

'That's my assigned job. It's as good a job as any.' I have no idea what made the Job Allocation Panel think I'd be a good nurse. I've heard that fifty percent of graduates are assigned to health-care jobs, so maybe it has nothing to do with the CV I submitted. 'But you already had plans. You were going to be a great artist.'

'What do you want me to do?' he asks again, slumping in his chair.

'Get angry. Do something.' I'm louder than I intend. Time

seems to stop for a second and all heads turn towards me. Ethan frowns and shakes his head ever so slightly. My nostrils flare. I curl my lips into a smile to show everyone that everything's all right. Don't stand out. Don't make a scene. Don't do anything to embarrass your dad. It's the way I was raised.

Ethan scoots closer to me. 'This opportunity with National Re-Design won't come along again for years, if ever. It's a good job. I start tomorrow and that's the last I want to hear about it.' He collects his sketches in his open sketch pad and closes the cover. He lowers his voice. 'I'll leave the protesting to you and Sanna.'

I can see the hurt in his eyes. He thought I told him everything. But he didn't know anything about my rebellious plans until Sanna's announcement at the Dark Party.

'I wanted to tell you,' I whisper. 'I'm sorry, Ethan.' I hear sniffles. It's Ethan's eye model. Tears dot the woman's cheeks. 'I should have told you, but I thought you wouldn't like it.'

I glance at Ethan and then back at the woman. I wish I could say something to stop her crying, but sadness seems infused in our recycled air.

'Neva,' Ethan says and draws my attention back.

'I didn't want you to feel pressured to join us,' I continue, trying to make him understand. 'If you didn't know anything then you couldn't . . . but if you want to . . .'

He holds up his hand to stop my string of excuses. 'I can't be a part of anything like that. Especially now.' The old Ethan would have joined us. I want my old Ethan back.

'You didn't tell me,' he pauses and scans the room, 'because you knew I'd try to talk you out of it.' And now the gap between us has widened again. Part of me understands. He's always felt torn, like I have. Our families are part of the problem. Generations of Harrisons have helped build and maintain the Protectosphere. Ethan's father and older sister are engineers. His uncle works in the plant that makes Protectosphere panels. His mother is employed as a weather monitor – maintaining the filtering system and monitoring the weather programme.

'But, Ethan, I think we can—'

'Not another word, Neva.' He looks around. 'I don't want to know anything about it. I wish you'd stop this nonsense with Sanna.'

The crying woman wipes her eyes on a lacy handkerchief and stands. She arches her back and I can see her full, round pregnant belly.

Ethan touches my chin and turns my face towards him. He whispers, 'Do you understand how dangerous it is? If the government finds out … My God, Neva, your father. What were you thinking?'

'How can you sit back and let them rob us of our future?' I try to keep my voice low, but the pressure inside me is building.

'They're not robbing us of the future I want.' He reaches for my hand and I let him take it. 'I want us to get married and start a family.'

'Don't be silly,' I say, but I can tell by the look on his face that he's serious. 'We just graduated.' I can't believe he wants me to give in. I try to withdraw my hand, but he pulls it closer to him.

'Let's stop wasting time.' He's kissing the place behind my ear. The place he knows used to drive me crazy. 'Courtney and Kieron. Sara and Neil. Jasmine and David. They're all getting married. Sara's already pregnant.'

I try to focus on what he's saying, not what he's doing. 'What about our vow? We promised. We can't give in to the government. Not now …' I stop talking because he's not listening. He's wrapping his arms around me.

'Ethan, please,' I say. He tries to kiss me, which makes me think of Braydon, and I twist away. 'Ethan.' I wriggle free.

He clears his throat. 'We're adults now, Neva. We need to start acting like it.'

Where's all this coming from? 'Some arbitrary date on the calendar and some ceremony doesn't mean—'

'Neva, I need to tell you something,' he interrupts. But he doesn't say anything. Instead, he removes his watch and places his hand, palm-side up, on the table. There's a thin red line, like a cat scratch, hidden among the blue veins in his wrist, the place usually covered by his watch.

'What's that?' I ask, and reach out to touch it, but he turns away. 'Ethan?'

'It's a tracking device. They implanted it after I was arrested.' His back is to me so it feels as if I'm eavesdropping. I can't have heard him right. A tracking device? 'They said that they will track my movements. If I go a year without any other incidents then they will remove the device.'

I don't want him to turn around. I don't want him to see the shocked look on my face. If I'm with him, the police know exactly where to find me. I feel as if he's contaminated. I cross my arms tight across my chest.

He's waiting for me to say something, but my mouth is dry.

'I can't be caught gathering with other people with tracking devices.' He's started talking faster. Bits of spit spray from his mouth in his frenzy to finally confess to me. 'If they see a cluster of us together, they'll bring us in.'

I look around. Are they watching us now? I want him to take it back. Tell me it's a joke. He used to have such a wicked sense of humour. He regularly reset the clock in our history class so that it was ahead by fifteen minutes and we'd get out of school early. He slipped in later and changed it back so the teacher was none the wiser. He was always playing little pranks like that. But when he turns towards me, I can see it's no joke. His eyes appear darker, haunted, next to his pale skin.

'How could you keep this from me?' I ask.

'Because of that.' He points to my face. 'That look.'

I try to change my expression, but my face feels set in stone.

'So much is changing, Neva. I wanted – no, *needed* – us to stay the same.' He moves in for a kiss. I am repelled, but I force myself to give him a quick peck on the lips.

'I love you,' he says.

'Why are you telling me this now?' I search his eyes for something familiar.

'I don't want this to happen to you,' he says, glancing at the thin red line on his wrist. I don't know if he means the tracking device or the way that it has drained the life out of him. 'What you and Sanna are doing is dangerous,' he whispers. 'I had to warn you. You have to stop. Please, Neva. I had to tell you. I couldn't let them do this to you.'

I caress his tiny scar with my finger. I can feel it there, right below the surface of his skin, a thin square. 'Does it hurt?'

He shakes his head.

'I didn't know that the government had started ...'

'Me neither.'

'We've got to tell everyone. The government can't do—'

'Please, Neva, no. I was forbidden to tell anyone.' He takes my hands in his. 'Promise me.'

I nod. I wish he hadn't told me. I can't look at him without wondering who else is listening and watching and tracking our every move. I want to tell him everything will be all right, but that would be a lie. I don't want to touch him any more, but my heart reaches out to him. Being watched so closely must be driving him crazy. I want to make him feel better, but I can't.

'Neva, eventually you're going to have to face facts. This is the future we get, and it's not so bad.' He fumbles in his tan canvas backpack, the same one he's carried since primary school. He removes a few crumpled sheets of paper and smoothes them on the table in front of us. It's a printout of the morning news. 'When are you going to realize you are in the minority?' He points to a headline. 'See, people support the Protectosphere. They want more government protection. Why can't you just be happy with the way things are?'

I read the headline: Nighttime Vandals Paint City Red with Plea for Help. I grab the papers and read as fast as I can. According to the story, these vandals wrote the words 'Protect Us' more than one hundred times throughout the City. The police are quoted as saying they believe it's a plea for the government to strengthen the Protectosphere. Some right-wing Protectosphere-loving group has claimed responsibility.

'Oh, my God.' I collapse into my chair. The government has transformed our protest into a statement of support. All our work last night – our planning for weeks – hijacked.

'Neva, what's the matter?' He's reaching for me, but I wrench myself away. I stumble backward, knocking my chair to the floor. Everyone stares at me.

'I've got to go.' I wad the story in my fist and dash out of the coffee shop.

'What the hell happened?' I ask when Sanna opens her front door. I shove the printout into her chest. She takes the papers and studies them.

'Don't know.' She shuts the door behind her, and we sit on the top step of her front stoop. 'This is a colossal catastrophe.'

'How did they erase ... I don't understand.' I shake my head as if trying to jostle the pieces into place.

'All that work for a big zilch.'

'*Worse* than nothing. Now it seems as if there's growing

45

support for the Protectosphere.' I can't stop picturing someone wiping away all our hard work, making our statement of freedom the government's rallying cry.

Sanna and I sit side by side staring at the boarded-up houses across the street. I remember when those houses had families. Someone has stolen the plywood from the lower windows. The houses don't seem solid any more.

We don't speak. I don't know what we expected to happen.

Sanna leaps to her feet. 'What we're forgetting ...' She's pacing as she's talking; I can almost see the pinwheels spinning in her brain. 'Oh, God, Nev, this is really awesome. What we're forgetting ...'

I'm leaning forward, feeling her excitement build. 'What? *What?*'

'Someone has seen our message. They had to coordinate the clean-up. There must have been these manic calls zinging back and forth last night. They cared enough to counter our attack. Don't you see?'

And the part of me that was deflated gets a breath of air. She pulls me to my feet. 'We've got to check it out. See for ourselves.'

We take a train and exit into the stale air of the City. I know where I want to go. I lead Sanna towards the embankment. I follow the same path that Nicoline and I took last night.

As we walk along, I'm almost afraid to look. I grab Sanna's arm. I can't believe it. 'Over there. On the bench.' We slow down, but we don't stop. We nudge each other again and again. We are trying not to smile, but we must look like we are in pain by restraining our euphoria. PROTECT US. Two of the words I wrote in red still remain, but since the government's clean-up someone has book-ended the red with bold, block capital letters – No and FEAR – in a brownish grey paint. They haven't managed to restore every slogan, but someone has taken up our rallying cry. They have littered the walkway with flyers that say 'No Protect Us Fear!', and someone has scratched the words into the stone of a statue and etched it on the wood of a bench. Our slogan has multiplied. If we had wings, we'd be flying.

CHAPTER SIX

'What have you done?' my mum asks as she bursts into my bedroom. It takes me a moment to wake up, but only a moment. Mum's eyes are wide, her face is flushed.

'What?' I sit up. It's morning already. Yesterday's events come flooding back. Sanna and I felt like superheroes, for a few hours at least. Until we saw the cleaning crews with their high-pressure washers and wire brushes removing our messages. Never mind. It was a small victory and that is more than most people ever get.

'It doesn't matter. There's not much time,' Mum says as she hands me a pair of faded blue jeans. 'Your dad called, and the police are on their way.'

'The police.' The euphoria from yesterday plummets. I scan my room for anything incriminating. My pink journal is peeking from under my pillow. I must have fallen asleep holding it. I catch the bra Mum is throwing at me with one hand and shove the pink journal further under my pillow.

'What do they want?' I toss my covers off, remove my T-shirt, and slip on my bra.

'Something about graffiti,' she says, and I freeze. I thought I'd got away with it. 'Keep your story simple,' she continues, not realizing I'm paralyzed with fear.

Why do they suspect me? The police officer Nicoline and I encountered that night couldn't recognize me. I've got no visible identity mark. Nothing's distinctive about me. Did someone turn me in? That has to be it. My body feels liquid.

She notices I'm not moving. 'Neva, get ready.'

'OK. OK.' I nod, but I can't move.

Mum gives me a quick hug. 'Don't get ahead of yourself. They can't ... They won't ...' Her voice falters. 'Calm down.' I don't know if she's talking to me or herself. 'Only answer the questions they ask.'

Since when does my mum give me advice on how to cover up a crime? I try to stop mentally fast-forwarding to all the terrible possibilities. Just get dressed. I pull on the grey shirt and light blue jacket my mum has selected. I hop around the room, squeezing myself into my jeans.

She grabs my arm to keep me from falling. 'You were never there, wherever.'

I start to respond, but she shifts me perfectly parallel to her. Her hair is swept back in a loose ponytail. Stray locks of hair fall in fuzzy stripes across her face. She's wearing one of Dad's old dress shirts. She's missed a button, which makes her look as if her body is off centre. 'You didn't do anything.'

I nod and tuck my snowflake necklace under my shirt. I touch it through the material and ask Grandma for strength. I'm going to need it.

'It will be OK. Calm down.' She's talking to herself again. She walks over to my bed and takes the pink journal from under the pillow. 'I better hide this for you.'

'Mum ...' I reach for it.

'I won't read it. We all need our secrets.' She tucks my journal under her arm. 'Just hurry. I'll buy you some time.' She closes the door behind her.

I slowly spin, looking for anything else suspicious. My room resembles your average recycling dump: clothes everywhere, half-read books on my nightstand, jewellery scattered on my dresser. I start to clean my room, but I'm afraid that will look more unusual. I check myself in the mirror. My upper lip is sweaty. My eyes are bloodshot. Even the way the tail of my shirt is stuffed into my jeans and the way the jacket sits stiff on my shoulders makes me look guilty. I flop on the bed and wait for the police.

'Would you state your name for the record?' The police officer looks up from the file folder in front of him. Something about him reminds me of Ethan. Their hair is the same length. He's got dark circles under his eyes too. The black police uniform obscures any other defining features. Only his face is exposed. I'm so busy examining him that he has to repeat his question.

'Oh, sorry.' I lean in to the microphone in front of me. 'I'm Neva Adams.' My voice trembles. I thought about the questions the police might ask and my answers on the car ride over. It was either that or imagine how easy it would be for them to make me disappear. They didn't take me to the Central Police Station. I'm in the building where my dad works. They made me walk down three flights of stairs to the sub-basement. They want me to know how trapped I am. I'm in a grey room with concrete block walls. I can see my reflection in what is probably a two-way mirror. I bet my dad is back there, watching. I can sense the tension he normally brings to a room.

'Your full name,' the police officer demands, and I instinctively search for his name badge, forgetting that the police are the only government employees that don't have to wear them. Their uniforms are a clean slate except for the crest of Homeland embroidered on their lapels.

'Neva *Elaine* Adams.' I emphasize the new piece of information. All the women in my mum's family for generations have had the same middle name. You'd think that would make me feel connected, but it's one more thing that makes me feel recycled.

'I'm going to ask you a few questions,' he says casually.

'OK.' I try to mimic his relaxed manner, but my heart is thumping so hard I'm afraid he can hear it.

'What can you tell me about the recent vandalism?' he asks, shutting the folder with his black-gloved hand.

'I read something about graffiti in the news,' I say after taking a few slow breaths.

'We believe that a gang of youngsters are responsible for this breach of patriotism.' He's watching my every move. My eyes reflexively widen. 'Do you know or have you heard of anyone participating in this or any other unpatriotic behaviour?'

'I thought the graffiti supported the Protectosphere. That's what the news said.' I have to deny it, but part of me is screaming to tell the truth.

'The graffiti wasn't all positive.' He looks me in the eyes. I force myself to hold his gaze. Only guilty people look away. Or do innocent people look away and the guilty maintain eye contact because they have something to prove?

'You know the consequence of such behaviour, don't you?' He increases his volume and his words bounce off the concrete blocks.

I nod.

'What is it?' he demands.

'Patriotic seminar,' I answer, ashamed that my voice squeaks and sounds so small.

'No.' He stands. He is an imposing figure dressed from head to toe in black. 'This type of behaviour borders on treason.'

My legs start to shake. How can painting a few simple words amount to treason? It feels as if all the blood has drained from my body.

He sits on the corner of the table and crosses his arms. I

remember my mum's advice, only answer the questions asked. He didn't ask a question, so I remain silent. I probably couldn't speak now if I wanted to.

'At a minimum, the person or persons will be sent to Community Farms.' He sits back to let that soak in. Sanna's brother was sent to a Community Farm for six months. It's the government's answer to food shortages and crowded prisons. He came back with calloused hands and an anger that radiated from his tanned, peeling skin.

The officer coughs and tugs at his collar. 'The maximum punishment ... Well, that doesn't bear thinking about.'

But I want to know. I want him to say it: the unpatriotic will disappear. But what awaits The Missing? Torture? Death?

A buzzer sounds, startling us. He exits through the only door. I rest my forehead on the cool metal table and roll it from side to side. I don't know how long I stay there. It feels as if I'm suspended in space and time, trying not to imagine what's next.

I sit up when the door clicks open. My interrogator returns. The tail of his shirt is sticking out on one side, ruining the straight lines of his police uniform. He sits across from me again. 'I'm going to ask you one more time if you know anything about the unpatriotic graffiti that was painted all over the capital city.'

I look down at the table and shake my head.

'We know there are groups planning more protests. We need good patriots, people like you, to help us uncover these plots. Your father is a member of the governing Council. You wouldn't want to do anything to jeopardize his position.' He looks at the mirror behind me. 'Can you tell us the names of anyone who has engaged or plans to engage in unpatriotic acts?'

I run my fingers through my hair. It's damp with sweat. 'No,' I say, a slight tremor in my voice, 'I don't know anyone.'

But even I wouldn't believe me. I must look as guilty as I feel.

'Neva, we know you are a good citizen, but we have reason to believe that you know who might be planning protests. For your sake, and theirs, give me their names and we can put an end to this nonsense. I promise we'll go easy on them if they stop all this now.' He pulls a small battered notebook and pen from his shirt pocket. He flips the notebook open and finds a clean space to write. Pen in hand, he's poised to transcribe my confession. Does he really think I'm going to give him names? He continues, 'The Protectosphere keeps us alive. There are dangerous levels of toxins out there. We are safer inside.'

I've heard it all before. My grandma and Sanna's mum didn't believe it. My grandma said there is no proof that everything outside the Protectosphere ended. The government never says what happened out there. They don't give any details that could be refuted. As far as the government is concerned, it's a fact: there's nothing but a dangerous wasteland beyond the Protectosphere. It's hard to refute a fact with no evidence. I try not to do anything to give away my true feelings. I force myself to nod in agreement.

'Any anti-Protectosphere rhetoric could cause some mentally unstable person to compromise our security and filtration system.' He sounds as if he's repeating a lecture he's given hundreds of times before. 'You wouldn't want that, would you? You wouldn't want the reckless words of you or someone else to cost good people their lives.'

'No, sir.' White-hot fear slithers over me, like a dry, scaly snake. What if Grandma was wrong? Are we doomed if we do nothing *and* if we open the Protectosphere? I don't know what to believe. I place my hands on the table and spread my fingers wide to steady myself.

'Are you OK?' he asks.

I nod, but I can feel saliva collecting in my mouth as if I might throw up.

'Neva, are you going to tell me their names?' He's leaning in closer, pen at the ready.

I've got to be careful. He's setting a trap. 'I don't know anyone who has done anything. Can I please leave now?' I tuck my hands under my thighs.

He slams his notebook and pen on the table. 'I've got to release you,' he says through clenched teeth. I relax a bit. 'But consider this your warning.' He walks around behind me and rests his hands on my shoulders. I want to scream. Every muscle in my body tenses. He bends down and whispers so that only I can hear and, if there is someone watching, they won't see his lips moving, 'I know you are mixed up in this. But Daddy saved you this time.' His hot breath sends chills rippling through my body.

I involuntarily jerk away from him. 'I haven't done anything wrong.' My voice cracks and I have to concentrate on every syllable. I can still feel him behind me.

'No one's accusing you of anything,' he says for the people behind the mirror, 'for the moment. You are free to go. Shall I call your mum or dad to pick you up?'

'I'm an adult now and I can get home on my own.' I try to sound confident, but I can see in his cold, hard eyes that he's not buying it. I stand on wobbly legs and walk slowly towards the door.

'I'll be watching you,' he whispers as he walks by. He leads me through a maze of underground corridors. We climb three flights of stairs and finally we are above ground. Windows line the hall. I am comforted by the sight of trees and sky. I'm almost out. As we turn a corner, I see someone being led down the corridor by another officer. The star on her cheek is bright red and nearly glowing. Nicoline must have retraced it. As we pass, she glances at me and tries to smile, but her lower lip quivers. I force myself to smile what I hope looks like a strong, confident smile. I want her to know her secret is safe with me.

Is mine as safe with her?

I can't stop walking; I can't even pause or change the speed of my step. I have to keep moving forward. As I leave the government building, I can still feel watchful eyes upon me.

CHAPTER SEVEN

'Sanna,' I stammer into the phone. 'They know.' That's all I can think to say when Sanna answers. The phone booth is humid and smells of urine.

'Nev, chill. Where are you?' The line crackles.

It takes me a moment to remember. The concrete steps. The massive stone structure ahead of me, which dominates the city block. 'I'm in front of the government building where my dad works.' People are sitting on the stone steps, drinking coffee from colossal mugs. Two runners in shorts and tank tops run by. 'Sanna, they asked me about—'

'Nev . . .' Her words are obscured by static.

'What?' I've got to tell her. I've got to tell someone. 'Sanna—'

She cuts me off. 'Nev, shut it. We need to talk' – she pauses – 'in per-son,' she enunciates.

Now I understand. She thinks someone could be listening. She's right. Of course she's right. How could I be so stupid? I'm not thinking straight. I glance at the two women in grey business suits who are standing nearby. One smiles; the other nods at me. They could have overheard. I pull the phone away from my ear. Are they listening? 'Sanna . . .' There's so much to say, but I feel gagged. Every word in my brain seems incriminating. I feel as if someone has turned a spotlight on me.

'Braydon's on his way.'

His name triggers a new level of panic. 'Wait, no,' I start, but I've got to get out of here.

'He'll be there in a few. He's got his motorcycle. He'll take you home. I'll meet you there.'

'Braydon rides a motorcycle?'

'Yes, that's why he wears the killer boots,' she retorts. 'There's a lot you don't know about him.'

I have no doubt.

❄

I hear the roar of his motorcycle before I see him. He's wearing faded jeans with holes in the knees and a black leather jacket with deep cracks around the elbows. He rolls up in front of me. His long wavy hair curls at his shoulders. He looks so confident astride that bike. I walk down the steps to meet him.

'I'm sorry, Neva,' he says in a low, steady voice. There's a sincerity I've never heard before.

Braydon closes the distance between us. He reaches up and tucks a stray curl behind my ear. He repeats the motion as if he knows that was what my grandma used to do. What is he doing? Don't touch me. Please. I want to move away, but something in his deep brown eyes keeps me there. I look at him and see everything I want to be. Strong. Self-assured. Free. His touch, the way he looks at me, it's as if he understands that I can never feel safe again. It's as if he knows what I need, knows me.

He wraps his arms around me.

'It's OK, Neva.' He presses his cheek to mine. I fold into him. I don't know how long we stand like that, but it isn't long enough. 'We need to go,' he says.

'OK.' I look up at the stone structure one last time. A dark-uniformed figure looms at the top of the stairs, glowering down at me. It could be the police officer who questioned me. It's impossible to tell. 'Let's go,' I say, hopping onto the motorcycle. Braydon climbs on in front of me.

'We'll ride for a while.' He shoves the motorcycle forward and releases the kickstand. We balance there. I'm suddenly scared to touch him. 'Hold on,' he says, and starts the engine.

I place my hands on his sides. He pulls me forward. I mould myself to him, my fingers connecting at his chest. He rests his hands on top of mine for a second, then he grips the handlebars and we speed away.

My cheek is pressed against his sun-and-sweat-warm leather jacket. My thighs are tense, gripping the bike. I'm trying not to hold on too tightly, but every inch of me wants to touch him. I can't tell if it's the vibration of the engine or something inside me that makes my body tingle. I am ashamed of how excited I feel. He pins his arms to his sides to keep my arms securely around him. Our bodies are pressed together with every turn.

We wind our way through the city streets. I notice him checking and rechecking his rear-view mirrors. I don't dare look around, afraid to alter our perfect balance, but I feel as if we are being followed. We dart into a tunnel and speed through. When we are back in the light, he takes a series of sharp rights. We duck down so we are hidden behind a row of shrubs facing the tunnel's exit. A dark sedan emerges and then slows down. Maybe it's looking for us. We wait until it passes and then head back into the tunnel.

Braydon's body relaxes. I pretend that he's kidnapping me. We will disappear together. I press my lips against his jacket. After a while, I recognize the streets and houses. I hug him tighter, not wanting this break from reality to end. He parks in front of my house. My life has been shaken like a snow dome, but instead of the happy figures and houses being covered with glitter, they have come undone and are floating free, crashing into one another and landing higgledy-piggledy.

He pries my hands from his chest before he dismounts. He

helps me off. My legs are weak and I lurch forwards. He catches me. We wrap our arms around each other. My cheek is pressed to his chest and I can hear his heartbeat, which is matching mine, beat by deafening beat.

That's when I know he feels it too – an undeniable attraction, but it's more than that, deeper than the kiss we shared. Whatever this is, it sizzles with electricity in the space between us. I pull away in surprise. I study his face. The way his eyes draw me in. Those lips.

He brushes hair from my wind-burned cheeks. Our faces inch closer. It takes every ounce of strength not to let our lips meet. I slip into his arms but turn my face away. Sanna is watching us from my bedroom window. The crack running diagonally through the window makes her look as if someone has sliced her in two. She waves and disappears behind the curtain.

'Sanna's coming,' I whisper, and turn my face towards him. I drink in the warmth of his stubble-rough cheek and his scent; there's a hint of cologne I hadn't noticed before.

'Oh, God,' I say as we part.

He looks at the ground, at his red boots. 'I know,' he says, and kicks a spray of gravel into the nearby grass.

'Nev, poor you.' Sanna races to me and tears me away from Braydon. She hugs me, but my body is rigid. I reinhabit my life and the guilt floods in. She grabs my hand. Braydon takes my other. Sanna tugs me towards my house. Fingertips on outstretched hands linger in the air and then the sensation that was igniting my skin is gone.

CHAPTER EIGHT

Sanna drags me into my house. I hear Braydon rev his engine and drive away, and a part of me goes with him. We pass the kitchen where I spot my mum stirring something on the hob. Her expression asks if I'm OK. I nod. She and Sanna have conspired against me. Mum's letting Sanna do the debrief while Mum follows up with a hot meal to make everything seem perfectly normal. I smell the turkey roasting in the oven, but I can't imagine how my life will ever be normal again.

'The police asked me about our graffiti. They have Nicoline,' I ramble as soon as Sanna has shut my bedroom door and flopped next to me on my bed.

'Whoa there, Nev. Slow down.' Our backs rest against my headboard and we stare out across my messy room.

'They were threatening me.' I tap my head against the wall. 'Talking about treason and toxic gasses. They wanted me to name names.'

She hops up and makes her way around the clothes scattered on my floor. 'What did you tell them?'

'I didn't tell them anything.' I watch Sanna pace, which only makes me more nervous. 'They said they would send me to a Community Farm, but I've also heard that they've been implanting tracking devices into people accused of unpatriotic behaviour.'

'Can they do that?' She peeks out my window and then closes the curtains.

I shut my eyes. 'I know someone who knows someone who is being tracked.' I don't tell her the whole truth. I can't tell her about Ethan. I promised. 'They inject this chip under your skin.' I rub my wrist as if to make sure there's not one already there.

I hear her manoeuvre around my room and feel the mattress lower as she sits at the foot of my bed. They've implanted something worse than a tracking device inside me. They've injected me with doubt. 'You don't think they're right? You know, about what's outside the Protectosphere? There's got to be something more than a toxic wasteland, surely? We have a right to know, don't we?' My grandma was so sure. But now, that faith in my grandma and her steadfast belief that there was life outside the Protectosphere is wavering, and I'm not sure how I can live without it.

'I don't know.' Sanna bounces on the bed. 'OK, enough of that.'

I open my eyes. 'So what do we do now? I was thinking we should get everyone together. Make a plan ...' I stop. Sanna kicks a pair of jeans out of the way with her bare feet. She seems more interested in excavating my wardrobe. 'Sanna?' I say softly and then raise my voice when she doesn't respond. 'What is it?'

'Nev, we've got to cool it. At least for a while.' She looks at me for a second and then back at the floor.

'Our Dark Party, our slogan, was only the beginning. We are doing something. Finally. We can't quit now.'

'It was ... It is ... I mean ...' she stammers. 'But we've got to go in slow-mo.' I stare at her. She's changing too, just like Ethan. It's like watching a roaring fire dwindle to embers.

'What?' I shout and then pinch my lips together. I don't want my mum to come running, but I'm overcome with anger. When I speak again, I try hard to even the tone of my voice. 'How can you give up so easily?'

'I'm not giving up exactly.' She curls and uncurls her toes in my frayed carpet. 'We've got to just take a little break. You're majorly disappointed. I am too—'

'I'm not disappointed,' I interrupt. 'I'm terrified. I was dragged in for questioning. They are going to be watching me. But we can't give up. We can't let them win.'

'My guardians are going mental. I had to sneak out to come here. My bro says we gotta lay low. He says the word underground is things are heating up. The police are twitchy. Something's happening, but he doesn't know what.' She flexes and points her toes and her bones click, setting my teeth on edge. 'And I promised Braydon.'

His name on her lips crushes me. Braydon's the real reason. Her guardians and all the rumours are excuses. Before Braydon, I know that type of pressure would have just fuelled Sanna's rebellious fire.

'Don't be mad, Nev.' She playfully knocks herself against my outstretched legs. 'He just worries about me. That's sweet, isn't it? He doesn't want anything to happen to me "Now that we've found each other". That's what he said. Isn't that ... well, a-maz-ing?'

I swallow the guilt and jealousy that have tightened around my throat. I pull my legs to my chest and nod. He's stealing my best friend and killing our rebellion.

'It's not forever, Nev. We've just got to play it cool for a while.' She wants me to tell her it's OK to give up for now. But I can't. 'It's just I didn't have anything to lose before,' she adds quietly.

'I understand.' Now I'm the one who feels as if I've got nothing to lose.

We sit there in a silence that is new for us.

'I gotta go, Nev. My guardians will hit the Protectosphere if they realize I'm gone,' she says after a while. I'm relieved. 'I'll call you later.'

'Yeah,' I mutter as she leaves. My feelings for Braydon have tainted my relationship with Sanna. Every tug of loyalty and love I feel for her is countered by my new feelings for her boyfriend.

❄

I'm startled by two quiet taps on the bedroom door. 'Neva, are you OK?' my mum asks. I check my clock; it's nearly dinnertime. I don't know where the afternoon has gone.

'Yeah, I'm fine,' I call through the door.

'Can I come in?' she says as she pushes the door open. She has a kitchen towel draped, like a burping baby, over her shoulder. Her shirt is still misbuttoned and more wrinkled than it was this morning. She walks over and scoots in next to me. 'I spoke to your dad. Everything's OK. Everything's going to be fine.'

'OK,' I say. 'I'm sorry.' I rest my chin on my bent knees.

'You've got to be more careful,' she whispers. 'You don't understand. This could have ended . . .' She pauses and bumps our heads together. 'But we won't think about that.'

I can see there's more she wants to say. 'What could have happened?' This is the closest we've ever come to talking about The Missing. I don't want to waste this opportunity.

'Just be smart, Neva.'

She doesn't tell me to stop or ask me what I was doing. It's as if she *wants* me to rebel. But how can she? We are Adamses, after all. My bloodline can be traced to the founding fathers. My grandfather was elected to Parliament four times. My dad's on the Council. I've got a pedigree that opens doors and keeps others from closing. But what she leaves unsaid speaks volumes.

When I look at my mum, I know what my life will be like in thirty years. She used to run a clothing store, but now she grows tomatoes in our greenhouse and runs the barter programme in our neighbourhood. Dad says we must do our part. His government role has expanded while Mum's life has shrunk. Even though she'd never say it, I know she wishes things were different.

'Your dad will be home soon. And Neva . . .'

'Yes?'

She rests her head on mine, and whispers, 'I put your journal back.'

'Thanks, Mum.' We stay here like this until we hear the front door open.

'Join us for dinner when you feel up to it.' She's up, rushing down the hall to greet Dad.

My pink journal is tucked under my pillow. I wonder if I need to add Nicoline's name. My family name saved me. But Nicoline has no connections. Her bloodline is muddy. And she has an identity mark. But she can't be gone; she just can't. I put my journal into its proper hiding place, deep in my mattress. I have to call her.

'Hello.' The voice is soft and hoarse, barely above a whisper.

'Hello, Mrs Brady?' I ask.

'Yes.' She sounds like I've woken her up. 'Who is this?'

I try to answer, but the static surges. I wait until the line clears. 'My name is Neva. I'm a friend of Nicoline.'

'Oh.'

'Can I speak to her?'

'No.'

I'm caught off guard. 'I'm sorry?' Something's not right. Why would she say no?

'You shouldn't have got my daughter involved in such—'

'I don't know what you're talking about,' I interrupt. I can't let her say any more. Someone might be listening. 'Is Nicoline OK?'

'She's . . . she's . . .' she pauses as if she's searching for words ' . . . grounded. You won't be seeing her for a while.' Her voice is fading in and out. I have to listen closely. 'Just stay away.'

'But, Mrs Brady, I just want to make sure Nicoline's—'

'Listen,' she talks over me. 'Maybe you didn't hear me or don't understand,' her anger is clear, even through the static on the phone line, 'just drop it – if not for Nicoline's sake, then for yours.'

The line goes dead.

I have to make an appearance at dinner. I've got to pretend everything is OK. We are in our assigned seats. I sit at the table across from my mum. Dad faces the empty chair. A family of three should really own a round table. The empty chair always makes me feel as if someone is missing.

'Neva.' Dad says my name as if it's a reprimand. Mum looks at her plate, cutting a small bite of turkey in half. She's made Dad's favourite meal. She must have bartered hard for the turkey. There's usually only a dozen or so each day from the turkey farm.

'Yeah.' I'm creating clusters of sweetcorn on my plate. I can't bear to eat another kernel. We have it almost every day.

'You have to stop this nonsense.' That's more words than he's said to me in days. 'I let you befriend that girl with that horrible scar on her face. It's her influence.'

He *let* me?

His hair is the only thing that disobeys him. The hair he has left forms a horseshoe around his balding scalp. He's clean shaven but always seems to forget a patch when he shaves, either under his lip or higher up his cheek. He has a few longer eyebrow hairs that look more like misplaced eyelashes. Sometimes a stray white hair peeks out of one nostril.

'I don't see why you have to mutilate yourselves; it's barbaric,' he says, staring at the empty seat. 'We've worked hard to create equality, and you undermine generations of effort with your little rebellions. You really should find more respectable friends from good families.'

'Oh, George,' my mother coos. 'They are kids doing what kids do. Leave them alone. It wasn't that long ago that you and I painted our faces.'

'Dad painted his face?' I can't imagine him any other way than he is right now – stone-faced with a permanent look of disapproval.

'He used to paint his face white with black stars around his eyes.' Mum traces stars around her own eyes.

'Really?' I try to picture him with stars for eyes.

'We were young and didn't appreciate our elders.' Dad frowns and I notice the deep lines around his mouth and eyes, as if he's painted this expression on his face.

'We all grow up,' Mum sighs. Her eyes focus on something beyond my dad.

'That's right. Neva is an adult now. She has responsibilities to this family and to Homeland.' He stands and heads into the hall. He returns with a manila envelope and lays it by my plate.

'What's this?' I ask, spooning mashed potatoes into my mouth.

'Your orientation pack. I got you a job.' He settles into his seat and smiles at Mum.

The potatoes congeal in my mouth. I can't spit them out, and I can't swallow. 'What?' I managed to lob the word around the lump of potato. I force myself to swallow.

'Your orientation pack.' He takes a sip of water. 'You'll be working for me.'

Mum seems to be concentrating on excavating something foreign from her potatoes with her fork.

'What?' I repeat, because he can't be saying what I think he's saying.

'It wasn't easy to arrange. Most people have to pass an

entrance exam and wait for a complete background check. But I placed a couple of calls and called in a few favours.' He picks up his knife and fork. 'You start the day after tomorrow.'

'Thanks, Dad, but no thanks.' I can't imagine a worse scenario. Not only would I be doing the most boring job under the Protectosphere, but my dad and his government cronies would watch my every move. 'I'm starting my nursing programme in a few weeks. That was my assigned job, remember?'

'Not any more.' He's eating his dinner again.

'So you're ordering me to take this job?' I drop my utensils and they clatter on my plate. My fork tumbles onto the floor.

'You need discipline and direction. This job will give you both.'

I kick back from the table and rise to my feet. 'I'm so sorry that I'm such a disappointment to you.'

My mum jumps in. 'That's not what he said, Neva.' She's crawling on the floor, picking up my silverware.

'That's what he meant.' I glare at him.

'Stop with the dramatics, Neva, and sit down and finish your dinner.' He doesn't even look up. 'We'll go through the pack later.'

My mind pulses with all the things I want to say to him. This is why I got off with a warning; I'm being sent to Dad prison. 'I will not.' I stamp my foot like a little child. I wish I hadn't done that.

'Is this the thanks I get for trying to help my daughter?' He's asking the top of Mum's head.

'I didn't ask for your help,' I say through gritted teeth. 'I am so tired of my life being planned for me.'

'Then start making good decisions about your future.' He leans back in his chair.

'What future? We don't have a future.'

His face flames red. His knuckles grow white from gripping

the arms of his chair. 'Never talk to me that way again.' He doesn't shout. He lowers his tone of voice and calmly selects each word. 'Don't ever blaspheme Homeland.'

I have so much anger and so much to say that I stand there, nostrils flared, mouth open but stunned into silence.

My mum jumps up and clamps her arm around my shoulders. 'Neva, your father is trying to help,' she says in a strange high-pitched voice. 'Maybe it's the best thing for now. He's gone to a lot of trouble.'

I storm to my bedroom and slam the door behind me. I throw myself on my bed, bury my face in my pillow, and scream. My day has gone from nightmare to disaster. The government has stripped me of my privacy, and my dad has stolen the little freedom I had left. This must be what a caged animal feels like.

CHAPTER NINE

It's my first day of work and the first time my dad and I have been alone together in any meaningful way in years. He grips the steering wheel. He's making me nervous. The electric hum of the car mimics the buzz of my nerves. He keeps opening his mouth like a goldfish gulping tank water, as if he is about to say something but thinks better of it. I wipe my sweaty palms on my frayed grey skirt. I tug at the hem. My legs feel naked. Dad demanded I wear a skirt or dress to work. Mum altered a few of hers. It's another way in which he's trying to turn me into something I'm not.

I can't believe this is the life I get. I want to ask Dad what it's like not to question your every thought and action. To make a decision and not wonder if the other option is better. To be so sure. Maybe Mum can teach me how to settle, to accept my fate and move on.

We stare out through the windscreen in a loud, awkward silence. The City looks like a film set waiting to come to life. People seem to lurk around the edges. Dad hesitates at each junction even though we rarely encounter a car. Dad has said this is the last car he'll salvage. I wanted him to teach me to drive. I liked the idea of controlling the vehicle rather than always being a passenger. But he said there was no point because total mass transit is the way of the future. More government propaganda to make us believe there's progress.

We head into the heart of the old city. Almost every building seems propped up by scaffolding, except for the mammoth government structures. Dad beeps his horn a few times to clear a path in the road, now dotted with people not differentiating between pavement and street.

'Where do I go first?' I ask with an exasperated sigh. This is really happening. I can't fight it any more. 'The letter in my pack said something about orientation.' The tufts of hair on his head and his wiry eyebrows quiver in the breeze from the open window.

'You'll need to go to administration first. They will give you your name badge. Then they will bring you to my office, and Effie will get you started on a few projects.'

Effie is part pitbull and part old-maid schoolteacher. I can remember her nasally voice when I used to call my dad's office: 'Ancient History Department, Minister George W. Adams's office. Effie speaking. How can I help?' She said exactly the same thing in exactly the same way every time I called. When I used to visit Dad's office as a little kid, before Grandma left and everything changed, Effie would put a bottle of antibacterial hand gel on the corner of her desk. I was instructed to use some every time I passed her desk as well as after I ate, drank, sneezed, coughed or sniffed.

Dad used to carry me into his office piggyback. He'd introduce me to everyone we passed as his 'little girl, Neva.' In his office, I would curl up on the leather sofa, the one with all the buttons that created diamond shapes, which I would trace with my finger. He'd tell me stories and end each day with a cliffhanger so that I would come back to work with him. He told of heroes and inventors and geniuses. 'Dr Ben polished each panel. Would it be ready in time? He had discovered a way to make see-through panels that could act as a barrier and a filter. He had to create a puzzle to cover the sky. The sky was so huge. Dr Ben worked day and night. He knew that the future of Homeland rested on his shoulders.'

'What happened, Dad?' I'd ask.

'Tomorrow, Neva.'

'How can he create a puzzle in the sky? Does he save everyone?'

'Patience, my darling girl.' He'd pat me on the head and make me wait for the happy ending.

I found out later that he had tricked me. Those tales weren't concocted from his imagination. The stories weren't fiction at all; they were history lessons. But he wouldn't merely recount dates and facts, he'd bring the stories to life. I'd fall asleep and he'd pat my hair every time he passed. Sometimes I'd only pretend to be asleep, so I could feel the warmth of his hand on my head and hear him murmur how much he loved me.

'Neva.' He clears his throat bringing me back to the present. 'You are working for the government now. You are working in my department.' He says the latter as if it's more important. 'You need to behave yourself and live above reproach.'

My blood feels like it is clotting and bumping through my veins faster and faster. I want to scream or do something to make this stop. This feels like a surrender, even though I've still got a lot of fight left in me. But all I say is, 'Yes, sir.'

He slows the car and stops for a cluster of men in grey business suits. He studies me. He knows about my party and the graffiti. I don't know how he knows, but he does. He's even robbed me of my secrets.

I have to watch a video about patriotism and my role as a member of the Central Government. A young woman about my age – Jessica, according to her name badge – hands me a five-page, single-spaced contract and tells me to sign on the dotted line.

'I'd like to read it first,' I say. She huffs. The contract states that I am first and foremost a government employee and everything else comes second. Jessica keeps glaring at me from her desk.

'Can you hurry it up ...' she glances at my paperwork '... Neva? I have a schedule to keep.'

I nod. She rolls her eyes and then begins typing on her computer keyboard. I read the contract again. The type is so small that I have to hold it an inch from my nose to read it. I feel as if I'm making a deal with the devil. I ask her about the confidentiality clause, and she doesn't even look up from her computer screen when she says, 'That means keep your mouth shut, sweetie.'

I must sign my name on the contract. It's odd that I feel a twinge of guilt at the thought of signing my name, signifying that I understand and accept all the terms and conditions outlined above. I understand all too well, and I one hundred per cent do not accept them. But why do I care if I lie to a government that has lied to me my whole life?

'You going to sign or what, honey?' she asks, hovering above me now.

'Yeah, sure,' I say, and let the pen's point touch the paper. I move the pen before the ink can pool on the page. I don't think of what I'm writing as my name. I think of it as linking lines and loops in a predetermined pattern. That way it doesn't mean anything.

Now I have a name badge and an employee number. Jessica takes me on a tour of the building. She points at each department and recites facts from some government propaganda handbook. 'Resource Management takes up the top two floors of the building. They are responsible for salvage and re-allocation as well as natural resource management,' she says with a swing of her ponytail. 'Hi, Bill,' she calls to a short, fat bald man. 'He's the head of Research and

Development,' she says to me, giving Bill her best toothy smile. 'And that woman over there' – she nods toward a woman in a yellow suit – 'she runs the collection and redistribution centres. She's a good person to know.' She waves at the woman in yellow. 'Hi, Joann!' She leans in closer. 'She found me a replacement part for my dad's old television and brought me a leather handbag that only needed the lining replaced.'

Each floor looks pretty much the same. Every available inch of space is occupied. It's as if someone opened the top of the building and poured furniture in. One man has an old, hand-carved wooden desk with what looks like a plastic kitchen chair. Two people share a desk constructed of two filing cabinets with a slab of wood on top. A few desks have old computers. We weave our way through the building and end up in the Information Services wing. I know it well.

She drops me off at Effie's desk. The women exchange nods but neither speak. The last time I saw Effie was ten years ago, a few weeks before my grandma disappeared. Effie hasn't changed. She still wears those stubbly wool suits. Her glasses have brown, almond-shaped frames and her hair is slicked back in a bun so tightly that her eyes almost squint. Her lips are drawn into a thin red line.

Effie has an old wooden desk that's been worn smooth and a metal folding chair, positioned just outside my dad's office. Mismatched desks and chairs are lined up as far as the eye can see up and down the hall. Men and women tap on keyboards and chat with one another without ever taking their eyes off their computer screens. Maybe the history department is called *ancient* because of the average age of its employees. I am the youngest person by at least thirty years.

According to Dad, Effie has been sick, and I'm supposed to help her with a major reprint of our history book. The history book is the only document that gets printed and mass produced any more. What a waste of resources.

Effie stations me at the far end of her desk. I've got the history book's master proof and, literally, a two-foot stack of edits from other Council members and Dad's key department heads. People have gone thesaurus happy. Someone crossed out the word *demanded* and replaced it with *requested*. As in: The government *requested* that every citizen sign the Pledge of Allegiance before the Protectosphere was sealed. It seems like a slight change at first, but there's a big difference between a request and a demand. The government changes everything in tiny shades of grey until what was white is now black.

I reread the opening chapter about The Terror. Someone – probably my dad – has even altered the first chapter, going a bit adjective crazy with his red pen. *Massive* explosion. *Extreme* panic. *Necessary* measures. A *superior* race. But not one word about what was outside. It's as if the slate was wiped clean that day. That terrible tragedy convinced our founding fathers that we needed to protect ourselves, seal ourselves away.

When we studied history at school, I asked Dad about what came before The Terror. He closed his eyes and took a deep breath. 'Everything has a beginning, Neva,' he said, and patted the top of my head.

Someone has crossed out two paragraphs on a man called James Washington. A chill threads through me. I'm helping the government erase people from history. Future generations will never know that James Washington stabilized the rubble of the Capitol Complex and helped create a memorial to those who perished in The Terror. One tiny gesture and he vanishes from the pages of history.

I'm not sure if I can do this. But I don't have a choice, do I? I become a good little government employee or disappear like James Washington. Is this why our country is spiralling slowly downwards? Because people like me do what they're told. No one questions. If I do this, then I'm no better than the police or my dad.

'Why are people editing ancient history?' I ask Effie as my pen is poised to erase James Washington.

She stops typing. Her hands hover above the keyboard. 'I knew this was a bad idea.'

'What?'

'Your job is not to ask questions, young lady.' She resumes typing.

I may have to do this job for now, but I still have a voice and I can question. 'What are you doing?' I scoot a little closer to her. My skirt twists, so I rise from my chair an inch and untangle myself.

She turns her back to me, trying to block my view of her computer. It only makes me more curious. 'If you must know, I'm managing the day's news,' she says begrudgingly.

'What?' I knew my dad was responsible for information management, but now I understand that it's more about censorship than dissemination.

She takes a breath that rattles in her chest before it is expelled. 'Information Services reviews all the news and sends me any stories that need attention.'

I peek over her shoulder. 'What does that mean? "Need attention".'

Effie tuts and gives me a disapproving look over the upper rim of her glasses. 'None of your business.'

I concentrate on my editing for a while. I consider making a few additions and deletions of my own. If Sanna were here, she'd see how many times she could fit the word *wacky* into a sentence or something like that. I want to disregard their rewriting of history altogether. I intentionally leave out a few of the smaller edits – an adjective here, a sentence there. It's a small rebellion, but it eases the growing outrage I feel for how the government, which I'm now a part of, manipulates information.

Effie's fingers fly over the keys rat-a-tat-tapping. Even her fingers seem agitated that I'm here. She only pauses to cough. I half stand and read over her shoulder.

'Um, Effie,' I say, but it's as if she's in some sort of trance. I try again. 'Effie, why does that ...' I point to an article that she immediately clicks closed. 'Why did you code that "action required"? Wasn't that an obituary?'

She clears her throat. 'Newspapers are no longer to report on deaths by natural causes.'

'But that guy was my dad's age.'

She continues working without answering my question. I settle back in my chair and try to resume my editing duties, but I can't.

I realize that Effie has stopped typing. Her face is pale. I shift in my seat so I can get a better look at the screen; my skirt is constricting me again. I scoot as close as I can without Effie noticing. I squint and try to read what's on her screen. The article is from a small town up North. It's one of the few places that has refused to relocate its residents to population hubs. They have fewer government resources, like power, water, and police, but more freedom. The headline notes: FIVE GIRLS MISSING. I gasp. More Missing.

Effie closes the article and highlights the entry in red. She picks up the phone and punches in numbers without even looking.

'Yes, another code eleven; I'm sending you the article now,' she barks, and hangs up. She punches in more numbers and repeats her cryptic message. She pounds on the keyboard and the red entry disappears. She taps another icon. I think it's titled GovNet. She types and clicks so fast I have no idea what she's doing. She rises and smoothes her hair. She knocks on my dad's office door.

'Enter,' my dad bellows.

Effie steps inside. 'Dr Adams. Sorry to disturb you. Another code eleven.' She pauses. 'Yes, it will be handled. I'll search the system and purge any necessary data.'

As she blathers on to my dad, I inch closer and closer to Effie's computer. I study her computer screen. There are two search boxes: one titled ACTIVE, the other INACTIVE. I scan the headings on the screen. I check to make sure Effie isn't watching. I quickly select ABOUT GOVNET. A small box appears in the middle of the screen:

> GovNet was established in 0010 to more efficiently catalogue citizens.
>
> Each citizen has a central file. To review a specific file, type the citizen's name in the appropriate field.

I look over my shoulder. Effie's back is still to me. I can hear she's wrapping up. I click the box closed and go back to my chair. This database knows everything about everybody. Why didn't I think of it before? It will be much easier to find answers working inside the government. Maybe I can find out the truth about the Protectosphere. Maybe I can find my grandma and all my Missing.

When Effie returns to her desk, red faced, I ask, 'Can you explain what just happened?'

She ignores me.

'How am I ever going to do this job—' I start, but Effie cuts me off.

'You,' she shouts, and then realizes that heads are turning. She lowers her voice. 'You are never going to do *this* job. You will do as you're told and nothing else.'

I flinch at the venom in her voice. I summon my courage. 'What happened to those girls?' Maybe if I can find out what happened to them, I can find my Missing.

She raises her hand to stop me. 'There are no missing girls. The news organization was misinformed.'

'But how do you know—'

Her open palm closes into a tight ball. 'No one goes missing in Homeland.' She smoothes her hair. 'The Protectosphere keeps us safe. How could anyone go missing?' she says sweetly.

'But the article said—'

Effie interrupts, 'I think you are mistaken.'

I open my mouth to contradict her.

'You are mistaken.' She takes a deep breath. As she exhales, she seems to return to her normal, controlled self. She hands me a stack of envelopes. 'Why don't you deliver these for me?'

'What are they?' I ask, checking the names and office numbers on the tattered envelopes.

She closes her eyes and shakes her head. 'That doesn't concern you.'

I open my mouth to ask for a map or something to help me navigate this maze of a building. But she just points a rigid arm and shoos me away. All eyes follow me as I shuffle down the hallway. But nothing, not even Effie, can squelch this new hope I feel.

Sanna is waiting on my front steps when Dad and I come home from work. Dad steps around Sanna as if she's rubbish that can't be recycled. The rosy S glows on her cheek.

'What's with the disappearing act?' she says when we are alone. 'I tried to call you a zillion times yesterday and today.'

I sit down next to her, tucking my skirt between my legs. We normally see each other or at least talk every day, but I don't know how to talk to her when I can't stop thinking about Braydon. 'It's just I've got this new job, and Dad's watching me like a hawk, and ...'

'Life's got all weird. I get it. Your mum told me about the new job. Major snore, I bet. But don't leave me hanging.' She rests her head on my shoulder.

I feel even worse, if that's possible. 'I'm sorry, Sanna.' She brushes the grass with the bare soles of her feet. 'What's wrong?' I ask even though I'm afraid of the answer.

'Braydon's acting strange. You're a ghost. Everyone's freaked out.'

I think about the wave of his hair and how he smelled of cologne. In my head, I know he's all wrong for me, but in my heart he feels right somehow. I try to think of something, anything, else. 'Come on, San. There's a lot going on. I've got this job. You're going to start school soon. We've got to find a new sense of normal.'

'You're right.' She perks up a bit. 'Tell me about your big job. You even look all professional. How does it feel to be all responsible-like?'

'It's like working in a minefield,' I say, and then the rest comes flooding out. 'I'm working with my dad's assistant, Effie. She hates me being there.' I don't tell Sanna about how my dad shapes the news and history. For some reason, I can't bring myself to betray him, even to my best friend. 'I'm supposed to update the history book and ...' I pause, look around and whisper, 'I think I may have a way to find The Missing.'

'What?' She leans in close. 'How?'

'The government has a computer system with files on everyone. There's got to be something in there about my grandma.' My pulse quickens. 'Sanna, I'm on the inside now. I'm sure I can find useful information. Maybe even something that will prove that the government should open the Protectosphere.'

'Nev, I thought we agreed to cool it for a while. Braydon says that it's too dangerous—'

I stop her. I don't want to know what Braydon says. 'Maybe we—'

Now she interrupts. 'Can't we go back to the way things were before our Dark Party?'

'I wish we could,' I say.

She loops her arm though mine and I feel the sting of guilt. I should be arrested, but not for crimes against Homeland. I should be condemned for sins against my best friend.

CHAPTER TEN

After a week of Effie-intensive training, I think I may lose my mind. She only leaves her desk to respond when my dad beckons. The woman must have a bladder of steel with all the coffee she drinks – from her own thermos, obviously, no unnecessary trips to the kitchen for 'pointless socializing', as she puts it. She hovers over me and randomly spot-checks my work. She clears her throat if I pause for one minute. I consider spiking her coffee so I can have a few minutes alone. I haven't had one second to check out GovNet again. It's like waiting to open a Christmas present, except Christmas never comes.

Today I decide to have lunch outside on the front steps of the building. Effie must have sprayed me with repellent because no one will come near me in the break rooms or the cafeteria. I sit nibbling my cheese sandwich on the front steps and inventing dramas for those around me. The two women a few steps away are signalling spies with some complex nail-filing code. The jogger has escaped from the Border Patrol Detention Centre and is heading up North. The man in a light grey suit has passed this way twice: at least, I think it's the same man, probably casing the joint for a heist of government secrets.

'Neva!'

It takes me a moment to realize that it's my name being called.

'Neva, is that you?'

I scan the spies and the convicts. Maybe I'm imagining friends like I did before Sanna came along.

'Neva!' The voice seems familiar but out of place. It's coming from behind me. I twist around. My insides tangle. I look at his feet to confirm my gut reaction. Red boots.

'I thought that was you,' he says as he sits next to me.

'Hi, Braydon,' I say. My face flames red. Our bodies are inches apart. It's as if he is radiating heat. 'What are you doing here?' My immediate instinct is to make sure no one's watching.

He studies his boots. 'I wanted to see you.'

God, I wanted to see him too, but now that he's a breath away, I want him to leave. He's triggered an almost unbearable ache inside me.

'Are you all right?' he asks. I don't see him move, but he feels closer to me somehow.

I shake my head ever so slightly.

'Yeah, right. Stupid question.' He notices a smudge on his boot and rubs and rubs and rubs it. 'How's the new job?'

'Fine,' I lie. I don't know how to act around him. Every word and gesture seems to give away my new feelings for him. He makes me feel safe and wild all at the same time.

He leans in close. I freeze, terrified he'll touch me yet wishing he would.

'Neva,' he whispers, 'please promise me you're not doing anything that could get you into more trouble.'

I know that he means stop protesting and looking for The Missing, but what I'm doing right now with him is much more dangerous.

'You're not going to stop, are you?' he says when I don't respond. He already knows my answer.

'I can't.' Everyone around me is going about their business. It's a typical day. They are eating and drinking and talking and laughing, but if I look closer I can see it: a dullness in the eyes. They all know their limits; I'm not sure of mine yet.

'Do you understand how dangerous it is?' He takes a deep breath as if he's about to launch into a sermon.

I shake my head. 'Don't bother. You may have convinced ...' but I can't say *Sanna*.

He exhales, exasperated. 'You know it's the smart thing to do.'

I nod. 'But the smart way is not usually my way.'

'Yeah,' he says. 'Nor mine.' He stretches his legs and leans back on the step behind him.

We sit in a silence that's begging to be broken. I can't look at him, can't speak. I try to casually scoot away from him, to create space between us. I can tell he notices, but he doesn't move. We both pretend to survey the crowd around us.

'How do they do it?' he asks me finally.

I don't see anything out of the ordinary. 'Do what?'

'Do this, day in and day out?'

I know what he means. I've watched them act out the same boring play every day. 'I have no idea,' I say.

'Don't you ever want to scream and run far, far away from here?'

'All the time.' I sigh.

'Yeah, me too.'

But we both know there's nowhere to run that doesn't dead end at the Protectosphere.

He glances at me and says, 'We won't end up like them.'

Something deep inside me still believes it. 'Yeah, as long as we know we're trapped, we still have a chance to escape.'

He looks at me as if he's really considering what I've just said. 'I never thought of it that way. These people don't even see the cell bars anymore.'

Funny, he doesn't sound like Braydon. I don't know if it's his tone of voice or the fact that we've never really had a conversation before. He still has the same mysterious edge, but it's as if I've got a glimpse of the man behind the mask. 'You better watch it,' I say, allowing myself a long look at him. 'You're starting to sound like a rebel.'

He smiles at me and the jittery feeling he's inspired turns molten. We move closer one painful millimetre at a time.

Something inside me snaps. 'Braydon, I can't do this.' I straighten.

'Do what?' He knocks his shoulder against mine.

Zap. That feeling again, like an internal lightning bolt. 'You know what.'

'We aren't doing anything, Neva,' he says, but we can't look at each other. We both stare at his red boots.

Maybe I've misjudged the whole thing. But I've got to know. 'Why did you kiss me?'

He shrugs. 'It was just ...' Our eyes meet, and I can see it meant something to him too. 'You kissed me back.'

'I didn't know it was you,' I protest. He's rested his hand on the step next to mine. Our little fingers touch. *Zap!*

'Braydon, stay away from me.' I stand and smoothe my skirt.

'You're right.' He looks up at me with those eyes.

I should leave. 'I would never hurt Sanna.'

He slowly rises to his feet. 'I don't want to hurt her either, but ...' He takes my hand.

'Please don't, Braydon,' I say, but I don't let go.

He steps closer. 'You can feel it. I know you can. Everything's all planned out for us. Then we kissed and I felt—'

'Alive,' I finish his thought.

'Yeah.' Our fingers interlace.

'Like we aren't living recycled lives,' I whisper. The electricity between us is powerful, a force like two Protectosphere-sized magnets.

His lips are dry and slightly cracked, but I want to close the gap between us and kiss him. God help me. It's as if I've been drugged.

'I can't do this,' I say, shaking the invisible hold Braydon has on me. 'I've got to get back to work.' I dash up the steps. I want to look back, but I know he's still staring at me. I can feel his eyes on me. It's as if that kiss in the dark cast a spell and I've got to find a way to break it.

I climb the steps, absorbed in my own thoughts. Too late I spot the jet-black uniform. A police officer is blocking the straight line away from Braydon and into the building. I change my trajectory, but he shifts so I can't pass. Fear wraps itself around my vital organs. How long has he been watching me?

'You should really watch what you're doing,' he says. What does he mean by that? I step back and prepare to walk around him, but he shifts so that his broad chest blocks my field of vision. My heart races. My eyes travel up his pressed shirt to his face. It's not the same man who interrogated me.

'Sorry,' I mutter. He steps aside and I bolt and don't stop moving until I'm back next to Effie.

I call Ethan and agree to meet him later at the National Museum. Maybe Sanna's right. I need to get my old life back. Ethan wants to celebrate our new jobs. He thinks I've given up my rebellious ways. I need to find what I've lost with Ethan and stop thinking about Braydon.

We walk into the museum's main lobby and stop in the centre of the space. Being with Ethan makes me feel like a traitor and a target. The government is tracking his every move. I'm painfully aware I'm being watched. Each room has a prism of cameras, sweeping electronic eyes. Even the eyes in the paintings seem to track us. Neither Ethan nor the government can see my betrayal, even though I feel it with every breath.

A mural covers the wall ahead of us. Ethan and I aren't the only ones admiring the expansive work. The artist appears to have captured Homeland in a snapshot taken from miles above. The Protectosphere glistens in the sun and the enclosed landmass looks lush green and the water sparkling blue. The image is reflected in the shiny beige tiles under our feet. The vivid colours change the hue on the surrounding walls as the sun streams in from skylights.

It's my dad's favourite painting. He brought me here a few times. I've heard him give lectures on Ancient History and the importance of the Protectosphere – 'the most advanced technological feat ever'. He smiled as if he'd been there, as if he'd connected each panel himself. I told my dad the painting makes us look small and insignificant. His body stiffened. 'You will never understand what it was like. We *were* insignificant. We *were* losing our identity, but our founding fathers reclaimed our proud heritage.'

The artwork in the museum highlights Homeland's history. The paintings show people and landscapes from hundreds of years ago. Buildings and fashions have evolved, but somehow remained the same, somehow it's still 01/01/01. My dad calls it 'elegant simplicity'. I call it stifling.

Ethan and I stare at the mural. I try to feel the pride that my dad and maybe even Ethan feel. But I look at that bubble and feel trapped.

Ethan kisses my cheek. 'Do you mind if we check out the young artists' exhibition?'

'OK.' I let him lead me up the stairs and through two galleries. The exhibition says it features young artists, even though the newest painting is more than ten years old. We've been here before. Ethan stops in the middle of the room, taking in each canvas. He walks toward the portrait of a couple looking in a mirror. I follow him. The painting is titled 'The Reflective Couple'. I watch his eyes dart back and forth as he slowly and systematically takes in every inch of the canvas. 'Do you see the way he's shown the whole picture, half in the mirror, half facing the viewer? Brilliant.' He pauses and reaches out as if he might touch it. 'There. Do you see how he's shown the light source without painting it?'

He's not really talking to me. I see two people who could be anyone and no one. He is bare chested; she's wearing a cream slip and nothing more. He's standing behind her, but they aren't touching. They have woken up together and can't look each other in the eye. So they survey what they've done in the mirror. She's regretting last night and he's reaching for her; his hand is barely in the frame but extended as if he wants to touch her.

'Why don't you sketch me?' All of a sudden I want him to study me, every line, every curve, so I can be solidly in this moment. 'I could model for you,' I say as I jut my hip to one side and pout my lips.

'Neva, you don't need to model. I could draw you in my sleep.' He kisses me on my pouty lips and moves on to another painting.

'Guess you're right. Portrait painters have it easy: make one painting and then copy it a million times.'

Ethan's eyes narrow. 'I never thought you'd be one of those people.'

'What people?'

'Those people who can't get beyond our physical similarities. We aren't identical.'

'But sometimes it feels as if we are.'

We move to the next painting. It's a portrait of an old woman whose face is a roadmap of wrinkles. 'So when you look at me, you don't see anything special?' he says.

'Yes, of course I do.' I feel hot, my skin tight.

'Then close your eyes.' He places his hand over my eyes. 'Describe me.'

I don't close my eyes. I stare at the pink parallel lines of light between his fingers. 'You have the softest skin.'

'No, Neva, what do I look like? Describe me like you would a painting.' He's standing behind me now.

'OK.' I pause to collect my thoughts. 'You have wavy brown hair, cut short. Your eyes are brown. You are wearing the striped shirt I gave you.'

'You're hopeless.' He removes his hand but stays behind me. He slips his arms around my waist. I wish it were Braydon holding me. 'Your hair is the colour of a sandy beach on a rainy day,' he says. 'The hair on your right side is wavier than on your left. You have full beautiful lips that grow a deeper shade of red when I've kissed you, almost the perfect shade of a June strawberry. Your body is pear-shaped.'

'Thanks a lot!' I say, and step away. I can't face him. He'll be intensely staring as if he's undressing me, and I'm thinking about Braydon. Kissing Braydon made me realize what I used to feel for Ethan. I wanted to believe that it was the police and his tracking device that had changed everything, but the truth is I changed. I don't want comfortable and easy any more.

'Come here.' He hooks his arm around my waist again. 'I'm not finished. Your waist is small and my arms fit perfectly around your middle. Your hips are round and dip in at the line where they connect to your thighs.' He starts to move his hands lower.

I shift out of his grasp. 'OK. OK, I get it. You are way better at this game than I am. You win.'

'It's not a game, Neva.'

I walk behind him and rest my chin on his shoulder. 'You may know the colour of my eyes and the shape of my butt, but I know you *here*.' Or at least I used to. I reach around and poke my finger in his chest. 'You are a brilliant artist, but you only draw parts of people because that's how you see them. A hand. An eye. A look. A gesture. You are scared to death to put them all together and draw something whole. You want to have a painting hanging here someday. You want it so much it hurts. I can see it in your eyes: the joy you have when you are surrounded by art. But instead you'll become an architect and remake their designs. To hell with originality. But you could be so much more.'

'Stop it,' he says, almost pleads. 'I love you.'

'I know you do.' He used to have a lust for life. He was the first one on the dance floor or into the pool on the first day of summer. God, I miss him, even though he's standing next to me. I walk over to the next painting. It has yellow, blue, and red shapes outlined in black. I prefer the abstract. I take it all in then let my eyes unfocus. It's the emotions that we keep walled away from ourselves and from one another. That's what I see. 'I like this one.'

'Yeah,' he says, walking over and stopping next to me, our shoulders touching. 'His precision and use of colour are amazing.'

I slip my hand into his. I'll be in this moment for a while. I won't think about the future or the police or Ethan's tracking device or Braydon, especially not Braydon. I'll hold on to this picture of Ethan and me, side by side, suspended in time like a painting. The Happy Couple.

'Marry me, Neva,' he whispers. The words shake me off centre. 'Let's not wait any longer. Let's start our life now.'

Marrying Ethan would be like stepping into my mother's recycled shoes.

He holds my hand a little tighter and keeps talking. 'We are perfect for each other.'

We are as imperfect as everyone else.

'I know about the police interrogation.' He draws me into his arms. I can't breathe. 'Sanna told me. She's worried about you and so am I.'

'I'm ...' I want to say 'fine', but I can't. I'm suffocating.

'It's the perfect solution,' he continues. 'We'll get married and find a nice place to live. I'm making good money. We'd get the government's marriage subsidy. We could start a family. The police would realize that we're law-abiding citizens.'

They'd leave us alone. We are a threat to Homeland until we settle down and start making babies. It's the answer. My parents would be happy. An image of Braydon flashes in my mind: us on his motorcycle driving into the sunset. My heart flutters at the thought of him. But nothing can ever happen between us. I try not to listen to the voice in my brain, Braydon's voice, that's screaming 'Run away, run as far from this ordinary life as possible.'

'Marry me, Neva?' Ethan asks again.

We've been heading for this finish line all my life. Why does crossing it feel like losing? 'I'm not sure, Ethan.'

He doesn't relax his grip. 'Just think about it,' he says in a panicked voice. 'Please.'

I surrender into his arms. 'OK,' I say, and feel the fight leave me.

CHAPTER ELEVEN

I throw myself into my work – well, as much as overbearing Effie will let me – so I don't have to think of the mess I've made of my life. The only thing that keeps me from going stark, raving mad is the thought that I might finally be able to find The Missing. I get a thrill every time I see the GovNet icon.

I get my first lucky break after nearly two weeks on the job. Effie gets a call. I don't know what is said, but she leaps from her chair. She skirts around her desk, but then the rubber soles on her sensible shoes squeak to a halt. She whips around. She's remembered her prisoner – me.

'Copy these handouts for Dr Adams's presentation this afternoon.' She points and taps her short, square fingernail on the folder at the edge of her desk. 'Under no circumstances are you to interrupt Dr Adams.'

'Copying? I thought there was a ban on photocopying.' I reach for the file and flick it open.

'That's only for nonessential, nongovernment personnel.' She slams her hand on the file, closing it. 'I want you to make these copies right now.'

Oh, I get it. She's not supposed to leave me unattended. I cannot be trusted. I pick up the file. She's got to think I'm going to obey orders. But there's no way I'm going to let this opportunity pass me by. I don't want to get my hopes up, but a chance to sneak onto GovNet like this might not come around for a long time.

'What are you waiting for?' She swats at me as if I'm a fly ruining her picnic. 'It's down the hall, next to the breakroom.'

We head off in opposite directions, her rubber soles squeaking on the tile floor as she takes short, clipped strides. I duck down the next hallway and wait for the squeaking to fade. Once I'm sure she's gone, I race back to our desk. I slide into her chair; the metal is cold against my bare legs. I quickly open GovNet. The flashing arrow hovers over ACTIVE. I move it to INACTIVE. I click. A dialogue box pops up and asks me to enter a name. My head is bobbing as my eyes constantly dart from computer screen to hallway, looking for Effie. My fingers tremble as I peck out the letters for my grandma's name: Ruth Laverne Adams. The computer thinks for a few seconds. I can't believe it's taking so long.

NO MATCHES FOUND.

The words seem to twinkle on the screen.

I hope this means she isn't dead. She isn't inactive.

But she is still missing. I scoot my chair closer. I position myself right in front of the screen to block the view in case my dad opens the door behind me.

I switch to ACTIVE. I type in my grandma's name again. The screen goes black. Red letters flash in the centre of the screen: CLASSIFIED.

What does *classified* mean? Already a dead end.

The monitor flickers and returns to the main GovNet screen. My hands freeze on the keyboard. If they can tap people's phones and track people's physical movements, then they could be monitoring computers. I move the cursor to the GovNet icon and close the programme.

But I can't stop. Not now. I'm too close. It's the chance I've been waiting for. I'll have to risk it. This is Effie's computer anyway. She must search for people all the time. I want to research someone else, but who? The red numbers on Effie's digital clock seem to flash as if counting down to Effie's return. Red reminds me of Nicoline's star. I click on the GovNet icon again, select the ACTIVE button and quickly type in Nicoline's name. The file has a series of subheadings, including Education, Family, Heritage, Address, Reproductive Status, Employment History, Identifiers, Associations, etc. It lists her address. I never knew she lived four blocks from my house. Her file notes the date she was interrogated. I recall the look in her eyes and the way her red star glimmered as if the ink was still wet.

Under Reproductive Status, there's a date a week after our interrogation and the word PENDING. What does Reproductive Status pending mean? There are a series of capital letters that don't spell any words I know: WEC and IVF.

I hear a rattle of the doorknob behind me. I quickly close down GovNet. I hold my breath.

'Where's Effie?' my dad asks.

I slowly turn to face him, but everything inside me is racing: my blood, my heart, my thoughts. He's wearing the white lab coat he always wears in his office. It makes him look like a mad scientist. Did he see what I was doing? I search his eyes but see nothing except his usual disapproving stare. Maybe he didn't notice. But my body feels jumpy, as if I've been caught. Remain calm, I tell myself.

'Neva, what's the matter with you?' He narrows his eyes as if he's trying to decipher a code. 'Where's Effie?'

I force the words out of my mouth. 'Um, some emergency. She'll be back soon.' For some reason I laugh. Not a real-sounding laugh but a fake laugh, as if someone has told a bad joke.

He stares at me for a moment as if he's forgotten what he was going to say. He walks back into his office and then stops and turns around. He scratches his scalp and his unruly hair quivers. 'Um, Ef—I mean, Neva.' He shakes his head. I wonder what's distracting him. His lab coat is unbuttoned, and he's only wearing one of his protective white cotton gloves. 'Tell her I need those copies for this afternoon's meeting.'

'Yes, sir.' I promised him I'd be more professional at the office. I messed up and called him Dad in front of Effie yesterday. He backs into his office but forgets to close the door. I pull it closed and collapse into the cold metal chair. I try not to think about what could have happened. I've got to be more careful. But I can't stop thinking about Nicoline and her 'Reproductive Status pending'. I've got to keep searching.

Instead of picking a name from The Missing, I type in my own name. The file notes that I'm Dr George Adams's daughter. I review the standard categories: Education, Family, Heritage, Address, Reproductive Status, Employment History, Identifiers, Associations, etc. Most of my boxes are blank. I haven't lived enough. Under Heritage, I'm a '+ +'. I'm sure that's good. I've got the correct past and present: my bloodline can be traced to our founding fathers and my dad is a respected member of the government, like his dad before him. There's a strange category at the bottom of the screen: Security Risk. I haven't noticed this before. The box is filled in with a percentage: 51.6%. I have no idea what that means.

In the notes section is a date and the words *interrogated on suspicion of unpatriotic behaviour.* Is this the reason government employees shun me? There's a letter and a numerical code that looks like a link. I try it. ACCESS DENIED.

I hear squeaking like rubber soles on a tile floor. Probably my nervous mind playing tricks on me, but it might be Effie. I scan the hall. No Effie. I take it as a sign to quit snooping.

This is only the beginning of my search. There will be other opportunities. I've got to pace myself.

I rush off to make Dad's copies. When I return, I'm surprised that Effie's not back yet. I knock and then burst into Dad's office, presenting his copies like a trophy. 'Your copies,' I say, expecting to see Dad's disapproving glare, but he's not behind his desk. I scan the room. It's empty. Weird. Dad rarely leaves his office. I'm surprised he hasn't turned into one of those underground creatures that shrivel and die in the sunlight. I glance at the coat-rack in the corner. His jacket is still there, but the white lab coat he wears only when in his office is missing. Strange.

I shut the door to his office and plop myself into Effie's desk chair. I flip open the manila file folder with Dad's copies. What's so important about this document anyway? Most of his reports are written in some government-speak with way too many words to say even the simplest thing. I flip through the pages. There's a sheet titled 'Agenda' with discussion topics: Historical Analysis, Structural Dynamics and Hypothetical Impacts, Perception vs. Reality, Next Steps. I only understand the first and final topics. The other document in the folder is eighty-seven pages long, twelve of which appear to be reference citations. *A Historical Analysis of Protectosphere Changes and Their Corresponding Environmental and Cultural Impacts* by George Adams. The date on the document is well before I was born. It must also have been before Dad earned his PhD. He'd never forget to include his title if he had it.

'What are you doing?'

I jump.

'Effie,' I say, and slap the file folder closed.

She nudges me out of her chair. 'I told you to copy them, not read them.' She sweeps the folder off her desk and checks its contents, probably to make sure I haven't screwed with the page numbers or lost a page altogether. 'Dr Adams will certainly be asking for these soon.'

'Dad— Dr Adams,' I correct myself. 'He's not even in his office.'

'Ridiculous,' she says. Now she can see through walls?

She's so convincing that I reach for the doorknob.

'You can't go in there!' Effie pivots so she's standing in the doorway, blocking my entrance. 'You are not allowed in here without Dr Adams's express permission. Sit,' she barks, and points to my chair. I obey but seethe at being treated like a dog.

Effie knocks twice on the door and then enters Dad's office. I sneak to the door and scan the room. Dad's not at his desk. I told you, Miss Effie-Know-It-All. As Effie places the file in the centre of Dad's desk, something catches my eye at the far end of the office. Dad seems to be walking out of the bookcase. I blink and look again. He's fiddling with something and part of the bookcase slides shut. It's a secret door!

I dive back into my seat. Through the open door, I can see Effie straightening the files on Dad's desk. She doesn't seem to notice that Dad has magically appeared behind her. But her back straightens in a way that shows she has sensed his presence. She slips out of the office and closes the door firmly behind her.

She sits down, back to business as usual, and she scoots her keyboard a half inch closer to her. 'Have you been using my computer?' Her question is more of an accusation.

I open my mouth to deny it, but Effie holds up a hand. 'Don't waste your breath with one of your lies.' She pumps hand gel in her palm and rubs her hands together so vigorously I think she may remove a layer of skin. She takes her time wiping down her keyboard with the handkerchief she keeps tucked under her watchband. 'Don't you ever' – her voice is low and shaking, she is so angry – 'use my computer unless you are specifically directed. Do you understand?'

I nod. A few strands of hair have sprung free from her bun. She smoothes them back. She glances in the direction of Dad's office and lowers her voice. 'We will not tell your father about this little breach of protocol.'

I can't believe what I'm hearing. I'm sure she's not doing it to spare me. I can only assume that she'd get in trouble too if anyone found out.

'Don't let it happen again.' Then she looks at me for what feels like the first time since I started to work with her. The hard lines fade from her brow. 'Neva, you don't want to know too much.'

What is she talking about? I'm tired of secrets, of living in the dark. I want to know everything.

'Once you know something you can never un-know it.' She turns to her computer screen and clears her throat. 'What are you waiting for?' Any softness from earlier vanishes. 'Get back to work.'

I drive home with my dad in silence. I want to ask him so many things. I hear Effie telling me I can't un-know anything. When he pulls up in our driveway, I hop out of the car.

'Where are you going? Your mum will have dinner,' he calls after me.

'I need some exercise,' I yell back.

At first I walk. Then I jog. Then I run as if I'm being chased. My lungs are burning. My eyes are stinging. Sweat is pouring down my temples and dripping into my eyes. I know what I've got to do.

I'm standing in front of Nicoline's house – at least it's the address listed in her GovNet file. It's a small brick house with boarded-up windows. I would think it was abandoned if there wasn't light seeping through a split in one of the boards.

Before I lose my nerve, I knock on the door. The second my knuckles hit the wood, I want to bolt. I force myself to stay. One phrase echoes in my brain and keeps me rooted to the spot: Reproductive Status pending.

The woman who opens the door looks like she's been in bed. Her clothes are wrinkled and baggy, but her bloodshot eyes look as if she hasn't slept for days.

I open my mouth to speak and get a whiff of her. She smells like our compost heap when my mum stirs it. I rub my nose and hold my breath.

'Mrs Brady,' I start, 'you said Nicoline is grounded, but I really need to speak to her.' The woman looks up at me blankly. 'Please – it's important.'

Her face creases as she makes this low guttural noise that doesn't sound human. She is sobbing, but there are no tears – only this hoarse moan.

'She's not here, is she?' I ask, but as soon as the words leave my mouth, I want to take them back. I don't want to know.

The woman shakes her head.

'Where is she?' I ask.

The woman takes a series of deep breaths. 'They. Took. Her.'

I don't have to ask who. 'I'm so sorry.' The memories of the night my grandma disappeared come flooding back. I know the loss she's feeling.

She looks around. 'I'm not supposed to say. I didn't say, OK?'

'OK.'

She notices my government-issued name badge.

'You!' she screams. 'This is all your fault. You and that other friend of yours. Why didn't they take *you*?' She slaps me across the face. The sting and force of it push me back a few steps. She slams the door shut. I cup my face where the heat of her anger burns.

Oh, God, how I wish I could un-know this.

CHAPTER TWELVE

When I arrive at work the next day, Effie's chair is empty. 'Where's Effie?' I ask Dad.

He looks as baffled as I do. 'I'm sure she'll be here in a minute.' He moves through to his office, leaving me alone to fill Effie's space.

Other employees start arriving. No one even looks my way. Effie has trained them well. After thirty-three minutes of sitting with my hands folded, staring at the red numbers on Effie's digital clock, I decide to take a break. While making a cup of tea, I think I hear Effie's name mentioned in hushed conversations, but I'm never close enough to make out the context. When I move closer people stop talking. I hope Effie's not sick. I didn't really mean it when I said I wanted to poison her. Effie is always here before Dad and I arrive, and still here when we leave each night. I'm not sure what Effie would do without her work, or what Dad would do without Effie.

After another half hour passes, I knock on Dad's office door.

'Come in,' he bellows. I push the door open. Dad is hunched over his desk. His lab coat isn't buttoned and the collar stands up on one side. His hair juts out in all directions as if he's separated his locks in fistfuls.

'Dad, Effie's still not here,' I say, and glance in the direction of Dad's secret hiding place. All my questions resurface.

'Yes, I know.' He leans back in his chair. 'She won't be coming in.'

'Is she OK? I know she's been sick and . . .'

'Effie has been fired.'

'Fired?' I rest against the door, it opens, and I stumble farther into the room. I have never heard anything so preposterous in my life. 'But why?' Being too efficient? Caring too much about her job? I can't imagine Effie stealing a paper clip.

'She misused GovNet?' he says as if it's a question.

My stomach drops as if I've been hoisted up and it's been weighted down. I used Effie's computer yesterday. Effie is missing and it's all my fault. 'What . . . w-what does that mean?'

'She had been sharing government information with a group that is suspected of unpatriotic behaviour.' He's saying the words, but he doesn't seem to believe them.

'Effie? Are you sure?'

He nods and stares off into space. 'I trusted her.'

My guilt subsides. This was not my fault. 'What will happen to her?' Effie a rebel? I can't believe it.

Dad clears his throat and that faraway look is gone. He is tense and in control again. 'She will be replaced as soon as possible. Until then, you will be responsible for all Effie's non-confidential duties. We'll have to forget this happened and get back to work.'

He means forget Effie. He must be good at erasing people from his life; he's had enough practice.

I sit at Effie's desk. They come and take her computer. They empty her desk. There is not one single personal touch in or on her desk, not even a scrap of paper with a doodle or partial grocery list. It's as if she were never here. They plug in a new computer for me. When I turn it on, the only icon on my screen is for the history book. That's it. There's no GovNet, no nothing. My search is over. I could scream.

Strange, but I miss Effie. Her efficiency and unwavering belief in her job and Homeland were the backbone of the office – and it was all an act. Dad walks aimlessly between his office and Effie's desk, my desk now. He comes out of his office or looks up from the book or papers he's reading when I come in and it's as if he realizes Effie is gone all over again. His face softens and then creases in a frown.

It's lonely without her exasperated sighs and steely looks of disapproval. I'm getting requests for information from all over the government. The Minister of Exchange's office wants an inventory of all stories related to recycling programmes. Someone from the Minister of Health's office calls to remind Dad about some doctor's appointment. I organize the requests and work up the courage to ask Dad what to do.

I tap on Dad's office door and hope he doesn't answer, even though I know he's in there.

'Come!' he shouts.

I step one foot across the threshold but keep most of my body on my side of the door. He's slumped behind his desk so that I am talking to his bald spot. Papers and folders are stacked haphazardly around him and threaten an avalanche. He's poised over a thick report with a highlighter in one hand and a pencil in the other. His wild, wiry hair vibrates as he scribbles on the paper and then makes broad yellow strokes with his highlighter. 'Um, Dad, I was wondering, if, well—'

'What is it, Neva?' he barks, looking up from the stack of papers in front of him. He's done an even worse shaving job than usual. He's got stubble on his chin and his sideburns are uneven.

'I don't know what to do.' That was the wrong thing to say. His jaw immediately clenches and his eyes narrow. 'What I meant was ... I've made all the edits you've approved to the history. Effie didn't tell me anything about the rest of her job.

I'm getting requests from all over and I don't know how to respond to them.'

His face relaxes a smidge. 'Give them to me, and I'll deal with them.'

I hand him a series of folders. 'I've organized them by deadline and importance – anything from one of the other Council members is in the first file.'

He looks almost pleased.

'The Minister of Health's office called to remind you about some doctor's appointment.'

His expression darkens.

'Are you feeling OK?'

'I'm fine, Neva. It's just ... routine.'

'Dad, I want to help.' I approach his desk. 'I could arrange this for you,' I say, gesturing to the mess of papers scattered in front of him. I pick up a thick folder with Women's Empowerment Centre scribbled on it in my dad's cramped handwriting. WEC. That's one of the acronyms in Nicoline's file.

'Don't touch that!' He snatches it from me. His voice is unnecessarily loud. I stumble back to put distance between us.

'I'm sorry. I was trying to ...' I want to get out of here.

His creased brow smoothes. 'I'm sorry, Neva. I'm a bit lost without ...' He tucks the Women's Empowerment Centre folder into his desk drawer. 'I deal with confidential information, and you do not have the security clearance.'

'What do I need to do to get clearance?' I'd love to know what's in that file and the other secrets my dad is keeping.

'That's not possible.' He straightens the piles of papers and folders around him. His touch causes one tower to topple. I rush forward and shuffle papers into folders as best I can.

'What is a Women's Empowerment Centre?' I ask, as if I'm reading it off one of the files.

He scoops the files from my arms before I even register his movement. 'None of your business.'

'I could get security clearance. I could be an even bigger help to you.' I could find The Missing.

He studies me. 'Not with your *history*. The only reason you were allowed here in the first place was because I promised that Effie' – he pauses at her name and clears his throat as if to erase the very thought of her – 'I promised that we would keep a close eye on you. I had to call in a lot of favours to get you sent here rather than ...' He clears his throat again.

I would love to know the end of that sentence. The graffiti and my interrogation seem so long ago. I feel helpless.

'That's all, Neva.'

Dad locks himself in his office for the rest of the afternoon. I leave at five o'clock on the dot without Dad. I call Sanna from a phone booth. I tell her to get everyone together. I am coming right over. We've got to do something.

What's happened to Nicoline and Effie? Why does Dad have a secret hiding place? I am a guppy swimming round and round in a glass fish bowl. Sanna wants to meet at 'our place'. That's code for where we first met. She's right. Of course, she's right. We can't meet at her house, not with her patriotic guardians listening at doorways.

The playground feels empty, but Sanna's already here. I can hear the squeak of the roundabout as it slowly turns. Three swings hang perfectly parallel. The slide stands like an outstretched tongue. The first time I saw Sanna she was playing on this roundabout. She held on to one of the bars and ran as fast as she could, then dived on. As her spin slowly dwindled, she'd jump off and race around again. She'd scared all the other kids away with her mad dashes. I watched her for a while until I knew the rhythm. Then, as the roundabout slowed, I hopped on.

'Whatcha doin'?' I'd asked when she looked at me as if I were the one with the dirty bare feet, the mud-streaked face, the ripped skirt, and hair barely restrained in four ponytails. I scooted into the centre of the roundabout where the pull of the spin was less fierce.

'Spinning,' she replied.

'Why?' I braced myself as she started to run.

'It feels a-maz-ing.' She jumped onto the roundabout and held on for dear life. She let the force pull her away.

'It makes me dizzy.' I only felt the tight rotation at the centre.

'Yeah,' she said, hopping off. 'I love it.' She fell to the grass laughing. I waited until the roundabout stopped and slowly walked over to her.

'Lie down and close your eyes.' She patted the grass next to her. She didn't know who my dad was and didn't care that the rest of the kids kept their distance. 'You can still feel it.'

I lay down and closed my eyes. I felt wild and dizzy, but it wasn't from the roundabout. That was from Sanna.

Sanna is slowly spinning on the roundabout, smoking a cigarette, creating a halo of smoke. This is the only way I ever know Sanna is anxious. She's a stress smoker. Her bare feet lazily push the ground away.

'So,' I say as she circles by. My feelings for Braydon have changed everything. Even if she doesn't understand it, she feels it.

'So,' she repeats when she comes around again. She flicks her cigarette to the ground.

'Where is everyone?' I ask, and check my watch.

She digs her heel in the dirt and the spinning stops. She's facing away from me. I sit down on the opposite side of the roundabout facing away from her. The wood and the metal feel less solid than when I was a kid. The wooden plank seems to sag under my weight.

'Nev.' I hear the click of her lighter and her deep inhale and exhale. 'It's over.'

My heart stops. Did she break up with Braydon?

'Our rebellion,' she whispers the words.

'What?'

'Everyone's heard about your interrogation. They know you are working for the government. And ... Nicoline's ... you know ... no one's seen her since you and she ...'

I sidestep, stretching one leg wide and bringing my legs together. We turn slowly. I can hear Sanna's feet responding, sliding in the dirt and gravel beneath our feet. My face cuts through her cloud of smoke.

'I know. That's what I was going to tell you. She's gone. They've taken her somewhere. She's missing. Missing just like your dad and my grandma and ... when everyone gets here ... I'll tell them. We'll think of something .... We can ...' My thoughts are coming faster and faster. I can't speak quickly enough to get everything out. I've got to make her understand. We are spinning faster.

'Nev.' She digs her heels in and stops the roundabout. 'You're not listening to me. Everyone thinks ... well ... Nic's gone and you're here ...'

I can't believe what she's implying. They think I'm the enemy.

'I didn't have anything to do with Nicoline's disappearance.' I kick at the dirt. 'No more than you did.'

'I know that, but they're scared,' she says softly, defeated. I hear her grind her cigarette out. 'I'm scared.'

'I'm scared too, but we've got to do something.' Even though the roundabout has stopped, I still feel as if I'm spinning. 'Did you tell them it's more important than ever that we fight back? Any one of us could be next. Have you heard of something called a Women's Empowerment Centre? What does that mean? My dad has a secret room – I haven't told you that yet. There's got to be something in there ...' I ramble on and on and on because my secrets are eating away at me. 'Maybe we should try to find Nicoline, but I don't know how.' I put my head in my hands. 'And not just Nicoline. Effie's missing too. They say she was working to undermine the government. Effie! Maybe she knows something. If Effie's working against the government – straitlaced, by-the-book Effie – then certainly we ...' I grind my palms into my eyes, trying to make everything stop. 'I can't stand by until everyone I love is missing, can I? 'Cause that's what it feels like.'

Sanna stands and my side of the roundabout sinks even lower. Someone is tugging at the roundabout, trying to make it spin. I lift my feet but keep my eyes shut tight. I rotate towards Sanna.

'Nev,' she says softly. When I open my eyes, Sanna is now flanked by Braydon and Ethan. I close my eyes. This can't be happening.

CHAPTER THIRTEEN

They know. They all know. That's all I can think when I see the three of them lined up in front of me. My boyfriend who wants to be my husband. My best friend who has finally found love. And the love of her life, Braydon, who I can't stop thinking about. The three of them stare down at me. My eyes flick to Braydon. He's wearing a pressed white shirt and tight black jeans. His long hair is smoothed away from his face. I lower my gaze and focus on their feet – Ethan's dingy tennis shoes, Sanna's bare feet, and Braydon's red pointy-toed boots.

'Neva.' Ethan sits down next to me. 'We are worried about you.'

Sanna kneels in front of me. 'You've got to stop this. It's too dangerous. We don't know what happened to Nicoline ...'

'And we don't want anything to happen to you.' Braydon finishes her sentence and sits next to me. He puts his hand on my thigh. I stare at it. His fingers extend over the hem of my dress so he's touching my bare leg. It feels as if everything is channelled into his touch, as if everyone is staring at the place where his fingertips merge with my skin.

Ethan rests his arm on my shoulders. I want to shrug it off, but I can't move. 'Neva, we need you to promise that you are going to stop searching for people you think are missing.'

'They *are* missing,' I insist.

'You work for the government, your father.' Ethan pulls me towards him. 'Sanna says she thought you might want to plan another protest. Neva, you can't be part of anything like that.'

'You mean *you* can't,' I say, and glance at his wrist. They could be watching us now.

'None of us can,' Sanna adds. 'Nev, please. This is for your own good.' She makes a fake stern face. She's trying to lighten the mood, but it's not working.

My body flushes with anger. How can she, above all people, ask me to give up? How can she give up on our secret rebellion? Ethan and Braydon are huddling closer and closer to me. Their thighs are pressed against mine. They are conspiring against me. I don't mean to, but I look at Braydon.

'Neva and I are going to get married and start a family,' Ethan announces. I whip around to face him. He hugs me away from Braydon. 'Isn't that right, Neva?'

'Is that right, Neva?' Braydon asks. He rests his hand on his own thigh, but the tip of his finger moves ever so slightly so he's touching me. He knows what he's doing.

Ethan nuzzles in close, and I feel the burden of his happiness. I feel the pull of Braydon. And Sanna is kneeling in front of me, silently begging me to let her boyfriend go. I am being torn apart. Everything I want to say, I want to scream, multiplies in my brain. The pressure is overwhelming. There's only one answer that doesn't destroy my best friend and my boyfriend.

'Yes,' I finally manage to utter the one word. I choke back the real answer and respond louder this time. 'Yes. I'm going to marry him.' It's the only answer. They won't leave me alone until they think I've given in. In books and films they lead you to believe that lying is difficult – that a lie gets caught in the throat. But this lie is easy.

Ethan kisses my cheek.

Sanna gives me a huge hug. 'Nev, that's big news. Congrats.' She hugs Ethan too. She pulls Braydon to his feet and gives him a comically noisy kiss.

Even though I'm surrounded by three people who supposedly care for me, I feel more alone in this moment than I ever have in my life.

I'd rather step outside the Protectosphere and take my chances, than step into this ordinary life with a man I don't love, in a job that I hate, with a future that will end too soon.

Ethan walks me home. He tries to make casual conversation, but I can't pretend that any of this is normal. Mum comes out the front door as Ethan and I approach my house.

'Hi, Mrs Adams,' Ethan calls a little too enthusiastically.

'Oh!' she says, hand to heart. 'You frightened me.' It's the first time I've seen her hair down in months. I almost forgot how her hair curls in spirals around her face. She looks younger. She holds her overcoat closed in her fist. 'I thought Sanna said you were going to be out tonight.'

'Change of plans,' Ethan pipes up when I remain silent.

'Are you OK, Neva?' Mum asks, and places her hand on my forehead. 'You don't look like you feel well.'

'I'm OK,' I say when she kisses me on the cheek. Since when are we the same height? Her lips and my forehead used to meet perfectly.

Mum opens her handbag and checks for her wallet and keys. 'Right. Your dad won't be home tonight. He's travelling up North on urgent business.'

'What?' He didn't mention anything to me.

'It was some last minute thing.' She fluffs her hair. 'I'll be home late.'

'Where are you going?' I ask.

'Out,' she says, and leaves before I can ask a follow-up. We used to tell each other everything, but I'm starting to feel as if I'm not the only one with secrets.

Ethan waves at my mother. The minute she turns the corner

he leads me into the house. 'Oh, Neva, you've made me so happy,' he says, snapping me to him like a rubber band. His mouth is on my mouth. We are twisting and turning down the hall but still connected. I wish it was Braydon, and for a moment I pretend that it is.

We fall onto my bed. He is on top of me. The sun is setting and the light from my open window gives his outline an eerie glow. He grabs my wrists and slowly raises my arms above my head. My dress inches up. The rough cotton of his trousers rubs my thighs. He kisses me and I try to kiss him back, but it's as if I can't get the rhythm right. His lips travel to my cheek and then my neck. I try to lower my arms. I want to tug at the hem of my dress, but he is stronger in a way I have never experienced before.

He is kissing me, but not softly and sweetly like at our Dark Party. His lips feel hard. He is crushing me. He releases my arms. Now he's twisting each button on the front of my dress between his fingers until it slips from the loop. I squirm under him, but I am trapped. His bicep is near my face, and I can see the curve of the muscle. He buries his face in my neck, kissing the line between my ear and collarbone. I grit my teeth.

We've done things before in this very room. We've kissed and taken things to the edge and back. But he's more aggressive and urgent now. He's never been like this before. Ethan is usually gentle and patient. This Ethan seems possessed. We are nose to nose. I press my head into the bed and gain a few more inches of space between us. Ethan's face is in shadow. His eyes are dark sockets.

'Ethan, stop.'

He stares at me, confused. 'Neva, I thought you ...'

I push away and scoot up the bed until my back is pressed against the headboard. I pull my quilt over me.

'We're getting married,' he says, and sits on the side of the bed. 'You said yes and I thought ...'

111

'Ethan, we promised we wouldn't.' I'm suddenly cold. I tug my dress closed. 'Please go,' I say, and pull my arms and legs in.

'But, Neva ...' He reaches up to touch me and I flinch.

I stare at his silhouette and try to remember what loving him felt like.

'Neva, let's tell our parents; let's set a date.'

I shake my head.

'OK, that's fine. Whatever you want. I can wait.' He scoots closer for a kiss, but I move away.

'No, Ethan, I can't marry you.' It hurts to say it, but I can't keep lying to him.

'OK, we don't have to get married. You're right. Why let the government think they've won? We'll abstain for a while longer. We can live together ...' He keeps stringing sentences together, not taking a breath.

'Ethan.' I place my hand on his. He stops talking. 'I care about you, but I can't be with you any more.' Saying it gives me a moment of relief, but then sadness rushes over me. We've been together so long. I can't imagine life without Ethan as my safety net. I have to remind myself that he's not that Ethan any more, and hasn't been for months.

He pats my hand. 'You've been through a lot recently. I understand. You don't mean it. It's OK. We don't need to decide anything now.'

Maybe I should leave it, but I can't. If I stop now, I may never have the courage again. 'Ethan,' I turn his face towards me. 'I want you to find someone and get married and have children. You deserve to have the life you want.'

Even in the half light I can see the tears in his eyes. I wipe one away and kiss his cheek. Why can't I pretend to love Ethan? It hurts me to see the pain in his eyes. I almost take it all back.

'Neva, please ...' His voice cracks and he can't finish his sentence.

112

'I'm sorry, Ethan.' I kiss his cheek and taste the salty sweetness of his tears.

He stands and tucks in his shirt. He bends over and kisses the top of my head. 'You're tired. This is all too much. I shouldn't push you. Take your time. It's OK.'

It's as if he hasn't heard a word I've said, but he's gone before I can work up the courage to break up with him all over again.

Later I dig out my journal. I sit on my bed and print Effie's name after Nicoline's at the bottom of my quickly growing List of The Missing. It feels as if everyone has surrendered and I'm the only one still fighting. Our secret rebellion was the only thing that gave me hope. I won't let Sanna give up on us either. I read each name on my list. Ruth Laverne Adams. I say her name out loud. She is the first on my list and the reason I'm still fighting. I promise Grandma that I won't give up.

CHAPTER FOURTEEN

I 'm tired of being pulled in so many directions. What Sanna needs. What Braydon wants. What Ethan asks. I decide to take a hiatus from all of them. I stop answering their calls and, because Mum tells them I am grounded, they stop calling.

Now I'm thankful for my job. Even without GovNet, I'm in the perfect position to find out why more and more people are disappearing. But I've got to be patient and smart. This is not the time for a sledgehammer. To open the Protectosphere, I need a pin. My new strategy is to poke a million tiny holes. The first thing I need to do is earn my dad's trust. I need him to believe I'm the best, most efficient government employee ever. In other words, I mimic Effie.

'Neva!' Dad bellows from his office. I don't have Effie's sixth sense for when Dad needs something, and it annoys him. Everything seems to annoy him these days.

I spring to my feet and am standing at attention in front of his desk before he can yell for me a second time. 'Yes?' I have to soothe my urge to rebel at being treated like a servant. Now Dad has to do most of Effie's job. All I can do are the menial, unimportant tasks, but I see every job as an opportunity. Getting his third cup of coffee from the cafeteria is an opportunity to explore another corridor of this massive catacomb. Delivering Dad's stack of mail is a chance to figure out who does what around here. I read every memo and every

114

file I can get my hands on. I can't be too eager, or Dad will get suspicious.

'This damn thing.' He whacks his InfoScreen on the top of his desk.

'Dad, you'll break it.' I swoop in and take the handheld device from him. It's his most prized possession. He salvaged it from his dad's belongings.

'It's not working again.' He rummages through the files on his desk as if he's looking for something. His phone rings. I go to answer it. He snatches the phone from its cradle. 'What?' He takes a breath and starts again. 'Dr Adams.' He pauses. 'I'm sorry I can't hear you … I'm losing you … I can't …' He throws the phone across the room. 'How am I supposed to work if everything keeps breaking?' he huffs.

'Dad, are you OK?' I retrieve the phone and put it back, careful not to get too close to him.

'Sorry, Neva.' He rakes his hand through his horseshoe of hair, and it's as if I'm watching an actor switch into character. He sniffs and straightens. 'I need you to take my InfoScreen to Allan in the annex and see if he can fix it,' he says calmly, back in control.

I turn the device over in my hands. It fits neatly in my palm. I've never held it before. Its screen is normally illuminated with words or images or both. He keeps a library full of documents in this tiny thing. It really is quite amazing. Most people have never seen one of these. 'OK.' I turn to go. He forgets I have no idea who Allan is or where the annex is. I could ask, but I don't want to agitate him further. It also gives me a chance to ask someone else questions and explore the building.

'Thanks, Neva,' he calls as I exit. That's a first. Another tiny success and another pinprick in the Protectosphere.

I leave the Information Service wing and look for a friendly face. Most people keep their heads down and don't make eye contact. I head towards the cafeteria. I've learned that I have more success getting answers outside of the Information Services wing. Everyone knows I am Dr Adams's daughter there and seems a bit wary of me. I've also discovered that people are more open to my inquiries when they are away from their desks, and the lower their rank the more likely it is that they will chat with me instead of just answering one question. I spot a lanky, grey-headed man in greenish grey coveralls: Tim, according to his name badge. Perfect.

'Ya want the tech graveyard,' he says when I tell him I'm looking for Allan in the annex. 'Follow me. You'll never find it on your own.'

I have to skip a few steps to keep up with him. He manoeuvres the complex like a mouse in pursuit of cheese. 'What ya need the annex for?' Tim asks, still snaking through the complex.

'My da— Dr Adams needs Allan to fix his InfoScreen.' I show him the device cupped in my palm.

He stops and takes it from me. 'I ain't seen one of these thingy whatsits.' He flips it over and taps on the screen. 'My grandpa said he had one of them. He said everyone used to have 'em. I thought he was fibbing, but he swore it was a phone and ya could listen to music, watch movies, and play games on it.'

Everyone of my grandma's generation likes to reminisce about the good old days when life was simpler. They had gadgets and technology to do everything. She would tell me stories of machines that looked almost human and were like a secretary, chauffeur, and maid all wrapped into one. She said her grandparents could take trips without ever leaving their house; she called it a virtual something. My grandma even swore that people before The Terror could fly in big metal birds. I didn't think she was lying exactly, but it's hard to believe.

'This baby's dead as a doorknob.' Tim shakes the InfoScreen next to his ear as if he's listening for loose parts.

I take it back from him. 'I hope not. Dr Adams won't be happy about that.'

He starts walking. 'Yeah, from what I hear Dr Adams ain't happy about much these days.'

I catch up to him. 'Why do you say that?'

'Well, that pinched-faced assistant of his got the axe. She'd bless him before he even thought to sneeze.'

I laugh. It's true.

'I heard he lost his temper over something at a Council meeting the other day.' We take a sharp left and then another right.

'Really?'

'Yeah, he's not one for yelling, but I guess he nearly blew a gasket.' We cut through a conference room. 'Almost there.' We take a sky bridge to another building.

'What was he so mad about?' I ask. That's not like my dad at all. He prides himself on being calm, cool, and collected.

'You think they tell people like me something like that, little lady?'

'You seem to know an awful lot.'

'That's what you get when you keep your ears open and your mouth shut. Ya got two of these' – he points to his ears – 'and one of these' – he smiles, and I notice he's missing a tooth – 'for a reason. And I think I've said too much.'

We take stairs all the way to the basement, and finally Tim stops. He nods toward the sign on the door: TECHNOLOGY RECYCLING CENTRE. 'Yeah, I know what it says, but, trust me, it's where gadgets go to die. I'll wait for you here,' he says, resting his back against the wall. 'Big Al don't like me much.'

I open the door, and a buzzer sounds.

'Can I help you?' a squeaky voice calls from some unknown place.

I'm too busy taking it all in to answer. The room spans two stories and is about the size of a football field. A counter stretches from one wall to the other and serves as a barricade, only letting people walk a few feet into the space.

'Can I help you?' The voice is closer this time.

'Um, yes,' I say and then speak louder. 'Dr Adams sent me. He needs his InfoScreen fixed.'

Floor-to-ceiling cages are packed with large, flat, black screens. Bins the size of dumpsters are littered with tiny capsules. There are piles of computers and cables coiled into mountains. The room is lit up like Christmas with tiny lights flickering and screens flashing with a strobe effect. The room hums, buzzes, and beeps. It's stimulation overload.

A man a foot shorter than I am seems to materialize in front of me. 'Can I help you?' His voice sounds like a hinge in need of oil.

'Are you Allan?'

He nods. He has thick-rimmed glasses. One half is a black rectangle and the other is a red oval. The two halves are taped together at the bridge of his nose. He's got some sort of electronic band that circles his head. He's so thin his translucent skin seems alive with blue veins and knobby bones.

I hand him the InfoScreen.

'You work for Dr Adams.' He sizes up me and then the device. He presses a panel on the counter and a screen pops up. 'Your name?'

'Neva Adams.'

He waves his hand over the counter and the image of a keyboard appears. He types my name on the flat surface.

'That's pretty cool,' I say.

'What seems to be the problem?' He lays the InfoScreen on the counter and keeps typing.

'Um, I don't know. It doesn't work.'

'Helpful.' The word is dripping with sarcasm. He pushes more buttons. A thin white line moves across Dad's InfoScreen. I can't tell where the light is coming from. It could even be projected from Allan's headband for all I know.

'What is all this stuff?' I ask, and nod to the warehouse behind him.

'Parts, basically,' he mumbles, paying more attention to the InfoScreen than to me.

I notice a cage full of surveillance cameras. My blood runs cold. There are enough cameras in there to cover every square inch of the capital. 'Are you fixing those?' I point.

He doesn't look up. 'No more parts.'

Is he saying that the government is losing its ability to watch us? 'Really?'

'Yep. I do the best I can, but with no new components and not many like me who know this old technology . . .' His voice trails off as the scan finishes and his computer beeps. 'Tell Dr Adams I'll have this back to him in a few days. He needs to back up everything on here. I'm not going to be able to patch this up for him much longer.'

'OK.'

The InfoScreen flickers on. Allan's bony fingers tap feverishly on the screen. 'Anything else?' he asks when he realizes I'm still there.

'No, thanks.' I slip out the door.

Tim is still waiting. His eyes are closed and I think he's snoring. When the door to the tech graveyard clicks shut, Tim's eyes flutter open, as if he's a machine flickering to life.

'Pretty amazing, huh?' Tim says, stifling a yawn.

'I don't know what half of that stuff is.'

'Progress.' He laughs. We start back the way we came. 'They want you to believe that the less technology we use the better off we all are,' he whispers. 'Poppycock. I used to love all my thingy whatsits.'

'But aren't they using more technology to watch us?' I ask, feeling like I can trust him.

'Nah. That's what they want you to believe. Half those fancy cameras they have looking down at us don't work.'

'What about tracking devices?' As soon as I ask it, I wish I hadn't.

He stops dead in his tracks. He looks around, swivelling as if he's a surveillance camera. 'Why'd ya ask something like that?'

I shrug.

'They got the technology, but they don't always use it, if you know what I mean.'

I don't.

Reading the confusion in my face, he continues, 'They implant devices, but they don't always track people.'

'Really?' His words drill tiny holes into the government's cool façade.

'They don't have the people or the parts to do half the stuff they tell us they are doing.'

I give him a big hug.

'What's that for?' he asks when I've set him free.

'Nothing.' I smile. 'Just thanks. I'll find my own way back from here.'

He raises his eyebrows in disbelief. 'Suit yourself. I've known better mortals than you to get lost for days in this place.'

'I'm not feeling very mortal at the moment,' I call as I race down the hall. The iron grip I thought the government had on me, on all of us, has loosened just a little.

CHAPTER FIFTEEN

D ad's been giving me more responsibility and more space. The last few weeks, since Effie disappeared, have been torture. I only speak when spoken to. I do what I'm told, when I'm told, as efficiently as I possibly can. Without Sanna, Braydon and Ethan in my life, all I have is my job – and my secret mission. I decide to take my spy efforts up a notch. I sit at Effie's desk with Dad's office door open a crack. He doesn't seem to notice. I watch him as he sits at his desk reading or staring off into space. He seems more and more distracted. He will ask for things and then forget that he asked when I show up with the requested item. He starts sentences that he can't finish. Human Resources sends over replacements for Effie, but between my sabotage and Dad's demands, they don't last for more than a few days.

I come to work with him every morning and leave with him every evening. I time how long it takes him to use the bathroom – one five-minute break in the morning and one in the afternoon, like clockwork. Every time I'm in his office my eyes are drawn to the back corner where I saw him walk through the wall. Nothing looks suspicious, but I know what I saw. Today he's given me a stack of books to re-shelve in his office. I wait until it's nearly time for his morning bathroom break. I put on the lab coat and white gloves I'm supposed to wear when I'm in his office. I go about my work quietly. He checks the clock. He glances at me as if he might ask me to leave, but I pretend to be hard at work. He slips out of his office. I think he's hoping I don't notice.

I don't take time to lay down my armload of books. I charge to the back corner of his office. I start pushing and prying each panel, glancing at the open office door every few seconds. I press the wooden trim at hand height and feel it give. I push it. Nothing. I slip a fingernail in the crack between the trim and the wood panelling and it slides. I can hardly breathe. I bend down and see a tiny keyhole. I quickly slide the panel back in place and am shelving the last book when Dad returns a minute later.

I finally know how to get into his secret space. I thought there might be a computer code or a magic word, but even Dad's security is ancient. Now all I've got to do is find the key. I keep my eyes open. I watch his every move.

One night when he's packing up to go home, I study him. I've learned most of his rituals. He straightens the file folders on his desk and thumbs through the title tabs. He stows a few files in his top right office drawer. That's when I know he's ready to go, so I usually start packing up too. But this afternoon, I watch him. He takes off his lab coat. He doesn't like to wear it outside of the office. Might bring unwanted toxins back in. He takes something from his lab coat pocket, something he pinches between his thumb and finger. If I wasn't watching so closely, I might have missed it. He tucks whatever it is in his waistcoat pocket. The pocket is the perfect size for a tiny key that fits a tiny lock. That must be it. It takes every ounce of strength to keep from leaping out of my chair and punching the air. Inside my head a symphony swells to crescendo.

Even after all that's happened, my first instinct is to call Sanna and tell her everything I've discovered, to share my little

122

victory with her. But I can't. She doesn't want to know any more. Maybe when I have something more concrete she'll listen and change her mind. Every thought of Sanna leads to thoughts of Braydon. No matter how hard I try, how I throw myself into work, he always lingers in my mind.

I'm beginning to think I'm never going to get the chance to test my theory about the key and Dad's secret room. Then a few weeks later I hear Dad talking to a colleague about some big emergency meeting scheduled for this afternoon. His InfoScreen is still broken, so I collect the books he needs for his meeting. He is flustered. He keeps getting phone calls, which is unusual. About ten minutes before the meeting, I stack the books in front of him. I've got to orchestrate this just right. My goal is to hurry him out of the office so he forgets to lock it.

'Shouldn't you be going?' I ask.

He checks the brass clock on his desk, the one with the funny mix of letters instead of numbers, lots of X's and I's. 'You're right, Neva,' he says, organizing the papers in front of him and tucking them into a leather portfolio.

As he stands, I gesture to his lab coat and then help him slip out of it. Before he can remember to transfer the key to his waistcoat pocket, I hang his lab coat on the coat rack.

'Have a good meeting,' I say as he hustles out the door, his arms laden with books and papers. I watch him scurry down the hall. Then I slip back into his office and lock the door behind me. I take the tiny key from his lab coat pocket.

I stand in front of the secret panel. I can't get the key into the lock. The tapping of the key aiming and missing and sliding seems to echo in my dad's wood-panelled office. I wipe the sweat from my forehead on the sleeve of my white lab coat. Dad and I have been getting along, which makes me feel majorly guilty about what I'm going to do.

The key slips from my fingers. The white gloves don't help

much. I should take them off, but I can't risk fingerprints. I must calm down. I pick up the key and squeeze it in my fist, letting the ridges dig into my palm. Dad said earlier he'd be in the meeting all afternoon. No one comes in here. No one dares to disturb Dr George Adams. I walk across the room to check the office door. It is locked. I wedge a chair under the doorknob. I can't be too careful. Dad will flip if he returns and can't get the door open, but it's better than him finding me in his secret room.

I concentrate, slip the key into the lock, and turn. The wooden panel clicks open. Warm musty air sneaks through the crack. With one finger I push the panel open further. The space is only big enough for one person to slip through sideways. I sidestep through the opening. A dim overhead light flickers on. I whip around, but the door must have triggered the lights, if you want to call them that. The room is barely illuminated. It's about the same size as Dad's office but much sparser. One wall is covered with metal filing cabinets, another wall has a glass display case; the final two walls are bookshelves. A large metal table is centred in the room.

I hear a faint click and air begins to circulate. My presence in the room has altered the balance of this space. To my right I see a control panel with tiny green and red lights. Everything about the room is monitored: light, temperature, humidity, and sound. As I move closer, my steps and breath seem to make the green and red lights twinkle. Sweat is dripping down my back. I don't want to set off any alarms. I study the control panel – there's nothing to indicate a security system. This is an archive. These monitors are to maintain old documents, not guard the room's contents. I take a tentative step forward and then another.

The books on the shelves look exactly like the books in his office. I wonder what makes them so special. I pick a volume at random and gently separate it from its neighbours. I don't even know how to pronounce the name on the spine. The book seems to vibrate in my trembling hands. I lay it on the table and crack it open. The pages in front of me show a landscape of some mythical place covered in snow. The images look like photographs, but they must be computer simulations. One image has icy white boulders jutting out of the ocean. Another has strange black-and-white bird creatures. I excitedly flip to the first few pages, expecting to read some fantasy tale, but instead the book reads like a history book about a land mass with a funny long name on the south of something called a globe.

I pull out another book. This book doesn't have any pictures, and the words are unfamiliar. I recognize the letters, but they form no words I've ever seen. Some words have funny hash marks over a vowel or silly looking squiggles under the letter *c*. Another language? It's almost too much to take in. I put both books back where I found them.

I don't have time to study each book. I don't even know what I'm looking for. My heart is racing. I walk to the display cases. Right in the centre is a big ball. The ball is decorated with green shapes in a field of blue. I recognize one green shape; it looks like the outline of Homeland. I lean in as close as I can without touching the glass. But the shape has another name on it. That's strange. It looks so tiny on this big ball.

I survey the other items in the display case, mostly old, yellowing books with frayed or missing covers. There is also a collection of devices that look like Dad's InfoScreen, only smaller. I slowly turn in a circle. I feel a tightness in my chest. I think I've discovered that my grandma was right. There was life outside the Protectosphere – a whole round ball more. But what *was* and what *is* are two very different things.

I want to stop and look at everything, read everything, touch everything, but there's no time. Think. The books are too old to give me any current information. The exhibit cases are locked. I skirt around the table and read the labels on the filing cabinets. Each drawer is labelled with a number and a letter. This coding makes no sense. It's as if the answers are right here in front of me and I don't know what questions to ask. Just do something, I tell myself, but the adrenaline coursing through my veins makes it hard to think straight.

I pick a drawer at random and open it. I flick through the old green file folders. The papers in the files are yellow and thin with words that have nearly faded.

I'm breathing faster. My sweaty hands are making my cotton gloves damp. I leave a smudge on one piece of paper as I return it to its folder. I need to calm down. I go to the first drawer of the filing cabinet and check the very first file. Fragments and dust is all that remains of whatever was in the folder. These must be the oldest files. If the files are ordered chronologically, then I need the last one, the last piece of information. The last three drawers are empty. The next one has four hanging files. I pull the last file out and lay it on the metal table. My hands shake and the file rattles as I open it.

The file is lying open on the table, but the rattling continues. It's the office door. Someone is turning the doorknob. Oh, my God! My heart stops.

I flip the file closed. But I can't leave empty-handed. I can't take the whole file. My dad would certainly miss an entire file. I open it again and remove the last sheet of paper. I fold it several times and stick it in my bra.

Now someone is knocking on the door.

I put the file away and glance around the room. Everything looks exactly as I found it, or I think it does. I slide out the door and pull it shut behind me. I push it once to make sure it's closed.

'Neva!' It's my dad and now he's shouting. 'Neva, are you in there?'

Think, Neva. How am I going to explain why the door was

locked? I pull two books from the shelves as I pass. I throw one on the leather sofa and one on the floor, accidentally ripping its cover. I yank off my lab coat and gloves and toss them behind me. I race to the coat rack and slip the key back in the pocket of his white coat. I remove the chair from where I've wedged it under the doorknob. I rumple my hair and pinch both cheeks. I half close my eyes as I open the door and answer, 'Oh, hey, Dad. Sorry.'

He pushes the door open and I slowly walk to the sofa and plop down. I pick up my coat and gloves.

'Why was that door locked?' he demands, walking the perimeter of the room.

'Yeah, I'm sorry ... really,' I say, and make a big production of fluffing the cushions on the sofa. 'I finished all my work. I was reading up' – I glance at the cover of the book – 'on *The Standardization of the Status Quo.*' I rack my brain for some titbit I learned in history class. 'Uniformity equals equality,' I say, recalling a familiar quote from one of our founding fathers, Dr Benjamin L. Smith maybe.

'Do you think I'm an idiot?' He's standing near the entrance to the secret archives.

'No,' I say, and fake a yawn. I stretch my arms over my head. I lower them when they start to shake.

He walks towards me. 'What were you doing exactly?'

'I started reading and then, well, I got a bit sleepy, so I thought I should lock the door. I didn't want anyone to catch me napping.' I scoot to the far end of the sofa.

He picks up the book from the floor, noticing the ripped cover.

'Oh, about that. Sorry. It slipped out of my hands when I dozed off, you know.' I go to take it from him, but he holds it closer to his chest and strokes the ripped cover.

'I'm very disappointed in you, Neva.' His words hollow out a place inside me. He finds the empty slots in the bookshelf for the two books and slips them into place. 'Please leave.'

'But ...' Why do I want to apologize? I want to make him understand. The grimace on his face looks as if he's in physical pain.

He runs his hands over the spines of the books. 'Just go home.' He bows his head as if he might pray.

How could he lie to me my whole life with stories of our perfect history? Now I know there's more, so much more that we don't know, and yet I feel as if I've lost something that I can never, ever get back.

CHAPTER SIXTEEN

'Meet me at your mum's,' I whisper into the phone. I walked two blocks before I felt safe using a phone booth. Even now, I keep turning in half circles, anchored to the phone, making sure no one is behind me.

'What, Nev, is that you?' Sanna's voice comes in loud bursts between the static. She says something else, but it's lost in the crackling air.

'Meet me at your mum's.' I speak a little louder and more slowly, hoping that my message won't get lost.

'Nev, great! You're ungrounded. Woohoo! Man, have I missed you. But no can do right now, I'm—'

'Just do it.' The static suddenly clears. 'Just you. No excuses. This is important.'

Sanna finds me resting against her mum's tombstone. 'Here.' I take the article from where I tucked it into my bra. The sweat, folding, and friction have turned the sheet of paper into sixteen jagged squares. I hand them to her.

'Whatcha got there?' She kneels down and places the pieces on her mother's grave. I sit next to her. I carefully arrange the squares to re-form the sheet of paper I stole from my dad's archive. I feel bad about the lying, the stealing, and the look on my dad's face. He didn't need to tell me he was disappointed. I see that look in his eyes all the time. But this time it was worse – much worse.

'I think it's an ancient newspaper,' I say quietly.

'A what?' She touches the crumbling paper.

'I stole this from my dad's secret archives.'

'His *what*?' Sanna looks at me in amazement. 'You stole something from the history guru?'

I nod. 'My dad almost caught me,' I say, and tell her about my heart-stopping escape from the archives.

'Nev, I thought we agreed ...' She moves closer to get a better look.

'Read it.' I should feel proud of myself. But this feels wrong. Even if he's a jerk, he's my dad. We read between the ripped spaces. The paper and the print have degraded. The headline is the only thing that's easy to read: COUNTRY CLOSES ITS BORDER TO PEOPLE AND IDEAS. The rest of the words are fuzzy as if water damaged. The photo under the headline is only a blur of grey dots.

The story, what we can read of it, talks about a mass exodus. People were thrown out or chose to leave when this country planned to seal itself off. I find myself scanning ahead, trying to find out more about the outside, but the story is more interested in what is being trapped inside. One scientist wagered that the experiment would only last a few years, until certain natural resources were depleted. Another doctor predicted that inbreeding and illness would eventually cause the country to re-engage. Sanna and I glance at each other when we read that.

We recognize one name: Dr Benjamin L. Smith. In the article, he defends the years, technology, money, and manpower necessary to protect his country and its way of life. 'Our culture is in danger of extinction. No cost is too great to ensure we are not swallowed by globalization.'

'What's 'glow-ball-a-zation'?' Sanna asks.

I shrug. 'Sounds like a disease.'

'You think that's why they closed us off?' Sanna goes on.
'You think everyone out there's dead of globalization?'
She shrugs.

The last half of the article has been ripped away. I run my finger along the article's jagged border and wonder what we are missing.

'What's this date all about? December 15, 2051,' Sanna reads. 'How can the article be from the future?'

But I know the answer. My grandma told me once. 'When we sealed the Protectosphere, we reset the calendar to 01/01/01. Life must have existed for two thousand and fifty one years before we sealed ourselves off.'

'Nev, this is a-maz-ing!' Sanna puts her arm around my shoulders. I wonder what Braydon would think. I try to shove him out of my thoughts.

'It proves there was something outside,' I say, pushing the puzzle pieces into a pile.

'What those people in the article said is happening. Our resources *are* dwindling. We *are* getting sicker,' Sanna points out.

'I could get in real trouble if this gets out. My dad could get fired or . . .' – I look at the scraps of paper – 'worse.' I lie back on the cool grass and Sanna stretches out beside me. We stare up at the Protectosphere. It looks different somehow, cloudier now that we know more about our history. All we are told is that we closed our borders after The Terror. But our founding fathers kicked people out. People outside were alive and well when we sealed the Protectosphere.

I sit up after a long time. 'You have to keep this for me.' I shove the scraps of paper at Sanna. I know it's asking a lot. 'Just until I can figure out what to do next.'

'This changes everything, doesn't it, Nev?' Sanna scoops up the paper and cradles it gently in her hands. 'It's proof.'

I nod. 'This is huge. Hide it somewhere safe. You can't

show this to anyone or tell anyone about it.' We share a meaningful look. She's back. Rebel Sanna is back.

I wander around until after ten. I want to hide in the shadows, but my fear keeps me tethered to the light. I move from one light source to the next. These streets that I've walked hundreds of times don't feel the same. The air that rushes past smells unfamiliar. I am lost even though I'm standing outside my house. I wait for a light in my parents' room. In the Adams's house, when Grandpa's old mantel clock strikes ten, then – as if programmed – my parents go to bed. Mum finds me and kisses me on the forehead. My dad calls from somewhere that I should 'sleep tight'. I'm never sure what that means exactly.

The light in my parents' bedroom window comes on. A silhouette steps into the frame; I can tell by the slump of the shoulders that it's my mum. She looks around before closing the curtains. She's probably looking for me. I wait ten more minutes before I head to the front door.

As I reach for the doorknob, the door is yanked open and I nearly stumble into my dad with the force of it. He's looming there.

'How could you?'

I regain my footing. I'm overcome with the urge to run.

He walks into the living room. I'm supposed to follow. I shuffle after him. I expect to see my dad commanding the centre of the room, expanding to fill the space. But, instead, he sits on the sofa, hunched forward, collapsing in on himself. 'How could you put me in this position?' he asks again, but the power has drained from his voice.

I don't know what to say.

'I know you went into the archives.'

'I don't know what you're talking—'

He shakes his head. 'Please don't make it worse by lying to

me. I know that room. I can tell when it's been violated.'

'I'm sorry, Dad.' The words slip out.

'You shouldn't have gone in there.' He doesn't look up. 'You can't come back to work. I don't know how I'm going to explain this without raising too many questions, but I'll think of something.'

You always do, I want to say. He's a master of making up stories.

'Why, Neva?' He absent-mindedly twists a lock of his hair around and around his finger.

'I can't believe you keep information about what's outside locked away.' I wait for him to tell me I'm wrong. To tell me he's not part of the conspiracy to keep us here.

'I should have got rid of it a long time ago. I was supposed to, but it's history, *our* history.'

'What is all that stuff?' Our eyes meet for a second.

'It's from before: a few books, a few artefacts. Nothing really. Things the government has confiscated over the years.'

It's the first time my dad has ever admitted there was a before. I want to know more, but I don't ask.

'Let me make this perfectly clear.' He begins to push himself off the sofa, but then he sinks back down. 'Forget about everything you saw in there. I've destroyed it all.'

'What?'

'You gave me no choice. I can't risk anyone finding out about those documents, those things. Not now.' He sighs. 'Neva, you can't know ... I hope you never know ... what I've done to protect you.'

I am ashamed. He destroyed generations of secrets to protect me. That's what he means, isn't it? He doesn't know. He hasn't guessed that I have stolen something. I wish I could take it back. Maybe I could have trusted him. Maybe he could have learned to trust me.

'Dad, things are getting worse.' I clear my throat and speak up. 'They are. I know you don't want to see it. The government is—'

'That's enough,' he shouts over me.

'Is everything all right down there?' Mum yells from the top of the stairs.

'We're fine, Lily,' Dad quickly calls back. 'Go back to bed.'

'Neva?' Mum calls.

Dad glares at me. I get the message loud and clear: do not upset your mother.

'I'm home, Mum,' I shout. 'I'm fine.'

'OK, don't you two be up too late.' We hear her retreat to the bedroom.

Dad waits to hear the bedroom door shut. He pulls himself to his full height and faces me. 'Neva, don't you ever say anything against the government again.' He seizes me by the shoulders. His eyes, usually an intense black, seem to have softened to a muddy brown and are pleading with me. 'Do you hear me?' He's shaking me now and my head flops back and forth in agreement. 'I can't protect you. I can't protect anyone any more.'

He releases me, but my body is still vibrating. 'You're scaring me,' I whisper.

He's scared too. I can see it in his eyes. He backs away. 'Get to bed.'

As I head for my bedroom, the floor and the ground beneath it feel less solid.

CHAPTER SEVENTEEN

I wake up to shouting. I sit bolt upright in my bed. My curtains are ringed with light, so it must be morning. It takes me a while to realize the voices belong to my parents. I have never heard them argue before. I can't make out words, and I don't even try to eavesdrop. I know too many secrets already. I don't want to know any more.

Mum comes into my bedroom after Dad has left for work. She sits on the edge of my bed. She's in her light-blue, fluffy bathrobe and mismatched slippers. She doesn't say a word.

'What's the matter?' I ask. She squints at me as if she doesn't understand the words that are coming out of my mouth.

'I'm sorry the job with your father didn't work out.' She clasps and unclasps her hands in her lap.

'I heard you and Dad arguing,' I confess.

She reaches into the pocket of her bathrobe and hands me a sheet of paper. It's an official letter from the Minister of Health. I have to read it and reread it. It's a lot of governmental mumbo jumbo. I think I know what's it's saying, but it can't be.

'Mum?' I need her to make sense of this. 'Is this saying . . .'

'That we are getting a baby? Yes.'

I scoot as far away from her as I can. 'Why didn't you tell me you and Dad were trying to adopt?' Dad's secret archives and now this. My reality is altering at an alarming rate.

'We didn't apply,' she says flatly.

'So you're telling me the government's giving away babies? I know you and Dad wanted another baby. I know you tried.'

Her face creases with sadness, but she fights back the tears. 'We wanted a brother or sister for you. Dad was getting a lot of pressure from the government. Bigger families have more opportunities, but we stopped trying and accepted that one perfect child was enough.' She touches me on the chin and tries to smile.

'So then why . . .'

'I've heard rumours about patriot families being asked to raise unwanted children.'

'Who doesn't want children? The government subsidizes and practically begs people to have kids.' I fold the letter and hand it back to her. She knows more than she's telling. 'What is it? What's the matter?'

'This is too much.' She waves the letter in the air.

'Don't you want another baby?'

'Look around. Things are getting worse. I don't want to bring another child into this . . .' Her voice trails off.

'Why don't you call the Minister of Health and tell her you don't want the baby?'

She shakes her head. 'Your dad's on the Council. And even if he wasn't, you can't really refuse a direct request.'

'How does this work? Where does the baby come from?'

'It's best not to ask too many questions,' she says.

I think we don't ask enough.

'So, I guess this means you are going to have a baby brother or sister,' she adds.

'Whether we like it or not,' I mutter. I want to tell her about the archives and what I discovered, but she looks so tired. She doesn't need another revelation today.

'I'm going out later,' she says, and heads to the door.

'Can I come with you?' I want to feel five years old, to reach up and grab my mum's hand and walk down the street feeling her tug me into a shop. I want to twirl in a frilly dress in front of a mirror for her. Our arms will swing together as we walk, and we'll eat ice cream cones and let the ice cream drip down our chins. She won't yell at me when the chocolate ice cream leaves brown spots on my shirt. We will come home and have a day's worth of secrets to keep from Dad.

Her back is to me. 'No, Neva, this is something I have to do for myself.'

I want to ask where's she's going. But everyone has secrets. She said so herself. So she leaves and I bury myself under my covers – my own personal Protectosphere.

There's a pounding in my head, in my dreams. Slowly I realize that this rhythm is outside of me.

'Nev.' Sanna's not just knocking on my bedroom door, she's playing her own special drum solo. She knows where we hide the spare key. Dad hates it when Sanna lets herself in, but, to me and Mum, Sanna's family.

I glance at the clock. It's nearly noon. All I want to do is go back to sleep. 'Give me a minute,' I whine.

But she doesn't. She bursts into the room. 'Rise and shine.' She looks down her nose at the grubby and probably slightly smelly mess that is her best friend. 'What's with the zombie routine?'

'I said, give me a minute.' I snuggle under my blankets, enjoying the weight of the quilt and the bubble of warmth.

She rips my blankets away. The cold air swirls under my big grey shirt. Goosebumps dot my arms. 'No time. Get dressed.' She throws a pair of jeans from the floor to me.

'Why?'

She searches for a pair of matching shoes. She gives up and hands me one pink and one grey tennis shoe. She opens my closet and pulls out a grey shirt. 'Here. Wear this.' More clothes are shoved at me. 'Nev, you want an engraved invitation? Get moving.' There's an urgency to her actions. She's rummaging in the pile of jewellery on my dresser. She loops my watch on one finger and the snowflake necklace on another.

'I'm not going anywhere.' I scratch at a crusty white spot on the leg of my jeans.

'Not like that, you're not.' She pulls off my shirt and throws it in the corner. I cover my bare breasts. 'Please, Nev, I've seen them before. Not all that impressive.'

I bend down and open the bottom drawer of my nightstand. I untangle a light blue bra and beige cotton underwear from the mass. I slip off my old underwear and put on the clean pair.

She's trying to act carefree, but I can tell she's *trying*, not just *being*. 'What's wrong?'

She waves off my question. 'Nice tat,' Sanna says, reaching toward my snowflake tattoo.

'Get off,' I swat her hand.

'Must say I do good work.'

'It hurt like hell,' I say, remembering the millions of tiny pinpricks. It took two hours to make my one-inch square tattoo, but Sanna was right: it looks pretty amazing.

I finish getting dressed. 'I don't really feel like going out.'

'I don't care.' Sanna slips my snowflake necklace over my head.

And it feels almost like old times, that effortless give and take, before Braydon created a wedge between us. I decide to play along.

Before I know it, we are at the train station. We take the two most secluded seats on the train.

'Sanna, where are we going?' I ask.

'I can't tell you.' She scans the passengers on the train.

'Why?' Now she's got me checking to see who might be watching us.

'It's mega top secret.' She's nervous; she keeps looking around. She's trying to act like her old self, but something's wrong.

'Sanna?'

She settles into her seat. She tucks her bare feet underneath her. It's as if she's been unplugged.

'What is it, Sanna? Talk to me.'

'My brother.' Her voice catches in her throat. 'I haven't heard from him in a few days.'

'Oh, Sanna, you know he has to go dark sometimes.'

'Yeah, he's disappeared before when the police were looking for him or something. But it's different this time.'

'You can't reach him whenever you want to, can you? I thought he was always the one to make contact.' Her brother is like this mythical creature. I haven't seen him since he went underground.

'I've asked around and no one knows anything.' She draws her knees to her chest, curling herself into a tight ball. 'We have a signal, you know. I've signalled and signalled and signalled, and nothing. That's not like him. He never ever hasn't come when I've needed him.'

Another Missing. 'He'll turn up. He always does.' I try to sound reassuring, as if I believe it.

'Yeah, you're right.' She brightens.

'Now, where are we going?' I bounce in my seat and try to lighten the mood.

She scoots closer to me and whispers, 'We are meeting some friends of my mum.'

'Why is that so hush-hush?' I say in my normal voice.

Sanna shushes me and pulls me closer. 'We have similar interests. I asked around; you know, looking for my brother. Seems as if we aren't the only ones planning a revolution.'

'What?' I feel a twinge of excitement.

'You were right, Nev. We can't stop. We have to do something. I figure if you can steal from the government—'

Now I shush her. 'What about Braydon?' His name tastes sweet and sour on my tongue.

'I've got to do this for my brother. Braydon doesn't have to know, right?' Now Sanna and I have a secret from Braydon. My web of lies continues to grow. Soon I won't know what the truth is.

Once we exit the station, she practically sprints. 'Where are we going?' I say, breathless.

'The Square,' she pants, and takes a sharp right.

I recognize where we are. 'Wouldn't it be faster to go that way?' I point left.

'I want to make sure no one follows us.' She speeds up. I'm not sure our evasive manoeuvres would fool anyone. She stops abruptly as we approach the Square. 'Here.' She thrusts a pair of sunglasses at me. 'Incognito.'

I almost laugh. Does she really think a pair of sunglasses is a great disguise? I put them on. Now she's walking really slowly, almost sauntering. The Square is swarming with people. Some are sitting near the fountain. Others are passing through on the way to the National Museum or the State Court, which border opposite sides of the Square. In the centre of the Square stands a bronze statue of Dr Benjamin L. Smith, who towers twenty feet high and looks down humbly upon the uniform masses.

'There they are,' she whispers. 'The one in the blue shirt and the one with the big yellow handbag.'

We approach two average-looking middle-aged women. Not my idea of revolutionaries.

'Sanna, look at you.' Both women coo and fuss over her.

The woman in blue introduces herself, Senga, and her friend, Carson. They look familiar. Maybe I met them at Sanna's mum's funeral, but that was so long ago.

'Congratulations on graduating,' Senga says. 'Studying science at the National Institute for Research and Development. Your mother would be so proud.'

Sanna shrugs off their attention. 'Yep, I'm all adult-like now. This is my friend, Neva—'

I clear my throat before she gives my last name.

Carson extends her hand. 'You must be Lily's daughter. She—'

Senga elbows her in the ribs before I have the time to shake her hand. The two exchange a knowing glance.

'You know my mum?' I ask. She's never mentioned them to me before.

'Yes,' Carson says.

'No,' Senga interjects.

'I mean, no,' Carson corrects. 'I know of Lily Adams, of course. Who doesn't? And Neva is such an unusual name.'

Carson's hands never stop moving. She fiddles with a loose button on her shirt then begins to bite her fingernails. Senga's eyes dart from side to side. They are making me nervous. I tug on Sanna's sleeve. I'm ready to go. Sanna brushes me aside.

'You have some information for us?' Sanna asks.

Senga nods. She whispers, 'Silent demonstration here tomorrow.'

'What do you want us to do?' Sanna asks without moving her lips. I understand, but Senga and Carson clearly don't. She repeats her question, but she still sounds like a stroke victim.

'Meet here at eleven thirty. Senga and I will be operating a sandwich cart. One of you come up and order a sandwich,' Carson explains.

This is ridiculous. These women are acting out some bad B movie. They don't look like revolutionaries. I'm not sure they could even rebel against hen-pecked husbands. Or maybe that's the genius of it. They naturally have the perfect disguises.

Carson continues, 'We'll give you some flyers. The demonstration starts at noon. You'll see what to do.'

'This is for you.' Sanna slyly hands a manila envelope to Senga.

'What is this?' she asks, and looks around again to see if anyone is watching.

'It's an article from outside, from when the Protectosphere was sealed.'

'Sanna, no!' I reach for the envelope, but Senga tucks it into her handbag.

'Nev,' Sanna says sternly. 'Chill.'

'But—' I start, then I notice heads turning towards us. I thrust my fists deep into my pockets. Anger boils inside me.

'Where did you get it?' Carson asks.

'See if you can use it.' Sanna puts her hands in her pockets too.

I can't believe she gave the article to these two women. They might know what to do with a recipe for applesauce cake, but how can they use the article without implicating me or my dad?

Senga elbows her friend.

'We'd better go,' Carson says, and hugs us, adding loudly, 'Great to see you.'

'Make sure you're not followed home,' Senga whispers in my ear. The pair disappears into the crowd.

'What just happened?' I ask, confused by the housewife drive-by.

'I know.' Sanna gives a little jump. 'Isn't it a-maz-ing?'

'How could you?' I punch her in the arm, not so playfully.

'Nev—'

'You put my life in danger.'

142

'Your life is already in danger, Nev. All our lives are. You know that.'

How does she do that? She does exactly the opposite of what I ask and then makes *me* feel bad.

She continues, 'This is the starting gate. They've got mega plans.'

'Those two? Those are the masterminds behind some plot to open the Protectosphere?'

'Shhhhhh,' Sanna hisses. 'Never underestimate the power of a mother. They're part of a network or resistance or something – oh, I don't know.' She roots around in her handbag. 'Nobody is supposed to know too much. It's for our own protection and theirs, I guess.' She pulls a slightly bent cigarette from the bottom of her handbag and pinches it between her lips. 'Want one?' she mumbles without dropping the cigarette.

'No, and you shouldn't have one either,' I say, and watch as she pats herself down for her lighter. 'Where are you getting cigarettes anyway?'

'My brother made them,' she pauses, realizing what she's done. She's spoken of her brother in the past tense. She swallows, erasing the sadness that flashes across her face. 'He makes them. Sells them. Started doing it a few months ago. You have a greenhouse for tomatoes. Some people choose to grow, well, other things to barter with.' She pulls a silver lighter from her back pocket. 'I'll let everyone know about the silent demonstration.'

'Yeah, I know. No one trusts me.'

'We could be the match that sparks the fuse that . . .' Lighter in one hand and cigarette in the other, she mimes a mushroom-cloud explosion. She repeatedly tries to ignite the old lighter, but her hands are shaking. *Click.* Spark. *Click.* Spark. The image of a skull is imprinted on the side of the lighter. It seems to be laughing at her.

'Where did you get that thing?' I gesture to the lighter. 'It's hideous.'

'My brother knows someone who knows someone.' Her voice catches. She's already missing him.

Sanna's brother is part magician, part angel and part ghost. I've always liked the thought of him out there somewhere watching over Sanna. He can't be missing. He just can't. I take the lighter and flick the wheel to produce a steady flame. Sanna lights her cigarette and inhales. She links her arm though mine.

'I'm still mad at you,' I say, but I am more terrified about what could happen next.

'I did what had to be done,' she says between puffs of her cigarette. She's right. I never would have used the article for anything. I would have kept it hidden just like my dad did.

We stroll to the centre of the Square. She exhales smoke though her nose, which makes me think of a charging bull. We gaze up at Dr Benjamin L. Smith's statue.

'Wonder what old Benjy would think about our silent demo,' Sanna says, flicking her cigarette at Benjy's knee.

'I don't think he ever intended for us to end up like this,' I say, surveying the earnest edges of his bronze face. I've seen photos of him. I know this is what he looked like, but he never looks real to me. It's as if someone has exaggerated his features.

'Look at him. Curly hair. Pointy nose. I heard he had blue eyes, can you imagine?' she asks, fumbling in her handbag for another cigarette.

I can't, not really. Eyes are brown, fact. How could people have eyes that are different colours? I look across the Square at a sea of sameness. Any extremes have been averaged out.

'He looks weird. Kind of ugly,' Sanna says.

But I am oddly attracted to his unique features. 'I know what you mean.'

As we leave the Square, Sanna removes her sunglasses. 'Do

you really think in a thousand years we'll all look like identical twins?'

I shrug. 'We look pretty similar now.'

'Yeah, but you're still you and I'm still me.'

'I don't think that will change.' I laugh and push my sunglasses onto my head. 'But what does it matter since we are never having kids?'

'Maybe not never,' she says.

She has never, ever mentioned wanting to have children. Her mum died in childbirth after all.

'Quit staring at me like I've got a scar on my face. Oh, wait.' She slaps her hand over her scar. 'I'm allowed to change my mind. I've been thinking that maybe I want a little Sanna. I don't want one now. And, no, before you go all inspector on me, Braydon and I have not broken the vow. It's just, with him . . .' she gets this dreamy, un-Sanna look on her face, ' . . . I start to see a future, you know?'

He has that effect on a lot of people. Maybe it's a game he plays or a gift he has that makes women fall for him.

'And now that you're engaged, I'm sure Ethan will want a little namesake sooner or later.' She elbows me in the ribs.

'I broke up with Ethan.' Even if he doesn't really want to believe it. I walk a little way ahead of Sanna.

She catches up and tugs on my arm. 'What? I thought you and the Big E—'

'Ethan's changed. You must have noticed that.' I don't want to have this conversation. What am I going to tell her? I broke up with Ethan because I think I'm falling for her boyfriend.

'Poor you.' She tries to hug me, but I shake her off. 'Maybe I can stay over like old times. Slumber party!'

I keep walking. 'I don't think so. Things are weird at my house.'

'We can't go to mine. My guardians removed my bedroom door. Can you believe it? They keep chipping away at my freedom.' She stops dead in her tracks. 'I've got a great idea. Why don't we meet up at Braydon's later? We'll forget about everything and just have fun.' It's as if she's read my mind. I would love to see Braydon – just see him – again. I am worse than the government. They keep us hostage, harm us, in some twisted urge to save us. But I know the damage I could cause and I long for him anyway.

CHAPTER EIGHTEEN

I take the train and walk to Braydon's. I don't want to be alone with him on his motorcycle. I remember how it felt to cling on to him. With every step I beg myself to turn around. This is a bad idea. I tell myself that it's harmless. I just want to see him. But it will be torture to see him with Sanna, to be so close to him. But that feeling he inspires in me, it's like a drug. I want to feel it again just one more time. And the way he'll look at me, it's as if he sees me – not government-issue Neva, but the real me.

I walk at an erratic pace. Sometimes fast, anxious to see him. Sometimes slow, unsure of what I'm doing. I speed up, hoping I get there before I change my mind. I stop a few times, preparing to turn around. I'm the rope in an invisible tug of war. My better judgment on one side pulling me to my senses, and my selfish, base desire on the other beckoning me onward – and winning.

The farther I get from the City, the fewer people I see. I pass houses that used to be grand and now crumble like castles of sand. It takes me more than an hour to reach Braydon's house. I turn into a driveway with wrought iron gates parted the perfect width for a motorcycle. The number Sanna gave me matches the number swirled into the pattern of the gates. Looming ahead is what can only be described as a mansion. As I get closer, the storybook image fades. The columns are grey with mildew and the facade is chipped, giving the house a polka-dot effect. I knock, and the door swings open into a two-storey foyer with a spiral staircase.

'Up here,' Sanna calls. I follow the sound of her voice. 'Look at what Braydon has,' Sanna singsongs as she swings a green glass bottle in one hand and a delicate crystal goblet in the other. 'Champagne. It's bubbly,' she says with a giggle.

'Where did Braydon get champagne?' I ask, trying not to appear to look for him.

'He says he found it in the wine cellar.' She sways as she greets me at the top of the staircase. 'There's a crate of this stuff. I think it's some of the last champagne produced by the National Vineyard. How cool is that?' Her words are running together. She's drunk. I've only seen her this way once. We went to one of her brother's parties. Some people brought homemade wine. It was sour and I didn't like the taste, but she didn't seem to mind.

'I've always wanted to try champagne,' I say, and hook one arm around Sanna to keep her from falling. I hope she doesn't get sick like last time. I follow her as she staggers to a huge room at the end of the hall. It has a four-poster, king-sized bed centred on the far wall. The ceiling is vaulted. Four of my bedrooms could fit into this room. To my right is a wall of glass with doors that open onto a balcony. To my left are two doors, both slightly ajar. One opens into a bathroom that appears to glow with chrome and mirrors. The other is a walk-in closet, where I imagine Braydon's collection of red footwear must be kept. But that's not the most striking feature. Masks are scattered around the room. Hundreds of empty eye sockets stare back at me.

Sanna pulls me farther into the room. 'Isn't this wild? He made some of these. The others I think were already here. That one is my fave.' She points her glass at a silver mask with sparkling multi-coloured gems embedded in it. There's a large emerald stone in place of one eye, which seems to wink in the sunlight.

'Where did he get the stuff to make all of these?'

'I guess he found some of it.' She points to a jewellery box with a tangle of necklaces spilling out.

'Where are the owners?' It feels wrong to be in someone's home uninvited.

'God, Nev, I don't know. Where has everyone gone?' She walks over to the bed and picks up a mask that's lying on one of the pillows. It's a delicate shade of pink framed by fuchsia feathers. Tiny crystals glow – in the same shape and spot as Sanna's scar. 'This one is me. Isn't it a-maz-ing?' Sanna strokes the feathers. She holds the mask up to her face and sticks the tip of her tongue through the slit between the mask's lips.

'He is quite the artist,' I say, taking it all in. A wooden mask where the grain of the wood creates a web of wrinkles. A white, glossy porcelain mask with distorted features as if the mask has been stretched in angry hands. Bright, coloured ribbons and silver and gold paint adorn a few masks, perfect for masked balls. Others are decorated with letters from keyboards and shiny computer chips that look like fish scales. Each one has a distinct look but all have dark eyes. There's a series of ten masks lined up like a headboard a few feet over the bed. Each mask is almost exactly the same. He's copied the same mask over and over, but each time he's added or subtracted something. You have to look closely to see the difference, but these subtleties make each mask unique.

I'm overwhelmed by his talent. I want to study every beautiful and disturbing creation. Each mask tells a different story. 'Wow!' is all I manage to say. It's as if the real Braydon is coming into focus.

'Do you get the signif?' Sanna asks.

I nod. I know exactly why Braydon creates these hollow images. I understand about the many masks we wear every

149

day. The row of similar masks is his expression of us. How we are all the same and all different. But I can't say that. Sanna knows me too well. She'll see right through me if I start complimenting Braydon now. 'Kind of creepy, don't you think?' I fake a shiver.

'Be nice, Nev.' Sanna swats at me and laughs. If she only knew.

'You've got to have some.' She pours fizzy liquid into her glass until it foams over. She hands it to me and licks the bubbles off her fingers. 'Drink up,' she says, nudging the glass towards my lips and tipping it back when I take a sip, so that the sip turns into a gulp that leads to me downing the entire glass. I didn't even taste it, only felt it tingle down my throat. My mouth feels drawn and dry. She pours me another.

'Braydon wants to make a mask of you,' she says. 'Isn't that a primo idea?'

No. I've never heard a worse idea. 'I don't think so. It's awfully nice, but—'

'Come on, Nev, he likes to collect faces.'

I bet he does. He has collected more than that from me.

'It won't take long.' She clumsily pushes me down on the bed. I try not to think about what they have done on this very bed. I spring up.

'It's perfect. You two can get to know each other better,' she stage-whispers in my ear. 'Do it for me, Nev. I want my two best peeps to get along.'

I empty the champagne from my glass.

Braydon walks out of the bathroom with a clear glass bowl full of white goo. 'Hi, Neva,' he says. It's already been decided. I can see from the twinkle in his eyes that he wants this. He wants to capture a piece of me.

'Nice house,' I say, unsuccessfully keeping the sarcasm from my voice.

Sanna looks from me to Braydon, then downs the last of the champagne from the bottle. She tosses it onto the bed.

'So, where does the artist want me?' I try to sound flippant and casual, so as not to give any hint of how excited I am to see him.

'Sit wherever you'll be most comfortable.' He waves his free hand in an arc. He's trying too. His smile is forced. We lock eyes, mine begging him not to make me do this and his begging me to let him.

I take a seat in a high-backed leather chair. Sanna brushes my hair back with an Alice band. She slathers thick, oily jelly all over my face.

'It feels a little yucky at first, but it will help the mask peel off when it's done. Close your eyes,' she says, and gently rubs the cold jelly over my eyelids. 'Keep 'em shut. Got it?'

'Neva, just relax,' Braydon says as he straddles my legs. I grip the chair's arms. His thighs are pinning my legs together. My whole body stiffens. 'Tilt your head back,' he says, and I obey. 'I'm going to start on your forehead. It will feel cold at first, but your body temperature will warm it up.'

He's right. The plaster is cold and gritty, but I can feel his fingertips through the chill. He's making tiny circles. His touch is light. He is hovering above me, so close that I can hear him breathing. The rhythm of my breath quickens to match his. We are once again connected. His fingers dance on my skin. We both know he's doing more than making a mask. There's a silent give-and-take between us. It's as if he can read my mind and I can read his. It feels more passionate than kissing. I pin my shoulder blades deep into the leather to keep from reaching for him.

I can hear Sanna singing softly to herself. The bedsprings groan. I assume Sanna has flopped onto the bed. I wonder if she's watching us. I shift uncomfortably in my seat.

'You need to stay still.' He cups my face and turns my head

151

to its original position. His fingers inch the cool goo down my temples and across the bridge of my nose. 'Your face is so tense.' He smoothes the tension from my jaw line.

I try to relax. I really do. But my body is betraying me. It wants to inch closer to him. My body is on fire, but my brain is frozen with guilt. He soothes the chilly mixture over my eyes. His fingertips outline my eyelids and wipe away the lines my anxiety has created.

Sanna is probably bouncing ever so slightly on the bed, excited that her boyfriend and best friend are finally getting along.

'How am I supposed to breathe?' I bat his hands away as they approach my mouth. I try to stand up.

'Nev, chill.' Sanna is at my side. I can smell the tart champagne on her breath. She is petting me and pushing me back down. 'He puts this straw-like thing in your mouth when he's done.'

'Would have been nice if he'd told me that.' Everything is closing in. My feelings for him sizzle below the surface. I feel as if I might explode. I've got to get out of here. 'Listen, I can't ... this is ... I'm just ...' I gasp for air.

Braydon backs away.

'Nev, it's OK,' Sanna coos. 'Just think, like, happy thoughts.' Her words are slurring a little. My mind is growing a little hazy with the champagne too. I let my thoughts fizzle away. I don't want Braydon to stop touching me. It could be, *should* be, for the last time.

'I'm sorry,' I say. I can feel the plaster beginning to harden on my forehead.

'Do you want Braydon to stop?' she asks.

'No,' I whisper. I don't want him to stop. That's the problem. I think I'll die if he stops. 'I'll be fine. Give me a minute.'

The air around me cools. They have backed off, but I can feel them there, a few feet away, watching me. Their voices and movements are muted into static. I think Sanna may be giggling.

'I'm OK,' I say. 'Let's get this over with.'

'Are you sure?' Braydon asks, and touches my arm with some part of his hand not yet covered in plaster.

I nod. 'But talk to me, OK?' I need a distraction.

'OK,' he says. He must know my agony. Does he feel it too? 'What shall I talk about?'

I have a million questions. *Why are you doing this to me?* being at the top of the list. A close second is *Who the hell are you?*, but all I say is, 'Anything. Tell me about yourself.' He's straddling me again, and his leg muscles tense.

'Fab. Story time,' Sanna chimes in. She thinks I'm showing an interest.

'I will if you'll sit still.' He moves in closer. 'I'm going to put this in your mouth so you can breathe.' He slips a flexible tube between my lips. 'Now close your lips around it.'

I do. I flick my tongue over the end of the straw.

'You OK?' he asks.

I nod and push air through the tube.

'I'm sure Sanna's told you this isn't really my house.' His meter is slow as if he's choosing his words carefully. 'My parents got into a little trouble and I was sent to live with a guardian. My guardian had about five other kids already living with him so I decided to, well, disappear. I don't think he even reported me missing. He'd lose the money the government gives him, and nobody really cares about one more missing person, do they?'

I try to ask if he's really a Bartlett, but the words are unrecognizable through the tube and with the plaster hardening on my face.

Miraculously Sanna translates, 'My nosy friend wants to know if you're actually a Bartlett.' She's farther away.

'Yeah, believe it or not. But my mum's last name was

Benzoni, so I'm only half respectable.' He laughs and Sanna echoes with a giggle.

He's tracing my lips. He's circling them again and again. I shift in my seat. He applies more goo to my left cheek. 'I found this house. Learned that the Council plans to turn the land into a graveyard. The house will be a mausoleum.' His answer sounds rehearsed, or maybe I'm making him uncomfortable.

I've got so many questions. I try to speak, but it's no use.

'Biz-zare. This place – a big funeral home,' Sanna says. 'Dead people planted like flowers out back.'

I wish she hadn't said that. I don't need that image stuck in my head.

'I'm almost finished,' he says. His hands are stroking my face, soothing away all the stress. And for a moment, it's as if everything will be OK. It feels as if I'm alone with Braydon in the dark again. Everything else has fallen away and it's just the two of us. Nothing else matters.

'Neva. Neva.' Braydon is whispering in my ear. I must have fallen asleep. I wiggle in the chair, feeling my body wake up. 'Are you OK?'

I nod.

'The plaster is dry, but I've got a few final touches I want to make to the mask. It won't take long.' I can feel a slight pressure on my face, and I can smell paint. 'Sit very still,' he says.

I do. I'm not ready to re-enter my life yet.

'OK,' he says after a few minutes. 'I'm ready to take the mask off.'

Me too.

He runs a finger around the edge of the mask and slowly pries it from my face. It prickles and pulls at my skin but slides free in one piece. 'Be careful opening your eyes.'

I raise my eyebrows and gently tug each eyelid open.

'Do you want to take a look?' he asks.

I nod.

He turns the mask around, holding it by its edges. The white underside gives way to a pale blue. He's painted it the most delicate shade. He's added only one artistic flourish. It's a snowflake in the shape and place of a teardrop.

'What do you think?' he asks.

I take it from him. 'It's perfect.' I study it, this face that I rarely see. The curve of my cheeks and lips. The line of my nose. The angle of my jaw. I don't recognize myself. 'Why the snowflake? Because of my necklace?' I say, and finger the pendant.

He stares at my hand. 'Your name, Neva. It means snow, right? That's how I think of you. As delicate and as unique as a snowflake.' He reaches up and touches my face.

'I better get this gunk off.' I slip past him. I notice Sanna asleep on his bed. She's snoring softly. Her limbs are cocked at odd angles, as if she's a puppet with her strings cut. Guilt floods back in. I'd forgotten she was here.

I duck into the bathroom. I wash my face more times than necessary. When I work up the courage, I head back to the bedroom. The setting sun is casting long shadows across the floor.

He's put my mask on some sort of display stand next to his bed. 'It needs to dry,' he says when he catches me staring.

'I've got to go,' I mutter, and glance at Sanna, who has turned over and pulled a corner of his shiny purple blanket over her.

'Stay.' He closes the distance between us.

I've got to get away from him. I run down the stairs and out the front door, into the cool evening air.

He races after me and grabs my arm. He spins me around

to face him. We are both panting. 'I've missed you.'

God, I've missed him too.

He searches my eyes. I am defenceless, hoping that he will be strong and walk away.

'I can't. I just can't,' I say. I can't leave him, and I can't stay.

'I've never felt like this before,' he whispers what I'm thinking.

With one move, his lips are on mine. Our bodies press into each other. I want to unzip him and slide inside. I can never be close enough to him. I'm utterly lost in his kisses. This feels so right.

Our lips part first. Our faces inch apart. Air finds the tiniest path between us. Our eyes are the last to break our embrace.

'How could you?' The voice severs the spell between us in one swift slice.

Sanna.

CHAPTER NINETEEN

I've been plunged from a white-hot fire into an icy bath. I open my mouth, but I can't speak. My head is still spinning from Braydon's kiss. The look on Sanna's face snaps me into the present. It's a collage of hurt, anger and confusion. I stumble backwards, away from both of them.

'Sanna, I'm so sorry,' Braydon says. But I want him to shut up. Please don't let him tell her. I have to be the one. I've got to make this OK somehow. This is Sanna. I'm the one who comforted her when her mother died, when her father disappeared, when she went to live with the Joneses. I'm the one she runs to when she looks like this. I'm the one who does whatever I have to do to pull her back from the edge. Now I'm the one who's pushed her to it.

'It's not what you think,' I blurt. But it's exactly what she thinks.

She glares at me. 'How could you?' she says again so quietly I can barely hear her, yet her words boom in my ears. Her anger has given way to tears. Her whole body is shaking. She looks from Braydon to me. She staggers between us and springs forwards. She falls, spitting gravel with her feet. Braydon and I rush to her, but she's up and running before we can reach her. She races out the gate. The sun has dipped behind the horizon and the last light is slipping away.

I grab Braydon's arm. 'Let *me* go.'

He nods.

'What have we done?' I ask myself more than him. I don't realize until he pulls away that I was digging my fingernails into his arm.

'We can't help how we feel,' Braydon says, eyes still fixed on the last spot we saw Sanna.

'But we can help what we *do*.' The urge to kiss him was overwhelming, but there were a million tiny choices between my thoughts and actions when I could have stopped. I should have stopped. One selfish moment and I've lost my best friend.

I run though the gate and strain to see which direction she took. I see her, still running, pumping her arms and kicking her legs as hard as she can. The look on her face when she discovered us kissing is emblazoned on my brain and will never, ever be erased. As I stretch each stride as far as my legs can go and swing my arms in high arcs, I know that I have ruined my relationship with Sanna forever. Even if she can forgive me, she will never forget. Even if she can forgive me, I can never forgive myself.

My lungs are burning and my legs are slowing from a sprint into a jog and then to a walk. I clutch the pain in my side. In the half light of dusk, I can make out a blur on the road ahead of me. Sanna is still running.

I force myself to keep moving through the pain. I've got to reach Sanna. I've got to make her understand.

Sanna's slowing, and I'm gaining on her. She's walking now in brisk, wide strides.

I stop when I'm in touching distance of her. 'Sanna,' I say, but she doesn't stop, doesn't turn around. 'Sanna,' I repeat, keeping my distance.

'Leave me alone!' she shouts.

'Sanna, please, talk to me,' I call to her. 'Or at least listen.'

She whips around and glares at me with hard, cold eyes. 'So talk.'

But I can't. I can see Sanna clearly, but everything around

us has faded to black. My skin prickles with fear. The darkness threatens to devour me.

'Talk.' She takes a step towards me. 'Talk!' she screams, and pushes me in the chest. The force propels me back a few steps, but she keeps coming. 'Talk!' she screams, and shoves me back. 'How could you?' She beats her fist on my chest. I wrap my arms around her, but her body still pulses with anger.

'I am so sorry.' I don't know what else to say. I repeat it over and over. She is sobbing into my shoulder. I am terrified of this nothingness that surrounds us and of losing Sanna.

Slowly her cries subside. 'Why?' she whispers in a voice drained of any energy.

I shrug.

She reinflates and pushes me away. 'Why, Nev?' she asks again, somehow regaining her strength.

'I'm sorry,' I say to the cracked tarmac beneath my feet.

'Oh, I know you're sorry.' Her tone is hard. 'He's everything to me. You're my best friend for God's sake.'

'It just happened.' But we both know that's a lie. Nothing just happens. Car crashes take two people making a series of decisions that will end in a collision. Even death takes a final breath and a surrender.

'You'll have to do better than that,' she says, her glare burning into me. 'Is this the first time?'

I shake my head.

'God!' she shouts, and her voice fills the darkness. 'Are you two seeing each other?'

'No!' Pure hatred is radiating from her. 'No,' I say louder. 'We accidentally kissed in the dark.'

'At the Dark Party? Is that what you mean? You've been going behind my back—'

'No, it's not like that. We kissed and . . . I don't know . . . we felt something for each other.'

159

'You felt something for each other,' she mocks me.

'It's hard to explain.'

'Try.'

'We've tried to stay away from each other—'

'Oh, you've tried,' she cries. 'Seems like you two suck at that.'

'We didn't mean to ... we just ...' I give up. There is no explanation. 'We never wanted to hurt you. It meant nothing.' It meant everything.

'Then why did you do it? How could you take Braydon away from me?'

'I haven't taken anything away from you.' It takes all my energy to add, 'You can make up with Braydon. You can forgive him.'

She stares into the darkness for a long time. 'I intend to try. I love him, Nev.'

I take a huge breath. Maybe this can be OK with time. 'Can you forgive me?'

She sort of smiles and, for a second, I think everything will be OK.

'Sanna?' I prompt when she doesn't respond.

'No,' she says quietly. 'I will never forgive you.'

I shatter into a thousand pieces.

'I hate you. I never want to see you again.' She speaks each word clearly. The words seem to reverberate in the silent night air. She walks away.

'Don't leave me, Sanna,' I say, feeling the darkness closing in. She keeps walking.

I'm frozen with fear. I hear a low rumble. Suddenly Braydon is beside me on his motorcycle. 'Are you OK?' he asks.

'Go make things right with Sanna.' I hug myself.

'Neva, I don't want Sanna.'

I back up so that he can't reach me. He's balanced on his

motorcycle, and he has to turn at an awkward angle to see me now.

'Go!' I shout. I run in the opposite direction – away from Braydon and Sanna.

The roar of his motorcycle draws my attention. I watch Sanna climb onto Braydon's bike. She wraps her arms and curves her body around him. They ride away. A sliver of the moon is breaking through the clouds. The light seems to reflect in the road surface, illuminating a path through the darkness.

CHAPTER TWENTY

I walk for minutes, hours. I don't know. The patter of my feet on the road is the only sound. I think I can see a real star glinting off the Protectosphere. It's only a dot of light. My grandma said that in the right light, if you focus your eyes, you can get a glimpse of what's behind the Protectosphere. One night like tonight, she took me outside. The moon was only a yellowing, hazy crescent barely visible through the Protectosphere. We laid on our backs in the wet grass. She led my finger to the faint spots of light in the night sky.

Skywriting with my finger, she'd say, 'That's a star. And another. There's another.' She said her grandma used to call them by name. 'And there' – she looped my finger in a circle – 'can you see it? It's just there.'

I told her I could. But I hadn't really seen the stars. I'd always thought we'd imagined them together. I wanted to see them, so they were there. We're told that the Protectosphere is clear, but Grandma always said that the sky's not as clear as it was when she was a little girl. She said the real sky is endless. I never understood endless. Everything in my life has limits. But tonight, in this darkness, I'm sure I can see real stars. And tonight I almost understand a place without end. I'm in an endless night with no job, no friends, and no future.

Two round points of light pierce the darkness. They grow bigger like eyes getting wider and wider. The light swallows the darkness until I am bathed in light. I squint and shade my eyes. The lights stop in front of me.

'Neva Adams, is that you?' the light seems to ask. I wonder if this is death coming for me. I would go with death tonight.

The light is extinguished and I see the shape of an old electric car, much older than the one my dad has. A figure emerges and comes towards me. 'Neva Adams?' it asks.

I nod.

'You're to come with me.' A man in a police uniform seems to materialize from the dark. 'I've come to take you home.' He opens the passenger-side door.

'How did you find me?' No one except Sanna and Braydon know where I am.

'Get in the car and I'll take you home.' His voice is low but not unfriendly.

I don't know how he found me. They must be watching me. The thought doesn't scare me any more. I am a rag doll, just skin and stuffing, no brain or backbone to hold me up. I could disappear into the night forever. No one would know why or how. I get into the car. I don't care.

He starts the car and we take off towards the City. 'It's not safe for a girl like you to be walking alone at night in the middle of nowhere,' he says, as if he knows what lurks in the dark. The hum of the road and the officer's deep voice lull me to sleep.

'Neva, wake up.'

I wake with a start and scramble away from the man in black. I am surprised to see that we are parked in front of my house. I hop out of the car. He drives off almost before I am on the pavement. Dad's car is not parked in the driveway. My house is dark. When I go inside, I call out for Mum and check every room. She's not home either. I try not to let my imagination lead me anywhere that has me adding my mum's name to The Missing.

I notice a blue envelope on the hall table with my name and address printed clearly on it. I don't recognize the handwriting. That's strange. I don't usually get mail. Almost nobody does any more. I've heard the government plans to phase out paper mail in a few months. The envelope is pieced together with tape. Names have been crossed out. Overlapping labels reveal its history.

As I walk to my bedroom, I slip my fingernail under the freshly applied tape. I pull out a postcard. The picture on the front is like something from Dad's ancient history books – the ocean and sky are a crystal blue and the sand on the beach a sparkling white. It's as if they have airbrushed the Protectosphere out. You can't see the red glow at the water line, warning you to stay back.

I flip the postcard over. 'Time to soar, my little snowflake!' is written on the back. The hairs on the back of my neck prickle. There is no signature, but I know who it's from. Everything in me swells with renewed hope. It can't be. But I need it to be, more than ever. I turn the card over in my hands, searching for more confirmation.

My grandma sent me this. I don't know how, but she did. Tears collect in my lashes. She is alive! I laugh and cry, overwhelmed.

In the bottom corner is tomorrow's date and a time. There's no meeting place. I suppose she had to be careful. The message says, *Time to soar*. I know where she'll be, the place she taught me to fly.

I've received a message from my long-lost grandma. Maybe she wasn't erased after all. Maybe she ran away. Maybe she's been hiding for the past ten years. I can't believe it. It's what I've wished for. She will help me clean up the mess I've made of my life. She's shone a bright light into my darkest hour.

CHAPTER TWENTY-ONE

I 'm standing on a pedestrian bridge in the middle of the river in the centre of the City in a bubble that protects me from the outside and the outside from me. Last night I couldn't go to bed until I heard my mum come home. I had to make sure she was safe. But I still couldn't sleep. I was afraid I'd wake up and my grandma's message would have been a dream.

This doesn't feel real. The bells of the big clock tower chime eleven times. I count the off-key notes one by one. No one knows how to fix them any more. Bellsmiths, or whatever they might have once been called, were reassigned to socially necessary tasks. So, every hour on the hour, the clanking flat tones ring out to remind us that all is not well.

Grandma would bring me here whenever I needed to talk, or when she wanted to tell me more of her secrets. We came here a few days after Grandpa's funeral. The City was covered in a blanket of snow. Tiny, glittering flakes fluttered from the Protectosphere. Everything seemed somehow new. Grandma told me she had arranged it especially for me, but I knew the weather monitors picked snow days months in advance. We stood here with artificially generated wind in our faces and our arms open wide as if we had wings. She said if we only looked up then we could pretend we were flying. So we stood there, the fingertips of our outstretched hands touching. A hush seemed to fall over Homeland in this swirl of white. It was as if we were gliding with the snowflakes.

166

Now I tilt my head upward. A flock of birds is flying overhead, twisting and untying themselves. I raise my arms, hoping Grandma will come soon and fly with me. But after a few minutes, I feel silly. My arms begin to ache and the illusion of flight is gone.

There is a group of school kids walking hand in hand across the bridge. Two men in business suits rest against the opposite rail and talk quickly as if they each already know the dialogue they will deliver. Farther down, a couple is kissing. I scan the length of the bridge. There is no one who could be my grandma, unless she's disguised as a teenager wearing roller boots, vibrating as she rolls over the metal grid floor. I haven't seen roller boots for a while. Sanna used to have a pair until she sold them when she was ten, to bail out her brother when he got arrested the first time he ran away from his guardians.

I check my watch. Nearly fifteen minutes have passed. Worry stirs my insides. Could I have been wrong about the location? The postcard said, *Time to soar.* This has to be the spot. It just has to. I'm getting warm. I unzip my grey sweater and tie it around my waist. I rub my snowflake necklace between my fingers. Maybe Grandma will recognize the necklace if she doesn't recognize me.

I try to remain calm. I practise what I'll say to her. I think of all the things that have happened since she left. She's going to show up. She's got to. But with every passing minute, I begin to doubt. No one else – not even my mum – knows that this was our special place. No one but my parents know she used to call me snowflake.

Sanna and I are supposed to meet Senga and Carson at noon in the Square. I haven't decided if I'm going to go or not. I'm sure Sanna doesn't want to see me. I thought maybe Grandma and I could go together. I started to call Sanna a hundred times this morning. I picked up the phone and even dialled the first few numbers, but I couldn't go through with it. Even if Sanna would talk to me, I don't know what else I could say.

Grandma is thirty minutes late. What if I missed her? What if she was at the other end of the bridge waiting for me? What if this was a trap to catch my grandma, and I'm the bait? What if the police spotted her and remembered her from years ago when they erased her? I pace in an ever-widening loop until I have walked the length of the bridge three times. The businessmen, the only constant occupants of the bridge, start to stare. One even asks me if I'm OK. 'Yeah. Yeah,' I say, but I can't focus on him because I'm searching for her. I keep walking.

I'm so busy looking behind me that I walk right into an old man. He grunts and his cane clatters to the floor. The force of our impact causes him to lean against the rail.

'I'm so sorry,' I say, picking up his wooden cane. He straightens his brown tweed jacket with lighter brown patches on the elbows. It takes a few seconds before he reaches for his cane. He smiles, giving his wrinkles wrinkles. He's bald. The sun is bouncing off his skin and I can see tiny hairs scattered across the surface of his scalp. You don't see many men this old any more.

'That's all right, young lady,' he replies, but I can see it's not. He rests his hand over his heart. He is taking slow deep breaths and I watch his chest rise and fall.

'Would you like to sit down?' I ask, but then I scan the bridge and realize that there's nowhere for him to sit.

'Yes, that would be nice.'

I wrap my arm around his shoulders. 'You could sit on the top of the stairs or I could walk down with you and we could sit on a bench by the riverside.' We are already walking towards the stairs.

'Ah, a chat by the riverside would be lovely,' he says.

I hesitate at the top of the stairs and look around one more time. My grandma's not coming. I choke back my disappointment. It's as if I've lost her all over again.

'Something the matter, dear?' he asks when he feels me resist.

'No, I'm sorry.' We take the first step down together. 'It's just I was waiting for someone and she never showed.'

'Oh, that's too bad,' he says, and takes the next few steps much quicker. 'You need to be careful,' he says when we reach the bottom.

'I'm sorry. I really am. I wasn't watching where I was going. I hope you are OK. I—'

He squeezes my hand to stop the flow of apologies. He's got deep brown eyes with the same sparkle Ethan used to have. 'I think I'm being watched.'

Great. Not only am I not seeing my grandma today, but I'm stuck with some nutty, paranoid old man. I try to pull away, but he squeezes my hand tighter. 'I knew your grandma,' he whispers.

My knees buckle and I lean into him to regain my balance. He's a rock and doesn't budge under my weight.

'Walk me over to that bench. Let's take our time.' We shuffle forwards. 'When your grandma left, I was supposed to go with her. But when the time came, I just couldn't. I was too scared. I was so stupid.' He smiles his warm wrinkly smile. 'She talked about you all the time.'

'You sent me the postcard?'

He nods. 'When she left, she gave me the postcard with instructions to mail it to you when the government renovated the Protectosphere again. I've just learned that plans are already underway and the renovation will begin soon.'

Maybe that's why the police are twitchy, like Sanna's brother said. Maybe it's also somehow connected to Senga and Carson's resistance. Maybe it's why my dad had all those meetings. I want to stop and take it all in, but he keeps coaxing me forwards.

'She wants you to join her.' He slowly lowers himself onto the bench.

'Join her where?'

'Out there.' He points skyward. 'Outside the Protectosphere.'

I plop down on the bench next to him. Is he for real?

He pulls me close. I'm surprised by the iron grip. 'In four days, meet at the Capitol Complex at midnight.' He pauses and looks around. 'Here.' He slips an envelope from his jacket pocket into my hand. He holds my hand with the envelope close to his chest. 'Do not read this now. Hide it. Find somewhere safe to read it, and then destroy the letter. It's from your grandma. She trusted me and so can you.'

This doesn't seem possible.

'Do you have an identity mark?' he asks.

I nod.

'I need to know what it is,' he continues.

I blush.

'You will only be identified by your mark, no names. Describe your identity mark.'

This is one of those moments that will change my life forever – and I'm not ready. I can trust him and tell him about my snowflake tattoo, or I can walk away right now. Trusting him means risking my life on the promise of escape. He could be working for the government. Or this could be the one and only chance I will ever have for a better life.

'So?' He is pressing the edges of the envelope into my palm. I fold the envelope in half.

'I've got a snowflake tattoo,' I say, and tuck the envelope down the front of my blue jeans. 'Right here.' I indicate the spot directly under the envelope.

'OK.' He clears his throat. 'Midnight. Four nights from

tonight at the Capitol Complex. Someone will approach you and ask to see your identity mark. Got that?'

'But that's right in the centre of the City.'

'That's why they will never suspect it. They send all their officers to patrol the borders. When you see your grandma, tell her that Thomas sends his regards.'

'Won't you be coming with me?'

He shakes his head. 'It's too late for me.'

'What if ...' There are so many what-ifs.

'You are Ruth Adams's granddaughter. You can do it.' He pats my cheek with his soft wrinkly hand. He looks me directly in the eyes. 'Tell no one about this' – he pauses –'no one.' His stare is not from a man in his seventies but a fierce young rebel. 'Neva, trust no one. Do you understand?'

I nod, but how can I keep this secret from Mum? She's lost so much already. What about Sanna? Will she even care what happens to me after last night? And Braydon. What about Braydon? How can I disappear without a word?

'You shouldn't be seen with me much longer. It's too dangerous.' He turns away.

I don't know what to do. My grandma has sent me an invitation to the great beyond. And I can't imagine accepting or rejecting it.

CHAPTER TWENTY-TWO

As I walk back across the bridge, the corners of the envelope dig into my stomach. It takes every ounce of restraint not to rip it open. When I'm once again in the middle of the bridge, I walk to the edge and hold the rail. I look up, arch my back and rise on my tiptoes. The wind whips my ponytail in circles and stray strands sting my face. Thomas is still sitting on the bench. He's resting his chin on his cane as if he's sleeping. From this vantage point, I notice a pattern of people spaced an equal distance from him. Were those people there before? I don't think so. We would have noticed, but I can't be sure.

A woman in a grey jacket walks over to Thomas and touches him, gently at first and then she's shaking him. She calls to the others who quickly surround him. Two men pull him to his feet. A black van drives up on the embankment. People have scattered like pigeons to make way for the vehicle. Thomas jerks his shoulders back and the two men release him. He straightens, takes his cane from the woman, and walks towards the van. As he bows to enter the van, he looks up and, for a second, our eyes connect. We both know too late that it was a mistake. Fear strikes like a fiery bolt of lightning and my body sizzles with it. The woman forces Thomas into the van. She bangs on the van and it speeds off. The woman is pointing to the bridge. Two men take off in my direction.

I back away from the rail and then run. My mind is racing faster than my feet. Who are those people? They can't be police; they aren't wearing uniforms. Maybe it's some special team like the people who robbed me of any trace of my grandma. Has Thomas been erased? It's that easy. The government wipes you away like a smudge on a window. If they catch me, I may also find out what it's like to be a smudge.

I run.

I stumble down the stairs from the bridge to the opposite embankment. I check behind me. I can't see anyone chasing me, but I can feel them closing in. They will have the better vantage point to find me. All they have to do is scan the area for a girl with a ponytail in a beige shirt.

That's it. Blend in.

I hide under the bridge. I rip the elastic band out of my hair and throw it into the river. I untie my sweater and slip it on, zipping it all the way up. I place my hand protectively over the envelope tucked into my jeans. I'm walking, but my legs keep speeding up. I have to slow down, but my pace bursts fast and then slows. Fast then slow. Fast then slow. I need to find a crowd and get lost.

The Square. It's only a few blocks away. I turn off at the next street. My neck throbs from forcing myself to face forwards. I desperately want to turn around to see if anyone is following me, but that would look too suspicious.

The Square is busier than I expect. I snake through the crowd with my head down. For once, I'm thankful for our similarities. I push myself forwards, but the friction of bodies seems to pull me back. Nearly every part of my body makes contact with someone else as I move. My heart is racing. I rise on my tiptoes and look around. The crowd is growing and it's harder to move, but maybe I'm safe.

A piece of paper is being forced into my hand. I make a fist and bat it away, but a hand is closing around mine. 'Read it,' someone whispers. I can hear paper crackling all around me as it's wadded and forced into hands.

'Our hope for the future,' someone else says in a low and steady voice. I curl my fingers around the paper.

It's the silent demonstration. I'd almost forgotten. I rise to my tiptoes again. I scan the crowd. Everyone is looking down. It's impossible to recognize anyone. I duck back down and aimlessly weave my way through the crowd. I pause and slowly unfold the paper. I read the headline: THE PROTECTOSPHERE IS KILLING US. I flip the paper over and freeze. It's the article from the archives. It's been pieced back together.

I am being knocked about in a human tide. I don't know if I'm more excited or scared. All these people know one of the government's secrets. Sanna and I have made a difference. But I've got the letter from my grandma tucked in my jeans. I think Thomas was just erased, and they – whoever they are – could be after me now. My survival instinct kicks in. I press the flyer into another hand when I bump it. I push through the crowd with my arms folded tightly across my chest. Anyone can see that I'm not distributing propaganda. I search for the quickest route out of the mass of people that is growing by the minute.

I need air. I climb up and cling to the Dr Benjamin L. Smith statue. I watch as the river of people flows from the Square and down towards the embankment. As people detach from the crowd, I can see papers being tucked into jackets and handbags, as well as dropped casually on the ground.

'Neva! Neva, is that you?'

I panic at the sound of my name, but I pretend I didn't hear it.

'Neva!' the voice is louder and familiar. I can't ignore it.

'Neva! Over here!' I see a boy waving his arms and rushing

towards me. My first impulse is to run, but I hold my ground. As he gets closer, I recognize the shape of his body. His short hair. The blue-and-grey-striped shirt I gave him for Christmas. Those deep-set eyes.

'Ethan,' I say when he reaches me, and throw my arms around him. I am safe. 'What are you doing here?' I don't really care. He's here; that's all that matters. If they come, he'll tell them he's been with me the whole time.

'I've been phoning you,' he says, and he strokes my hair, smoothes out the wrinkle where my elastic band was.

'I know.' Mum has given me all of his messages. I realize what I've just done. He will misunderstand and imagine that I've missed him and want him back. The truth is when I saw him I saw an alibi. I feel bad that after all those years together I can't conjure up a deeper emotion than feeling safe. I move away from him. 'What are you doing here?' I ask again.

He kisses me on the cheek and whispers, 'The demonstration.'

'Really? I thought you said—'

He takes my hand. 'I thought you'd be here.'

'You can't do this for me,' I say. 'It's too dangerous for you. What if—'

'I love you, Neva.' He tries to draw me closer, but I stand firm. 'You know that, right? I can't live without you.'

Maybe they aren't tracking him. I should tell him what Tim said about the government's haphazard approach to surveillance, but Ethan would probably only chastise me for snooping. And maybe he is one of the few they watch. Maybe everything would be different if they weren't tracking Ethan. But it doesn't matter any more.

I notice that the police have surrounded the crowd and are closing in. 'Let's go.' The police are after me. I'm a fugitive and a thief. I gave the demonstrators the stolen newspaper article. I have a letter from my long-lost grandma in my underwear.

We walk away from the Square. We travel side streets until we are at the train station. I kiss him on the cheek. 'I really need to go home.' I've got to read my grandma's letter.

'I'll go with you.'

I don't know what to say to him. Part of me wants him to take me home. It's Ethan. I can trust him. We've known each other forever. Everything around me is shifting, but Ethan still loves me. 'That's OK. You don't have to.'

'But I want to.' He smiles this sweet, warm smile, and there's a hint of the old Ethan, the one I fell in love with. The guy who picked his neighbour's flowers when he was twelve and brought them to me with the dirt still clinging to the roots. But I can't keep hoping. The old Ethan is never coming back. I can see it in his eyes. He's given up.

'Ethan, we broke up, remember? You have to move on.'

His face reddens and tears swarm his eyes. 'I thought if I showed you I could change . . . I can be the person you want me to be—'

'No, Ethan,' I say firmly. I don't want to leave any room for doubt. He can never be the person I want him to be. He will never be Braydon. 'I'm so sorry, Ethan, but I . . .' I'm not sure I can say it with him staring at me as if his life is ending. I blurt what I have to tell him, 'I don't love you any more.' Now that it's out there, a part of me wants to take it back so I won't have to see the way his eyes are deadening. But I may be leaving in four days. I don't want him to miss me or search for me. I don't want him to feel the anguish I've felt for my grandma every day for the past ten years.

I walk away. This is for the best, I reassure myself.

'I won't let you go,' he calls after me.

I stop. It sounds like he knows about my grandma's invitation to escape, but he couldn't. I walk on.

'I love you, Neva!' he shouts. His words have the impact of stones. I never knew I was capable of hurting someone so deeply. I want to comfort him, but I can't; I'm the source of his pain.

I hurry onto a departing train. I don't care about the train's destination. I've got to get out of here.

CHAPTER TWENTY-THREE

When I get home, the living room is dark. I can barely see the mum-sized shape slumped on the sofa.

'Mum, what are you doing?' I flip on the lights. Her eyes are rimmed with red. Streamers of hair hang loose around her face. She has a dish towel over her shoulder. Her beige shirt looks like a paint-splattered canvas. There's a brownish blob in the centre of her shirt and polka dots of a darker beige. 'What's wrong?'

Mum fiercely hugs me. I can hardly breathe, she is squeezing me so tightly. 'Where have you been?' she demands, suddenly breaking our embrace.

'What?' My mind is still processing the day's events. I could escape. I could see my grandma again. Four days. Her invitation has started an internal clock ticking.

Tears are streaming down Mum's cheeks. She covers her face with the towel from her shoulder. I press my hand hard into my stomach and feel the edges of the envelope.

'I ...' She's sobbing so hard she can only get one word out at a time. 'Thought.' She pants for air. 'You.' Her sobs are more like the low moans of a wounded animal. 'Were.' She holds her breath and cries, 'Gone.'

'Oh, Mum. Why would you think that?' But I could have been erased so easily, like Thomas.

'You don't know what's going on. What can happen to young girls. I saw Sanna.'

'What about Sanna?'

'I saw her today. You're always with her. I was so afraid . . .'

Did Sanna say something to her? 'Mum, Sanna and I had a fight last night. She's not speaking to me. She may never speak to me again.'

'Oh, thank God!' She throws her arms around me.

Not the reaction I was expecting.

'When the police were taking her away—'

'What?' I break free.

'At that thing at the Square.'

'You were there?'

'But you're safe and that's all that matters.' She's hugging me again, but I don't want to be hugged.

I pull Mum parallel. 'Mum, what about Sanna? Where did they take her? I've got to help her.' Sanna's missing.

'I know this is hard, Neva. But you can't do anything. You can't get involved. You don't understand the stakes. You were damn lucky last time. Your dad had to call in favours and practically beg them to release you. If you get mixed up with this again . . .'

'But, Mum, this is Sanna. I can't . . .' What? I can't what? I've betrayed her with her boyfriend. I didn't think things could get worse.

'They will probably interrogate her like they did you.'

I haven't told her about Nicoline. They will send Sanna away. I know it. 'I've got to do something.' I release her.

'Let me see what I can find out.' She holds my face so I am forced to look her in her bloodshot eyes. 'But you have to promise to stop whatever you and Sanna have been doing.'

'OK.'

Mum grabs her coat and leaves out the front door. I can't just stand here. I feel so helpless. I decide to make one call. Maybe Sanna's home already. She won't talk to me, but if I hear her voice, I'll know she's OK. I dial.

A deep voice answers the phone. 'Jones residence.'

'Hi, Mr Jones. This is Neva Adams. Can I please speak to Sanna?' I ask in my most polite voice.

The phone line crackles.

'Mr Jones, are you still there?' I ask after what feels like an eternity.

'Yes. I'm still here,' he says clearly. He knows me. I've spoken to him hundreds of times. He used to think I was a good influence on Sanna. He liked that Sanna hung out with the Minister of Ancient History's kid.

'Can I please speak to Sanna?' I ask again.

'I'm sorry. There's no one here by that name.' The phone goes dead. Not Sanna. Please, God, not Sanna. I double over to squelch the pain in my gut. The corners of the envelope hidden in my jeans dig into my snowflake tattoo. I'd almost forgotten.

As I head to my room, I remove the now-wrinkled envelope from my jeans. I turn it over and over in my hands. What does it matter now? If Sanna is missing, I can't leave until she's safe.

I sit on my bed and carefully slice the envelope open. There's just one sheet of paper; I rub the paper between my fingers. It's cream-coloured, nearly brown, rough with bits and pieces woven in. I'd forgotten the feel of my grandma's handmade paper. I unfold the letter.

My dearest Snowflake,

Leaving you was the hardest thing I've ever done. But if you're reading this then my fondest wish will be granted and soon we will be together again.

This message has to be short. I can't risk any more. You will have one chance to escape. No one must know what you are planning. Leave everything behind. If there is any way possible, I will be waiting for you on the other side.

It's a lot to ask. I can't make you any promises. But I believe that a better life awaits. I love you, Snowflake. Hope to see you soon.

Was this always her plan – from the moment I was born? My parents let her name me – her one and only grandchild. She chose to call me Neva. She told me once that she wanted my name to hold promise. 'The government can manage the snowfall, but it can't make two snowflakes the same,' she said.

I stare at the letter for a long time. I may have found my grandma and lost my best friend. I dig out my journal and flip to the pages filled with the memories of my grandma. The postcard she sent marks the spot. All I ever wanted was her back in my life, but I never expected that I'd have to choose between her and everything and everyone else.

I turn to the last page, make a note of the date and write: Thomas. I don't even know his last name, but he's gone. I re-read the names of the people I've lost. My pen hovers on the next blank line. I can see Sanna's name there, but I can't let that happen. I've got four days to decide if I want to accept my grandma's invitation, which means I've got four days to rescue Sanna.

I read the letter again. With everything else spiralling out of control, I want to hold on to the spark of hope it ignites in my gut. I want to save the letter with the other memories of my grandma, but it's too risky. I've got to destroy the only evidence I've ever had that my grandma is alive. I can't put it in the recycling bin. Dad has a shredder, but I can't put it in his office – even shredded in his bin. I stuff the letter and postcard in the front of my jeans and head to the bathroom. I lock the bathroom door. I rip off a few tiny pieces of the postcard and a few pieces of the letter and watch them flutter into the toilet. I flush the toilet and do it again. The scraps of paper look like tiny boats floating on a calm sea, then I flush and suck my fleet to a watery grave.

I make the pieces really small – only a few letters per piece. I decide to eat the key phrases in Grandma's letter. I put the paper in my mouth and grind the pieces. The paper fragments cling to my teeth. I stick my mouth under the tap and gulp water to wash away the evidence. A few more flushes and the evidence is destroyed. I sit down on the toilet. I can feel a lump of paper slowly making its way to my stomach where the acid will melt it into pulp.

I'm startled by two quiet taps on the bathroom door. 'Neva, are you OK in there?' my mum asks.

'Yeah, I'm fine,' I call. But my stomach is rolling.

'Neva, we need to talk.'

I search the bathroom for any stray fragments of paper. I glance at myself in the mirror before I go. I check to make sure there are no words stuck to my teeth. How would I ever explain that?

I open the door. Her cheeks are wet with fresh tears.

'You need to leave.' She grabs me by the arm and practically drags me to my bedroom.

'Mum, you're hurting me.' I wrench my arm free.

She's got a duffel bag. She's stuffing my underwear and a pair of jeans into it. 'You'll need a coat.' She rifles though my closet.

'Mum,' I say, but she doesn't hear me. She's too busy ripping shirts off hangers and jamming them in the bag. 'Mum!' I shout, and snatch the bag out of her hands. 'What are you doing?'

'You've got to go. They've taken Sanna and they are preparing to round up anyone they suspect might have been at the demonstration.'

'What?'

'You've got to get out of here.' Her eyes are wild. 'Do you have somewhere you can go?'

There's only one person who might help me: Braydon. I nod.

'Good. OK.' She hands me a tiny scrap of paper. She closes her hand around mine. 'This is contact information for someone called Senga. Find her tomorrow and she'll help you get out of the City.'

'How do you know Senga?' I ask, opening my hand and reading the address on the paper.

'Don't ask, just do it. Pack a few things and I will take you wherever you want to go. I'll make sure we're not followed.' Her voice is calmer, almost cold. 'There's not much time. We need to leave before your father gets home. He can't know I had anything to do with this. He can't know where you're going.'

I'm starting to see my mum in a whole new light or maybe it's that I'm seeing everything clearly now. I let the duffel bag fall to the floor. 'Come with me.'

'I can't. We are getting a baby. If I left, they would come after me. But you. You could disappear. Go up North somewhere at least for a little while.' She lifts my chin. 'We've got to be strong.'

If she can, I can. But I'm not going to run away. Not in the way my mum thinks. I've got to find Sanna and make sure she's safe.

By the time I get into the car, my life fits into a duffel bag. I've got the clothes on my back and the worn shoes on my feet. I rub the snowflake necklace between my fingers. When Mum pulls up in front of Braydon's house, we cling to each other as if we may never see each other again – and we may not.

CHAPTER TWENTY-FOUR

The crusty cream paint flakes away as I beat my fists on the door. No one comes. Maybe he's gone too. I pound harder. Slivers of paint and wood prick my skin. The door opens slowly.

'Neva? What are you doing here?' Braydon asks. He's wearing a pair of faded blue plaid pyjama bottoms.

'They took Sanna.'

'What? When?' His face creases with worry.

'There was a demonstration today—'

He doesn't let me finish. 'No, Sanna wasn't there. She said she had to—'

'She didn't tell you, did she?' I interrupt. 'She knew you'd be against it, but the police ... she's ... and now, I think they are coming after me.'

'Let's get you inside,' he says, wrapping a strong arm around my shoulders. He takes my duffel bag.

I'm exhausted in a way I've never felt before. My body feels heavy, but my head is floating above me. 'Sanna. We've got to rescue her.'

'We will,' he says in such a calm, reassuring way that I believe him. We are different people from the ones we were a few days ago, but that electricity still fizzes between us. It's painful and sweet all at the same time. It doesn't feel right to be with him when Sanna is locked away somewhere. But at the same time, I feel as if I'm exactly

184

where I belong. There's a pressure building between us.

He leads me up the stairs. When we reach his bedroom, I notice his bare feet. For some reason seeing him without his boots makes me almost giddy.

'I thought you slept in your red boots.'

He laughs, which breaks the tension, and I laugh with relief. I don't know what's so funny, but I can't stop. My stomach aches. We tumble onto his bed laughing, his arm still around me. Our laughter subsides into a whimper.

'I'm really sorry about what's happened, but I'm glad you're here,' he says.

'Thanks for letting me stay. I'll be gone tomorrow.'

'What?'

'I've got to find Sanna.' I want to tell him about the message from my grandma, but I guess there's still a part of me that doesn't trust him. I'm not sure I can leave anyway. I can't decide until Sanna's safe.

'How can we find out where she is?'

'I think I know someone who can help.' I don't tell him about Senga either. I decide to keep my secrets for now.

I finally work up the courage to ask, 'What happened between you and Sanna after she caught us?' Funny that I can't say the word *kissing*. It hurts to remember last night. It feels a lifetime ago.

He moves away from me. 'I took her home. She was crying and begging me not to go. I couldn't leave her like that.'

I told him to go to her, but I feel a pinprick of jealousy at the thought of them alone together. I hate myself for it. 'I can't believe her guardians let you stay.'

'They didn't know or didn't care.'

'I wonder if her brother knows she's been arrested.'

'Sanna found out this morning from some underground

contact that her brother has been sent to a Community Farm again.' He glances at me. 'For a year, maybe longer.'

I sit up. 'Now no one will care if she's gone. We have to find her.' I'm all she's got.

He narrows his eyes and sets his jaw. Suddenly he seems far, far away.

'Braydon.' I poke him in the side to get his attention. He looks at me as if he's forgotten I am here.

'Neva, Sanna was so angry and hurt and confused last night.' He looks out the window into the darkness. 'Even if we can find her, I'm not sure she'll want to talk to you.'

'She doesn't have to talk to me. She doesn't have to like me.' I walk to the window. I need distance from him. 'Even after everything, she'd risk her life to save me. I know she would.'

He walks up behind me. 'Let's get some sleep. We'll figure this out tomorrow,' he whispers in my ear. Electricity ripples through my body.

'I'll sleep in the other bedroom,' he says, turning to go.

I can't bear to be alone. I grab his hand. We don't say a word. I scoot into his bed, and he follows. He nudges me onto my side and cuddles my back. We fit perfectly together. I don't let myself think of Sanna. For the first time in a long time, I don't feel that dark solitude in the pit of my stomach.

'I'm not sure this is a good idea,' Braydon says, squinting to see house numbers. We've parked his bike and are looking for Senga's house on foot. I haven't told him everything about Senga and her rebellious ways. All he knows is that she's someone who might be able to help us find Sanna.

'I think 10978 will be on this side of the street.' We cross the road. 'Are you sure this is Blue Sky Crescent?' I look around even though I know I won't find a street sign. Most of them are long gone or weatherworn to the point that you can't read them any more.

'That's what the map said, I think.' Braydon rotates the map a quarter turn. 'It's either that or Starry Night Lane. Who came up with these names anyway?'

Most of the houses look abandoned. Some have boarded-up windows. The doors of a few houses stand open, like gaping mouths ready to scream. They all look alike – two storey brick structures. Some have different-shaped windows or garages attached, but they are fundamentally the same.

'I think it's this one.' I point to a house up the road. Its shrubbery has been trimmed into neat boxes. Chipped clay pots with red geraniums frame the front door.

'How do you know we can trust her?' he asks, his pace slowing.

'Just trust me.' I take his hand and pull him forwards. When I realize what I've done, I wriggle my hand free. Our whole morning has been like this. We'd get close and then one of us would remember Sanna and we'd create distance.

I knock on the door to 10978. Braydon stands behind me, like a bodyguard searching for threats. The door opens and Senga waves us in.

'We're friends of—' I start as soon as she has closed the door behind us.

'I remember you,' she interrupts. 'Follow me.' The woman has her hair in pink foam curlers and wears a threadbare grey bathrobe. She's shuffling her feet, and that's when I notice the tattered bunny slippers. They make me smile but somehow feel less safe. But surely Mum wouldn't have sent me here if it wasn't safe. Sanna wouldn't have taken part in the silent demonstration if Senga couldn't be trusted. I look back at Braydon and can tell he's got the same reservations I have.

She leads us to her backyard. 'Take a seat.' She gestures to a rusty metal chair, a lounge chair missing half its canvas ribbons, and a tricycle. I take the bike and Braydon chooses to stand. Senga gingerly sits in the lounge chair. 'Sorry I can't offer you something to drink; with three kids we don't have any to spare.'

I'm thrown off by the *we* and the kids comment. I wonder where her family is.

As if she can read my mind, she adds, 'My husband's at work and the kids are at school.'

'Sanna's been arrested,' I blurt. Her full, round face seems to elongate when she frowns. 'I was hoping you could help me find her.'

Senga glances at Braydon. I can tell she's not happy he's here. 'Not sure,' she says hesitantly.

'Where would they take her?' Braydon asks. He's not comfortable either. He's shifting in those red boots of his.

'Listen,' Senga says to me. 'I'm doing this as a favour. I told your mum I'd help you escape up North.' Braydon gives me a pointed look. I haven't been completely honest with him and he knows it. Senga doesn't seem to notice the temperature rise between Braydon and me. 'But no one told me about him.' She gestures towards Braydon.

'He's Sanna's boyfriend,' I say by way of explanation.

'I don't care who he is. As a matter of fact, I want him out.' She points to her back door, but her rigid arm tells me she wants him farther away than that.

'Yeah, all right.' He kicks at the dirt with the toe of his boot. 'I'll wait by the motorcycle. Don't be long, OK?' He squeezes my shoulder as he passes.

Senga waits until she hears her front door shut before she speaks. 'I wish I'd never told that girl anything about the resistance, but her mum was fundamental to the movement. I felt I owed it to her. Sanna begged me to tell her about the silent demonstration. Gave me some big dramatic speech about her friend counting on her. You know Sanna.'

'She was arrested at the silent demonstration yesterday.'

'Damn it!' Senga falls through the missing canvas strips with the force of her anger. Her bottom is now on the ground and her legs are bent and sticking up in the air, but she doesn't move. She continues as if nothing has happened. 'I thought the younger girls had got away.'

'Where would they take her?' I stand and help her out of the chair.

She stands really close to me and whispers, 'I've heard rumours, but it's just rumours, mind you, of a Women's Empowerment Centre.'

I remember those words. They were on a file on Dad's desk. 'What is it? Do you think that's where Sanna is?'

'I don't know exactly, but I think it's where they are taking young women when they get arrested.'

'Do you know where this centre is?'

She shakes her head. 'But maybe I could find out. If you're sure?' She's staring at me, sizing me up.

I look her directly in the eyes. 'I've got to find Sanna.'

'It's going to be dangerous; and I mean dangerous. I don't mean some patriotic seminar or time at a Community Farm. This is serious business, and if the rumours are true . . . Well, let's hope people are exaggerating.'

I want to ask her about these rumours, but I don't really want to know, not right now. It doesn't matter what the consequences. 'I've got to do it.'

'Well, OK then.' Her face is getting red and beads of sweat are forming on her brow. 'Let me ask around and see if I can get a location. I'll see if any of my contacts can confirm that that's where they've taken her. Come back tomorrow morning.' She looks behind me. 'Alone.'

CHAPTER TWENTY-FIVE

M y body is rattling. I have become one with Braydon's motorcycle. I can't feel my butt or my legs any more. I press my cheek into Braydon's back to keep my teeth from chattering. I think I'm still holding on to him, but I am disconnected from time and space. The landscape is barren: a line of trees borders the highway, then fields. Everything is dry, brown, and dying. They don't operate the precipitation programme very often this far north any more. The road is an endless black line ahead of us. We pass a car every half hour or so.

At first I was caught up in the excitement of it all. Braydon and Neva to the rescue. Braydon drove me to Senga's house early this morning. We watched her husband and three kids leave. My heart ached when I noticed that all three of her children were girls. I understand exactly why Senga is doing what she is doing. She is risking everything to give her girls a future.

She gave me vague directions to what she had been told was the location of the Women's Empowerment Centre. Senga said she couldn't promise that Sanna was there, but someone had told one of her contacts that Sanna had been transported to a facility up North. She told me to take the main highway out of the City. She said to look for a newly paved exit ramp. One of her friends in Resource Management said that nearly three years ago funds had been diverted by the Minister of Health to renovate a big complex up North.

'This has to be it,' Senga said. 'What is the Minister of Health doing creating roads? It's going to be well guarded. Good news is there are only portable generators up that way.'

'Why is that good news?' I asked.

'Means they won't use power for nonessentials like electronic fencing or surveillance systems,' Senga replied. 'They will guard the facility the old-fashioned way. Are you sure you want to do this?'

I nodded, but everything inside me screamed to call the whole thing off. What did I think I was doing? Braydon wanted to wait, but I said no. He doesn't know I've got no time to waste – only three days. Also, if I took time to think about what I was doing, let the reality of it sink in, I'd probably never have the strength to go through with it.

He gathered some supplies: food, water, blankets, and an extra battery for his motorcycle. There are no official charging stations more than one hundred miles north of the capital. If Senga's directions are right, we are going well beyond that.

The highway is vacant and never ending. It is as if we've escaped to another place. Braydon and I are held together by the pull of the road. Braydon elbows me in the ribs and points. I see it. Up ahead there's a black diagonal line angling off the highway. As we drove, if I looked hard, I could see where other roads branched off. Most of those roads were overgrown with weeds that sprouted from fissures in the tarmac. But as we approach, the dark line becomes an uncluttered, new road, almost an arrow, beckoning us to follow it.

We exit and feeling comes rushing back into my body. It's only then that I realize that I was beginning to like this no-man's-land that Braydon and I are inhabiting: the low mellow hum of his bike, the sun-warm feel of his leather jacket against my cheek.

The highway felt open and expansive. This road, which

cuts through a forest, feels as if it endlessly narrows. The black, oily asphalt is only one car-length wide. Tall trees with thick trunks create a staggered wall around us. Their branches reach crippled fingers across the road and block out the sky. The sun pokes its slim rays through the treetops and we travel through thin columns of light.

The sound doesn't register at first. I think I've imagined it. But as it gets louder, I realize it's outside of me. Braydon's body stiffens; he's heard it too. I look around wildly. Our balance is unsettled, and the motorcycle wobbles. I mould myself to Braydon to help steady us. But I've glimpsed something behind us, a van maybe.

Near his ear I yell, 'We are being followed!' I'm afraid the wind rushing past has stolen my voice until Braydon nods. He accelerates and I'm jerked back. I dig my fingernails into his jacket and he leans us forward. The sound behind us gets louder. It's gaining on us. I don't have to turn around to know that it will be there, looming large behind us. We speed up. The bike shudders between my thighs. It's as if it's straining every gasket to propel us faster and faster.

Braydon's looking for another exit, but the trees create a barrier around us. Braydon edges to the left. It's the wrong angle to get us safely over the lip of the road, but I've got to trust him. He steers the bike to the right. We are airborne for a moment and then slam down to the ground. It's only by Braydon's strength and skill that we manage to stay upright. We are off the road and into the forest now, and we slow down as Braydon weaves through the trees. The uneven ground jostles us. I bounce out of sync with Braydon. The trees are so close that I can almost feel their rough bark on my skin. I look behind us. The white van has stopped on the road. Maybe we are safe.

The obstacle course ahead seems impossible, but Braydon twists and turns us. We bounce over the ground, lined with tree roots. My head snaps back and forth with every jolt. I hold tighter to Braydon. We are well away from the road. The bike is slowing down at an alarming rate. The chase must have drained the battery. We roll to a stop.

I hop off the bike. 'That was ...' I start but can't find the words. 'You were ...' My legs falter underneath me. Braydon drops the bike and rushes to me.

We scan our surroundings, ears burning to hear the crack of a twig or the pounding of feet. But there's only a cool, eerie silence.

He pulls me close and kisses the top of my head. I can hear his heart pounding. My heart feels as if it's reaching for his in heavy, hard beats.

He rests his head on mine. 'We can't stay here.'

'We've got to be close.'

'Yeah, and they know we're here. They might come looking for us. Neva, I think we should go back to the highway. We didn't think this through.'

'We can't go back now.'

'I agree.'

I cock my head, confused. He picks up the bike and checks it out as he talks. 'We've got one battery. We should keep heading north. It's nearly deserted up there. We can camp out in the woods, live off the land for a while. Braydon and Neva can disappear forever.' He's removing weeds from the engine and battery.

I let his proposal sink in. I wouldn't be the Minister of Ancient History's daughter. He wouldn't be my best friend's boyfriend. Until this moment, I never imagined a future, not a future that makes my heart lighten the way Braydon's idea does.

He raises his eyebrows. 'What do you say?'

I want to say yes more than I've ever wanted anything. But I'm silent. It feels so right to be lost here with Braydon. It would be so easy to ride off into the sunset. But I can't desert Sanna and forget about my grandma's invitation.

'We should get moving,' he says when he sees my indecision. 'I've got to change the battery and then you need to decide.'

I watch him hook up the new battery. I let myself think about a life of only Braydon and me. I try to imagine living in the wild, in a place the government has all but abandoned. No one watching us or telling us what to do.

But then I think of Sanna. I see her face when she caught Braydon and me kissing. The look of confusion and then despair. I can't abandon Sanna, but I'm not sure I'm strong enough to rescue her either. It doesn't feel like there's a right answer.

When Braydon's finished, black grease is smeared on his cheek. He seems to have lost his polish. Even his red boots don't seem as shiny.

When we climb on the bike, I desperately want to tell him to drive north and keep going. It's probably the smartest thing to do. We have a better chance of survival if we run away. But I can't. 'We can't leave without Sanna.' I could never be happy knowing I abandoned her.

His shoulders sag. 'I don't see how this can end in any way that means we'll be together. We've got this chance to start over, to leave everything behind.'

He's right. We won't be together. If we go after Sanna, the government will come after us. If we somehow manage to free her, then she'll need Braydon more than ever. If we get home again – which seems like a very big if – I have an invitation to a new life outside the Protectosphere.

'I can't abandon Sanna,' I say softly.

'We may not find her. And if' – he pauses and raises his voice – 'if we find her, we might not be able to rescue her.'

'We've got to try,' I say, and hug his back. He starts the

engine. We slowly drive up one of the hills that surrounds us. Maybe we'll be able to see where we are and where Sanna might be. The hill is steep and we have to walk the bike to the very top. He lays the bike on its side.

The forest goes on forever, but at the base of the hill in the middle of this valley is a huge, square brick structure with a lush green courtyard in the middle. It looks like an old manor house. I can see shapes that must be people milling around. It's hard to tell what they are doing, but their pace is slow. Beyond the main structure is a square building with no windows. It could be a barn. Four dark figures orbit the building, security guards, no doubt. It has to be the Women's Empowerment Centre. If it weren't for the security guards travelling a well-worn pattern, this place wouldn't look sinister at all.

Women's Empowerment Centre. It doesn't sound so horrible. *Empowerment* isn't a bad word. *Women* has become the word that isn't so great recently. Being female makes you more likely to disappear. What are they doing to these women? Brainwashing them? Making them accept that the greatest gift they can give their country is children? They wouldn't torture them, right? They want them healthy so they can return to society, find partners, and make babies.

We notice movement on the gravel road leading to the cluster of buildings. It's the white van. Braydon and I instinctively duck. From our crouched position, we can see the van pull around to the far side of the building and park. We shift so we are sitting. Five people exit from the back of the van. They disappear behind the building. We watch for a while longer.

'It's getting dark,' Braydon says. I hadn't noticed. 'We can't do anything tonight. Let's find someplace to sleep and then figure out our next steps tomorrow.'

He leads me and the bike down the hill. We almost don't

notice it because it's made of forest trees and covered in brown, dying grasses. It's a small wooden shack. 'You stay here. I'll go check it out,' he says.

I'm too exhausted to argue. The shack is only a little taller than Braydon. He waves me forward after a few minutes. Once we and the bike are safely inside, I realize there is no roof. There are beams crisscrossing from wall to wall but nothing between us and the Protectosphere. There are no windows and only one door with a huge plank that rests in a solid latch.

Braydon secures the lock. 'I think we'll be safe here for the night,' he says, and begins to empty the contents of my duffel bag, which has been tied to the back of the bike. He hands me a piece of cheese and a hunk of bread. We've been sipping water from his canteen all day. There's only a little left. We are too tired to talk. We eat standing up on opposite sides of the shack.

The floor is overgrown with weeds that in places nearly reach my knees. Braydon stomps them flat and spreads a blanket on the floor. I take off my jacket. It feels as if it's moulded to me with sweat. He turns his back to me, carefully slides off his boots and lies down. My skin is damp and the night air is cold. I shiver. He pats the place next to him. I stretch out beside him. The dry grass and weeds crunch beneath me.

We are afraid to touch. We stare up at the sliver of moon, the only thing keeping us from being shrouded in complete darkness. It feels as if we are at the end of everything. My fear of the dark is trumped by a million other fears.

'Neva,' he whispers, and rolls on his side, facing me. It's a question and a plea all wrapped tightly in my name. He lowers his face to mine. I kiss him tenderly on the lips, giving him my answer. We kiss with eyes wide open. I want to see and feel this moment.

He pulls away painfully slowly. I follow, not wanting to

lose touch. His hands explore my body. His eyes follow his touch and he works his way down, removing each piece of clothing and then kissing my bare skin. He lingers at my tattoo. I cover it with my hand, suddenly embarrassed. He laces his fingers through mine.

I feel as if I'm imploding and exploding. I don't want to be scared any more. But I am. I'm terrified of what might happen next. I want him to stop, but I'm equally terrified of stopping and never feeling this way again.

'Are you OK, Neva?'

I kiss him, manoeuvring him until he's on his back. Now I undress him with trembling fingers. Our bodies are pressed together. I can't get close enough to him. There's a rhythm to our passion. Our hands, our lips flow instinctively over each other's bodies.

I want desperately to break our vow, but something keeps us from crossing the line. We don't speak. We both know breaking the vow means letting the government in, and tonight there's only Braydon and me.

CHAPTER TWENTY-SIX

I open my eyes, but my body is still heavy with sleep. Braydon is draped over me like a blanket. We are lying in shade, but the sun is shining brightly. I stare at him for a long time, wanting to recapture last night. In the harsh light of day, I see my best friend's boyfriend and someone I barely know lying naked next to me. But that's not how it felt last night.

I can't change what happened. If I'm honest, I don't want to. I won't regret it. I'll keep those memories trapped in a bubble away from labels of good and bad and right and wrong.

I slip out of his grasp and dress quickly. I lift the latch a millimetre at a time. Braydon has rolled over and wrapped himself in the blanket. His bare shoulders and feet are exposed. I feel a rush of the emotions we shared last night. My life is divided into before and after our kiss in the dark.

I have two more days. One day to save Sanna, and tomorrow at midnight I can escape. I don't know how I will ever say goodbye to Braydon now. But I have to. If I'm to have any hope of succeeding, I need to take it one moment at a time. I retrace our steps to the top of the hill. I watch the buildings in the valley for a long time. I notice how people move in and out of the main building. I figure out how the guards patrol. A dark car with what I think is the crest of Homeland pulls up. A man in black delivers what looks like a cool box and then drives away.

I hear steps behind me. I turn to see Braydon walking

towards me. His hair is sticking up on one side and his faced is creased from sleep. I realize I must look equally dishevelled. He slips his arms around my waist. We sway slightly as if moved by the gentle morning breeze.

He kisses me. 'You OK?'

I shrug.

We are cheek to cheek. 'What's the plan?' he asks. 'I can practically see the cogs turning.'

It's funny to feel his jaw forming words against my face. I put my hand on his cheek and hold him there. I have been thinking. I know the first part of a plan, but the middle is going to have to be down to a little luck and a lot of improvisation.

'Absolutely not,' he says when I've explained as much of a plan as there is. 'I should be taking the risk. I won't let you do it.' He breaks the connection between us.

'This is a place where they take women. I can blend in. And ...' I swallow ' ... if I get caught' – I talk faster. I can see his face getting redder – 'It won't happen. I won't let it, but if I do, you can tell my parents. My mum won't leave me here.'

'What are you thinking?' He raises his voice and it feels too loud.

'I've got to do this, Braydon.' I survey the Women's Empowerment Centre, nestled in the valley below us. I think of my grandma and my mum. Of Sanna and her mother. Senga and her three daughters. 'I'm doing this with or without you. But I have a better chance of success if we work together.'

We stare out over the treetops. I lean into him and we are kissing again. But this kiss isn't passionate like last night. It's sad and tender, a long goodbye. I pull away slowly. I can't give in to this now.

'OK, let's go over this again,' I say when I find my voice. We run through my plan over and over and over.

Braydon runs up the hill towards me. The sun is setting and flickers in the trees behind him. 'OK, Neva, the van's on its way.' He collapses at my feet, panting. He found a vantage point on a nearby hill that let him see the main road. He's run all the way to alert me. Today the only thing we allowed ourselves to talk about was my plan. We discussed every detail and worked out a strategy for everything we could think of.

'I guess this is it,' I say.

He hugs me. 'We can still walk away. We don't have to go through with it.'

But I can't let him make me emotional or frightened. There's so much we both want to say tangled in the air between us. I kiss him one last time and race away.

I watch the guards from a little way up the hill. I time it just right and sneak behind the barn-like building. I hear shouting.

I look towards the place where I left Braydon. A finger of black smoke winds its way skyward. Our plan has been set in motion, and so far everything is going as we envisioned. Braydon has started a fire to distract the guards. I flatten myself against the wooden building and count: one, two, three, four, five guards charging up the hill. That's all the guards on perimeter duty. My thoughts shift to Braydon. I pray that he's OK. He was supposed to set the fire and then drive a safe distance away and wait for some signal from me.

We dug a pit around the shack, the only home he and I will ever share. The wood was dry and the grasses hiding it brittle. Braydon had one of Sanna's discarded lighters in the satchel of his motorbike. We hoped it had a spark or two left. It was an ancient white plastic lighter, which still had the shadow of a smiley face.

I am hot and sweaty, but it's not from the fire Braydon set. I have never been so scared and exhilarated. All the possible outcomes spiral before me.

A girl screams. I check left then right. The coast is clear. I dart behind the brick building and peer around the corner. Four girls my age climb out of the back of the white van. I am thankful they are dressed in everyday clothes. It's possible that I could be one of them.

One girl is crying uncontrollably. Her mouth is open wide in an unnatural shape. She's batting at the other girls. One girl slaps the hysterical girl across the face. I cringe at the sound of skin on skin.

The girls stare at one another in shock. They seem to notice for the first time that they are unguarded. One points in the direction of the fire. The guards have disappeared into the forest. The girl who was hysterical seems to collect herself, sniffling and wiping her eyes. She bolts away from the fire and the van, deeper into the forest.

The girls call to her and then look at each other like puppies waiting for their master to issue a command. Another guard appears from inside the building and races into the forest after the escapee.

Now's my chance.

I step around the corner and into the open. Even though my legs are shaking, I stroll over and join the other girls. Their eyes shift from me to the building to one another, but no one says a word. I can see their fear and confusion.

'Please,' I whisper. They seem to understand. My lips twitch nervously.

A man in a blue-and-tan-striped shirt appears in the doorway to the main building. 'Hey, what the . . .' he exclaims when he notices us huddled together. His face softens. 'Welcome, ladies,' he says, directing us inside. He reaches a hand to help me, but I slip past him. He mouths the numbers as he counts us. Satisfied, he shuts the door behind the fourth girl. The light in the room is dull, and my eyes have to adjust. We are in a windowless room with hallways ahead of us and to our right. We cluster in a tight ball.

'Welcome to the Women's Empowerment Centre,' the man says, and smiles warmly at us. 'My name is Mr Jefferson. I am the director here. It's my job to get you settled into your new surroundings.' Why is a man the head of a place for women? He has an easy manner from his bushy, unkempt curls to his untucked shirt. He gestures to a cluster of sofas. 'Have a seat and relax. I know your journey was long and uncomfortable. My apologies.'

I look at each girl; they all have the same confused expression. We move in a pack and sit too close together.

Mr Jefferson takes a few steps down the hall ahead of us and calls, 'Can we get some hot tea for the ladies?' but doesn't take his eyes off us.

Two women dressed in faded blue doctor scrubs appear in the entryway. One holds a tray with mismatched ceramic mugs. The other hands a steaming mug to each of us. I cup it in my hands and inhale the peppermint steam.

'Go ahead,' the woman encourages. 'Drink up. You'll feel better.'

I take a sip and then another. The peppermint warms as it flows through me. The other girls are also enjoying the treat of hot tea. I scoot back into the sofa and wiggle some room free from the girls on either side of me. I take another sip and another, but this time I taste something sour through the peppermint. I notice a white grainy substance at the bottom of my cup. I give the mug to one of the women in blue.

She glances in my mug and nudges it back towards my lips. 'You'll want to finish it.'

She pulls her lips into a tired smile and waits and watches

until I put the mug to my mouth and pretend to sip. She steps closer to me. She doesn't say anything, but I know the tea isn't an option and this is no party. I drink slowly, trying to keep the settled matter at the bottom of my mug. The woman casually inspects each mug as we place them on the tray. I swirl the remaining liquid in my mug so the grainy flakes dissolve before setting it on the tray. My brain's getting fuzzy. I could be imagining it, but I don't think so. The girl to my left is swaying slightly.

The women in blue remove the mugs and bookend Mr Jefferson.

He smiles again. 'OK, I hope you are feeling better. Let me introduce Dr Ann and Dr Beth.' Both the women in scrubs wave at the same time, so I can't tell which is which. 'We have a few induction duties, and then you can go and relax in the garden. I need you to line up, please.'

We shuffle until we are one behind the other. I'm second in line.

'That's right. Good girls.' He snatches a pen and a clipboard from a hook next to the door. 'I'm really sorry about this next part, but we need to track all of you lovely ladies. It's the best way we could think of. Roll up the sleeve on your left arm.' He's writing on the first girl's arm with a big black marker. He reaches for my wrist next and I flinch. 'It's not going to hurt, I promise.' His fingers circle my wrist. His grip is firm. 'Hold still.' The marker is a cool dot on my skin until he roughly drags it in big bold strokes. He writes the number 1133 on my arm and 1134 on the next girl.

'Don't you want our names?' the youngest girl asks. 'I'm Crystal.'

'Hi, Crystal,' Mr Jefferson says, but writes 1135 on her arm. He marches to the front of the line. 'One simple rule and we'll all get along just fine. Please do as you are instructed by myself, Dr Ann, or Dr Beth. Remember this is for your own good and for the future of Homeland. Follow Dr Ann and Dr Beth now and I'll see you later.' He winks at us and disappears down the hall.

The doctors stride ahead of us, and we follow somewhat sluggishly. My feet feel heavy, as if encased in cement. They lead us to a big bathroom like we used to have at our school.

'We need each of you to shower please,' one doctor says, and points to a bank of showers on the far back wall, but none of us move.

I look at 1132, 1134 and 1135. Their eyes are half closed. I suddenly feel tired too. My skin tingles. I scratch my forearm and notice that 1134 is doing the same thing. They must have drugged us. My brain registers panic, but somehow my body doesn't feel it.

'Let's go, girls,' one of the doctors says. 'This is not very pleasant, we know, but it's necessary.'

The girl next to me obediently starts to undress. She slips off her T-shirt. Her large breasts sag in her ill-fitting bra. 'Guess this is better than a Work Camp,' she mutters.

I turn away from the doctors and struggle with the buttons on my shirt. My fingers feel thick. 'Work Camp?' I murmur. I've heard of Community Farms but not Work Camps.

'You don't want to go there,' she says, tugging her trousers past her hips. Her grey underwear is dotted with holes. The other girls are starting to undress too. We all look anywhere but at each other's half-naked bodies. I kick off my shoes and hop on each foot to pull off my socks. The new recruits are still wearing their underwear.

'Everything, ladies,' one of the doctors says in an almost apologetic tone. 'Let's get this part over with.'

I am unable to move. The bigger of the doctors walks over to us. She slips a bracelet off the young girl's wrist. I'm thankful Braydon made me give him my snowflake necklace. Now she's

205

standing in front of me. She nods at my underwear. I can't bear the thought of being completely naked in this place. My knickers and bra have been recycled so many times they are merely shadows shading my caramel skin. She reaches behind me and unfastens my bra. I force myself to remove the last shreds of clothing along with my dignity. I instinctively cover myself, but not before the doctor glances at the valley between my stomach and pelvic bone. My snowflake tattoo. I cross my legs and spread my fingers to obscure her view. Tears sting my eyes.

I hear the hiss of water as the other girls turn on the showers full blast. One doctor shoos us over to the showers while the other doctor hands us gritty lumps of soap. The water is freezing, but I almost don't feel it. I want to wash away the dirty feeling that's come over me.

I lather and lather and lather my body, trying to generate warmth. I am shivering. I scrub at the number on my arm until one of the doctors wags her finger at me.

'Rinse,' she says.

I wrap myself in a stiff towel that doesn't want to bend around me. My teeth are chattering. We are led to a bench with combs and brushes scattered on top. We dutifully yank the tangles from our hair. I slick mine away from my face. We are given hospital gowns with sleeves that don't reach my elbows and a hem that doesn't cover my knees. I wrap it around me, clutching closed the gaps between the series of ties on the front.

'We'll give you each a quick exam and then we'll show you to your room,' one doctor says, taking 1132 as the other doctor takes my arm and leads me to a door at the far end of the hall. As we get closer, I drag my feet. This isn't right. The doctor pulls me forwards.

'It's a little uncomfortable, but it's not going to hurt,' she tells me. 'It will be easier if you relax.'

'W-what are you g-going to do?' I ask as we reach the door.

She pauses with her hand on the doorknob. 'It's a simple female exam. You've had one of those before, haven't you?'

I vigorously shake my head. Some mothers take their daughters to doctors for female exams, but I've always been healthy. Mum got a letter in the mail from the Minister of Health when I turned sixteen. She read it and threw it in the bin. I'd rarely seen her that angry, so I dug the letter out when she wasn't looking. It was a doctor's appointment for me at the main medical facility. I didn't go, and Mum never mentioned it.

'Please, no,' I say when I see the examination table with two big metal arms at one end. I don't understand why they are doing this. I've got to get out of here. I think of Sanna, but only for a fleeting second. I don't have the strength to struggle, and the doctor's grip is firm. She pulls me inside the room.

'This is a simple exam. I promise you. A few tests. That's it. Hop up here and it will all be over soon.' She pats the exam table.

Braydon was right. This was stupid. What choice do I have now but to see my plan through? I summon all my strength and climb up on the table. She pushes me into a lying position. She stands at the end near my feet and pulls my hips forwards. She places my feet in the metal arms. My legs are spread wide around her. I try to close my legs, but she eases my knees apart.

'Relax. Take a deep breath. Close your eyes.'

I do as she says. I try to conjure up Braydon's face, the way he touched me so tenderly, but I can't. My body was so alive with sensations last night. Now my body is limp and lifeless. She pokes and prods between my legs. She's telling me what's she's doing. Some kind of test. Checking for something. I can't bear it. I wonder if I will ever be able to feel like I did last night. At this moment, I can't imagine it. I disappear into the darkness behind my eyes.

CHAPTER TWENTY-SEVEN

After the exam, they draw a tube of my blood. The lady who told me to call her Dr Ann leads me to a huge room with wall-to-wall cots. She tells me to lie here and rest until I feel strong enough to come outside. I pull the scratchy, thin blanket around my shoulders, fold my knees into my chest, and dig my heels into my buttocks.

My mind goes black. Maybe it's sleep. I don't care. I don't want to think.

I hear voices; people are talking loudly. I imagine it's Braydon. My eyes pop open. A face looms large in my field of vision. I think it's one of the girls from earlier because her hair still looks damp. I glance at her left forearm: 1132.

'Get up. Come on. There's a fire.' She's dragging me to my feet. I sway for a second, trying to find my balance. Sitting by a fire would be nice. Maybe it can take off the chill that has seeped into my bones, but I don't see a fireplace, just row after row of empty cots.

'Fire.' I say the word and think of Braydon and the smiley-face lighter. Fire. Fire. 'Fire?' I say again, but this time I'm beginning to understand. Number 1132 is ploughing a straight line to the door. Cots bang against my legs and I trip, but 1132 won't let me fall. Guards are shouting as they race past us. I think I hear a baby crying. I can smell smoke, but it can't be. They would have put out our small fire by now. Braydon should be waiting for my signal. Number 1132 is dragging me down the hall and towards the same door we came in. At least I think it's the same. My head feels foggy. I'm forgetting something. Something important. I almost remember, but it slips away. Then it comes flooding back.

I stop. Sanna. I break free from 1132. She glares at me and then darts out the door.

'Sanna,' I shout, and run through the building, punching open every door. The building is empty. I hesitate at the double doors at the end of the hallway. I push them open and look inside. It's an operating room. Silver surgical instruments are scattered across the floor. The room still looks sterile, except for a pool of blood, glistening red in the artificial light. There are red footprints that stop at the door I'm holding open. What are they doing to these women?

'Sanna!' I scream even louder and race back down the hallway and outside. It's night, but the sky glows. A wall of fire is blazing down the hillside. Did we cause this? How could our little fire be burning so wildly out of control? I pray that Braydon is safe. I want to run towards the fire and let it cleanse me. I feel dirty and raw. I imagine the warm flames licking my skin.

I am surrounded by a swirling sea of girls, dressed in the same flimsy nightgowns as I am. Their bare feet kick up dust from the dirt road. My ears are filled with the crackling sound of fire and popping as the heat consumes trees.

'Sanna!' I call. No one responds to the name. Maybe no one can hear me. I shout her name again as I weave through an ever-shifting mass of bodies. I turn girls to face me. I'm looking for Sanna's scar, but every face I see is rosy red and smooth. I shout her name again and again. Maybe she can't remember her name, and I don't know her number.

I am being drawn farther and farther away from the brick building. I can't leave without her. I stop and slowly turn, checking every face as it passes. Everyone's screaming. The girls form an uneven line and disappear down the road.

I race back to the brick building, the dust and smoke scratching my throat. I cough once to clear my airway, but I can't stop coughing. Black flecks of ash dot the hot air. I'm almost back where I started. I shout for Sanna again. I double over. I'm trying to catch my breath, but my body seems to reject it. I close my eyes and try to calm myself. Even though the air is thick with smoke, my mind is getting clearer. I must find Sanna.

I can see guards and women in blue pounding at the fire with blankets. They form a line from the brick building, and buckets and bowls and pitchers of water are being sloshed from hand to hand. The fire inches forwards, burning a black line in the brown grass. The smell of scorched earth is overpowering.

The door to the big wooden barn-like building is open, and girls in long, pink balloon-like nightgowns are staggering out. I race over to help them, to point them in the right direction. They are tripping over their gowns. One girl falls onto her hands and knees. I rush over to her. She looks up at me with a mixture of alarm and confusion.

'It's OK,' I tell her. I notice her number. It's 367+. I wonder why she has a plus by her number. 'What's your name?' I ask as I help her to her feet.

Her eyebrows narrow, and she squints. She can't understand what I've asked.

'What's your name?' I say again but realize now isn't the time. I point to the road. 'You need to follow those girls. Follow them.'

She nods and staggers forwards. She stops and turns towards me. 'Christy,' she calls. 'My name is Christy.'

'You need to run, Christy,' I yell, and wave her away. She starts walking, a little more steady on her feet now.

A few more girls in pink are exiting the barn. They look

around with half-open eyes. There's something else that doesn't seem right. Another girl drops to her knees. She doesn't cry out. I rush over to her. Her gown is pulled tight under her knees, and that's when I notice she's pregnant. She looks down at her bump as if she's only just noticed it. I help her up and instruct her to head to the road. I don't think she understands what I'm saying, but I point to the other girls in pink who are waddling forwards, like plump, round zombies.

I make my way to the barn's opening. The inside is bathed in a fiery glow. It's stark white like a hospital ward, dramatically different from its rustic exterior. Many hospital beds are lined in neat rows. Two women in scrubs are unhooking sleeping girls from the masks, tubes and needles that seem to pin them to their beds. Two other girls dressed like me are following behind them and waking the girls and hauling them to their feet.

And it all makes sense.

My whole body starts to shake. I think of my new government-issue brother or sister. A prison just for women. Our government's need for more citizens. The government is hijacking girls' bodies. I can't believe it's true, but the proof is all around me. My stomach convulses. The *what* and *how* are too awful to think about. I swallow back the bile rising in my throat. The horror of it refuses to sink in. I can't just stand here. I've got to help them.

With renewed energy, I press forwards. The farther I move into the building the hotter and hotter it gets, as if I'm walking into an oven. Sweat is dripping down my temples. I flick the sweat from my eyes so I can see more clearly. That's when I notice that the back of the structure has caught fire. Flames are eating black holes into the white walls. Two guards are beating the flames with blankets.

A girl my age walks towards me. She's so small that she's

swimming in the large pink gown. I rush up to her. She squints up at me.

'Nicoline.' I lunge for her and hold her close. I see the faint red outline of a star on her cheek. 'You're all right.' I hurry her forwards. 'Have you seen Sanna?'

She shakes her head.

'Sanna,' I say, and trace an S on my cheek.

'Sanna, I'm so glad you're safe.' Nicoline pats my cheek. She thinks I'm Sanna.

'No, where *is* Sanna?' I'm desperate to make her understand, but it's no use. I drag her outside and point.

She squints at me again. There's a flicker of recognition in her eyes. 'Sanna was here,' she says and walks away.

What does that mean? Does that mean Sanna was taken somewhere else? Or . . .

I won't let myself fill in that blank. I check every bed and every face. I'm ahead of the team waking the girls now. Only a few more beds to go.

Then I see her. Her scar shines brightly between the mask covering her nose and mouth and the tubes hanging from clear bags looped on hooks on the side of the bed. I watch the other women for a second and mirror how they are disconnecting the other patients. I check to see if the bed has wheels. Maybe I can wheel her out of here. But the beds are bolted to the floor.

'Sanna! Sanna! It's me, Neva. Wake up!' I'm shouting at her as I pull her to a sitting position. I lower the rail along the bed and swing her feet over the side. I shake her gently at first, repeating her name and mine. Then I slap her full in the face. Her eyelids pop open. She stares at me for a second and then rests her head on my shoulder. She's trying to speak. I can feel her lips moving.

I hug her close, and I hear her whisper, 'Nev, you came.'

'We've got to get out of here.' I half drag, half carry her out of the barn. The roof is on fire and the barn is filling with smoke. All the beds are empty and the last few girls are stumbling out along with us. At this pace we'll never make it. The fire is stretching out around us and closing in like a fiery hug.

We keep moving. We pass nearly all the girls in pink. I want to stop and help all of them, but I can't. I've got to save Sanna. I spot Nicoline and call to her. She waves and waits so we can catch up. Her eyes are open wider, but she's still a little unsteady on her feet. Her pink nightgown is dragging on the ground. I balance Sanna on my hip and bend over to pull up Nicoline's gown. I bunch a section of the hem in my fist and tie it into a big knot so she can walk without tripping.

'What are we going to do?' she asks. 'We'll never make it out of here.'

'We will. I promise. Braydon's here somewhere.' I look around as if hope will make him appear. Sanna perks up at the mention of his name. 'He'll get us out.' I say this like it's a fact, but my gut tenses. The fire is out of control. I've got no way of knowing where he is or if he's safe. And if, dear God, he *is* OK, we've got hundreds of women and one motorcycle.

As we walk, Sanna and Nicoline get stronger. My thighs feel slick with the gel the doctor used to examine me. The memory causes another wave of nausea. These girls have been through worse, much worse. Smoke and ash swirl around us. I pull my gown up to cover my nose and help Sanna and Nicoline do the same. Girls all around us are faltering. We stop to help and give encouragement, but words are hollow. Even the half-awake girls in pink understand our situation is pretty grim. My plan has gone so horribly wrong.

Sanna's nearly able to walk on her own by the time we reach the freshly paved road. Maybe it's my imagination, but I think I can hear the roar of the van that zoomed up behind Braydon and me yesterday. I turn in time to see a white van heading straight for us. I shove Nicoline and Sanna out of the way. As the van parts the smoke, I can see it is crammed with guards and other staff from the Empowerment Centre. They have stopped fighting the fire and are abandoning us. I help Nicoline and Sanna to their feet. We are miles from civilization. Without any means of transportation, we will die.

Girls are clustered in twos and threes. Everyone is helping one another. The sight makes me think of the Minister of Health's name for her baby-making prison: the Women's Empowerment Centre. Maybe she's done it after all. I'm surrounded by girls of all shapes and sizes, battered and bruised and coated in dirt and soot, but we don't give up.

'Come on!' I shout. 'Keep moving.' We walk. The fire flickers behind several rows of trees. It illuminates our path. Waves of heat push us forwards. I urge Nicoline and Sanna ahead of me. There's a fist-sized red spot on the back of Nicoline's gown. The stain, like the fire, seems to spread out at a rapid rate. Blood is dripping down her legs, leaving a trail of red spots for me to follow.

'She's miscarrying,' a young woman next to me whispers. 'She needs medical attention, in case there are complications. If the fire doesn't get her, she could bleed to death without the proper medical treatment.'

'What?'

The woman crosses her arms over her full round belly, as if she might catch whatever Nicoline has. 'You know what they've done to us,' she says.

I nod.

'Well, she doesn't. I had two miscarriages before I was sent here.' She hugs herself and sways as if rocking a baby. 'I knew what they were doing to me. Most of these girls don't have a clue. It's not like they tell us much before they send us off to dreamland. What's the date?'

I tell her.

'I've been out for seven months.' She starts to cry. 'Seven

months.' She grabs my arm and now I'm pulling her along.

Up ahead the girls seem to disappear. It takes me a minute to realize that we've made it to the highway. We could survive. Someone could spot us and get help.

'It's the highway,' I tell the woman. 'Up there.' She lets go of me and starts to run.

I find Nicoline and Sanna and wrap my arms around their waists. 'We've almost made it.'

Nicoline looks down at her blood-soaked gown.

'We'll get you help,' I tell her.

'What did they do to me?' she asks.

I can't tell her. 'You'll be OK.'

We've nearly reached the on-ramp to the highway. We hear screams. Has someone found us? We surge forwards.

Nicoline staggers and falls to the ground. 'Go on!' she shouts, and waves us on. How can we leave her? 'Go!' she demands.

'We'll come back!' I yell as Sanna and I run forwards. I can see them now – a fleet of white vans coming from the highway. A wave of hope shoots through me. The vans are skidding to a stop, barely missing the girls who have flagged them down. Two men in black hop out of each van – police! They shove the nearest girls into their vans.

I can feel a collective swell of anger. Our limp, defeated bodies straighten. Our hands clench in fists. We attack.

Sanna and I lunge at one policeman. We kick and claw and bite. He easily bats us away, but more girls join our fight, and soon he is overpowered. We move on to the next one, who has his arms full with two young girls. The girls are scratching his arms and face, and the man is howling. I punch him in the nose. Sanna jumps on his back and squeezes her arms around his neck until he releases the girls.

I am grabbed from behind; a strong arm wraps around my waist. 'Sanna!' I shout. I kick at his legs and elbow him in the face. He drops me and I land hard on my hands and knees, jarring every bone in my body. I'm stunned with the pain. I scream when he seizes a fistful of my hair and lifts me to my feet. Sanna charges, knocking him to the ground. I kick him hard. My foot makes contact with a satisfying thud. Now he's the one screaming.

'Nev, come on!' Sanna's pulling me off, but I want to keep kicking, even though the man has stopped fighting back. He's curled in a ball with his arms wrapped protectively around his head. I give him one final kick before Sanna can tear me away.

Girls are piling into the vans. A few of the vans are full and are pulling away. I notice the passengers in the van – all female. Sanna and I seem to get the same idea at the same time. We head for the nearest empty van. Two policemen are under attack from all sides. 'You load the van,' I tell Sanna. 'I'll get Nicoline.'

It's hard to see now; the black smoke is intense. The fire is hopping from tree to tree, advancing fast. I see a body on the ground up ahead. 'Nicoline!' I call, and race towards her. The bottom half of her gown is a solid red. The brown dirt underneath her is stained with her blood. I am only a few feet from her when I'm tackled from behind. I crash to the ground with the force of a body on top of me.

The weight is lifted and I am flipped onto my back. My attacker's face is a patchwork of dirt and bruises. His policeman's shirt and trousers are ripped and his red, raw skin is exposed.

Before I can react, he's lifted me off the ground and has locked my arms to my sides. I am pinned but facing away from him. I squirm with all my might, hoping to knock him off balance.

A loud crack splits through the chaos, and I stop fighting. A flaming tree is falling towards us, towards Nicoline. 'No!'

I shout, and flail in the man's arms as he carries me away. I watch the tree fall as if in slow motion. It erupts into a cloud of flame and ash when it hits the ground, engulfing Nicoline. A scream travels from my toes and radiates through me, filling the night air. The fire is now feet from me. The tree is spitting fire. Tiny pinpricks of heat sear my skin. My nightgown is covered in black, burned spots.

Nicoline is dead.

The policeman half drags, half carries me away from Nicoline's burning corpse. As we approach the van, Sanna stares wide-eyed at me from the driver's seat.

'Go!' I shout. 'Drive! Get out of here!' I deserve to die here with Nicoline.

The policeman drops me and pounds on the windscreen. Human shapes, some in black, some in pink and some in the same gown that I'm wearing, lie lifeless on the ground. 'If you don't let me in, I'll kill her.' He grabs me by the throat and lifts me. He presses me to the hood of the van. He'll kill me no matter what.

'Go, Sanna!' I shout before his hand tightens around my throat. The engine revs underneath me.

I turn so she doesn't have to see my face as he kills me. I am choking, eking out a few threads of air as he rams my head against the hood of the van. The pain explodes in my brain. He's screaming and the engine is roaring around me.

I must be dreaming.

Because I see Braydon.

He's on his motorcycle, heading straight for me.

He's off his bike before it stops. He punches the policeman in the face. The force of his blow releases me. I gasp in the smoky air. The policeman stumbles back, and I fall into Braydon's arms. He holds me up with one arm, bends over and pulls something from his boot. When he raises his arm, I see he's holding a gun.

218

'Stop!' Braydon demands, but the policeman is on his feet. He slowly walks towards us. 'Stop!' Braydon shouts again, but the man keeps coming.

Braydon squeezes the trigger and I hear the bang, but I don't understand until I see the policeman drop. A red hole opens in his chest.

Braydon opens the van door. 'Move!' he shoves me in, on top of Sanna, and she and I push girls out of the way to make room for Braydon to drive. Sanna sits in the passenger's seat. I end up on the floor between them.

'Are you OK?' Braydon asks as he slams the van into gear.

Sanna looks blankly from me to Braydon. She nods.

Braydon turns the van around, and we make our way over the uneven ground. As I rise and fall with each bump, I can't think about what's below us.

CHAPTER TWENTY-EIGHT

Rain taps angry fingers on the roof of the van. The raindrops started falling as soon as we left. The government's firefighters. We stare out in amazement as water blurs the landscape. It hasn't rained here for weeks. The weather monitors focus most of the rain showers on the population hubs. The government must know about the fire and our escape. They are probably looking for us already. The melody of the rain and the hum of the road numb my fear.

We've been driving for hours. I haven't moved from the floor between Sanna and Braydon. I can tell we are in the capital because the van is slowing and stopping and turning. I've been staring at the dashboard, watching the miles click by. I can't look at Sanna or Braydon or the girls who have quietly cried for hours. The smell of sweat and smoke is nauseating. Someone rolled down the windows, but the sour smell won't dissipate.

I see Nicoline's face when I promised I'd save her. My reckless actions got her arrested and sent to that awful place. My stupid, naïve plan killed her.

'Neva.' Braydon touches my shoulder and I flinch. 'Neva, we are at Senga's. I'll be right back. You keep everyone calm and in the van.'

Lovely, smart Braydon.

When the van door closes behind Braydon, everyone begins to stir.

'Where are we?' someone asks.

'I want to go home,' a high young voice squeaks.

'Everyone sit tight.' I lift myself into the driver's seat and survey my fellow passengers. There aren't as many girls as I imagined. Nine girls about my age are crammed into the space behind me. Their arms and legs intertwined.

Sanna adds, 'Senga will help us.'

'She's how we found you,' I tell her.

I look out through the windscreen. The Protectosphere is glowing pink in the early morning sun. Braydon has parked on a dead-end street lined with rubbish and recycling bins. It's a fitting spot for us.

'I want to go home. Please take me home.' It's the young voice again. She starts to cry.

'That's not possible, sweetie,' another girl says. 'If we go home, they will come and get us. You don't want to go back, do you?'

'But it's gone,' she says with a sniff. 'Everything's gone. The fire.'

'They can't let us out. Not like this.' I look at the girl in pink who is speaking. She's stroking her protruding belly.

'But I'm not like you.' The girl looks my age but sounds younger. She's wearing pink and has a plus sign by the number on her arm, just like the pregnant woman.

'Listen,' I say, turning to take my place in a circle of sorts. 'We are going to get through this.'

'How do we know we can trust you? Trust him?' the girl next to me asks, and jerks her head at the driver's seat as if an invisible Braydon is there.

'He saved us, didn't he?' I half smile, remembering the sight of him riding to my rescue.

'He shot that man,' the girl interjects.

My smile fades. Braydon has a gun. I try not to show the hint of fear I feel.

'He had to,' Sanna says. 'And his name is Braydon. I'm Sanna.'

Everyone hides their numbered forearms and speaks their names: Margaret, Kate, Karen, Bronia, Elizabeth, Sandra, Emily, Vinita and Ashley.

'I'm Neva,' I say, but I feel more like 1133.

I jump when the van door opens. I automatically ball my hands into fists, ready to fight.

'It's me, Neva.' Braydon slips into the seat with me. I lean back into him. I want his arms around me. I want him to tell me that everything will be all right, but Sanna's looking at us with a blank stare. I slip back onto the floor between them.

'OK,' Braydon says, looking at the scared girls' faces. 'Senga and her friend Carson are going to be here in a minute. They are going to take you someplace safe.'

The girls start to fidget and protest. I hold up my hands. 'Senga is the one who told me how to find the Women's Empowerment Centre. She's on our side. She will help you. I promise.'

Senga and Carson arrive with armloads of blankets. The girls file out. Sanna and I remain in the van. Senga opens the passenger-side door. 'Time to go, Sanna,' she says, handing her a blanket.

'I'm staying with Neva and Braydon.' Sanna hugs the blanket and settles back in her seat.

Senga looks from me to Braydon. 'Will you be OK?' she asks me.

'I'll take care of them.' Braydon reaches out a hand to each of us. Sanna takes his hand and tugs him closer. I let his hand dangle in the air.

'We'll be fine,' I reassure Senga. 'Just take care of them.' I nod towards the huddled group of girls.

'You know I will.' She closes the van door. Braydon and Sanna's hands are clasped above my head. I know Sanna needs him more than I do, but it's as if last night never happened. I slip into one of the empty seats in the back. I remember my grandma's invitation. Now it's my only option. Tonight I will escape and leave all this behind.

The sun is high in the sky by the time we arrive at Braydon's mansion. He hides the van in a garage behind the house. We file into the kitchen, unsure of what to do next.

'I'm sorry, Sanna,' I say, collapsing into one of the kitchen chairs.

'What do you have to be sorry for?' She looks down at her bare feet, nearly black with soot. 'You and Braydon came for me.' She laughs and wiggles her toes. The sound seems strange after all we've been through. 'I knew you would. I kept telling myself, "Neva won't forget me. She won't write my name with the others. She won't let me go missing".'

Braydon and I exchange a glance. I can tell he's thinking about what we shared last night. It seems a distant memory now, like the illusion of real stars beyond the Protectosphere.

'I almost forgot,' Braydon says after another awkward silence. He reaches into his jeans pocket and pulls out a long, thin chain. My snowflake charm twinkles as it dangles in the air. 'You don't want to forget this.' He slips the necklace over my head. I look down, not wanting to betray what I'm feeling. His fingers brush my cheek, and the tiniest spark from last night fills me.

'Thanks for keeping it safe,' I say.

Sanna's studying us. Her eyebrows are pinched together. Maybe she remembers catching Braydon and me kissing. She looks confused for a moment, then hugs Braydon closer to her. 'Our Neva's definitely one of a kind,' she says, smiling until her face creases unnaturally.

I finger the snowflake pendant and wish I could melt away.

I stand in the cold shower for ages. I let Sanna go before me. She had more she needed to wash off. I use soap and shampoo, but I can still smell the smoke. I can still feel the places where the doctor examined me. My arm is red and raw from where I tried to remove the black ink from my forearm. I can still see the number. Sanna comes in and makes me stop scrubbing. My arm is bleeding in tiny tears, like when I fell off my bike and scraped my knee when I was five. Sanna turns off the water and hands me a towel.

We dress in Braydon's clothes. She chooses one of his crisp white dress shirts. I select the shirt he was wearing at the Dark Party when we first kissed. I find a pair of cargo pants for each of us. We cinch them up tight with belts. Sanna pulls on a big, blue woolly sweater she finds in one of the closets. She also finds a scarf and swirls it around her neck, but she's still shivering.

'Go get in bed,' I tell her. She leaves me alone in Braydon's closet. His leather jacket is draped on a hook. I touch the rough, cracked leather and remember our motorcycle ride. I hug the jacket to my chest. I can smell him. I close my eyes and bury my face in the leather and lose myself in the memory of being moulded to Braydon with wind whipping past us and the open road ahead. I drink in his scent and then I smell the smoke and see the fire in my mind's eye. The image of the policeman at the moment Braydon shot him flashes into my mind. Fear flickered in the policeman's eyes before they went dark and dull. Then I see Braydon pointing that gun. The image should comfort me, but it doesn't. His eyes were as cold and dark as the policeman's had been when he was choking me. My eyes spring open, and I toss the jacket onto the floor.

Sanna and I curl up in Braydon's big bed. Braydon has drawn the curtains, but they are threadbare and don't block out much light. We huddle together for warmth and for fear that someone will come and take us away. Sanna's hair smells sweet from the strawberry shampoo. I place my arm around her waist and wonder if she is carrying a government-issue baby. I shudder.

'Sanna,' I whisper in her ear.

'Yeah.' The word slurs with sleep.

'Are you OK?' It's a stupid question. Of course she's not OK. None of us are or ever have been.

She scoots closer to the edge of the bed.

I don't press the issue. 'Sleep well, Sanna.'

She rolls on her back. She stares at Braydon's mask collection. Their expressions look horrified, as if they know what she's been through and what I've done. We lie there blinking at the faces that stare blind-eyed at us.

I wonder where Braydon is. He has given us a little space. It's too hard to be in the same room with Braydon and Sanna together. My loyalties feel divided and my guilt multiplied. How can I leave them like this? Sanna won't make eye contact with him. Braydon tried to talk to her, but Sanna mumbled something and eventually walked away. I want him here holding me. I want to feel reconnected to my life. My life has no borders now, no Protectosphere to keep me grounded.

'Nev? You still awake?' Sanna asks.

'Yeah.'

'I . . .' she starts, but forgets what she wants to say.

I wait.

'I can't remember. One minute I was being dragged away by the police and the next minute you were waking me up.' She looks around at Braydon's masks. Their mouths are open as if they want to speak, to tell our story. 'I feel like one of Braydon's masks.'

'Maybe it's best you don't remember.' She doesn't need to know. Not now. Maybe when she's stronger.

'Yeah.' She snuggles deeper under the covers. 'Braydon was great, wasn't he?'

'Yeah.'

'A real hero.' She sighs.

Tears slip from the corners of my eyes and trickle down my temples and into my ears. I try not to think about what's next. We are safe for now and that's all that matters. I sniff and wipe my eyes on the pillow. I've been living in a carefully constructed house of lies. I'll let Sanna live there a little while longer. I was much happier not knowing.

I think she might have fallen asleep. I don't want to disturb her. I want her to forget everything that has happened to her for the past few days. I hope she's forgotten our fight.

'Nev,' Sanna whispers. Her voice surprises me.

'Yeah,' I murmur, trying to act as if I've been asleep.

'I forgive you,' she says.

It's more than I could have hoped for. A sob collects in my throat. I swallow it back. The centre of my chest aches. She grips and nearly crushes my hand.

I've got to get out of here. Death would be better than lying here, holding my best friend's hand but wanting her boyfriend. I will break out of this shell and find out what's beyond. I can survive anything if my grandma is waiting for me. At least I only have to live with these lies until midnight.

CHAPTER TWENTY-NINE

I 'm exhausted, but I can't sleep. The light is ebbing from the house as day turns to dusk. Sanna is still holding my hand, but she's softly snoring. Every time I close my eyes, I'm back at the Empowerment Centre. I can feel the doctor examining me. I can see Nicoline's trusting face. I slowly withdraw my hand from Sanna's. Her grip tightens as she rolls over to face me, but her eyes are still shut. I try again. This time I move only a fraction and then count to twenty before I move my hand a little again. My mind is focused on getting free. Her breathing has a slow and steady rhythm. I count, using her breaths, and decide to move only on her exhale. The process is painstaking. When I'm finally free, she rolls away from me. I wait a few minutes before I sit up, and another before I shift my feet off the side of the bed.

My first thought is to sneak away. No one can know I'm leaving. How do I say a final goodbye, especially to Sanna? After everything she's been through, everyone she's lost, how can I desert her? Seeing Braydon will only make me want to stay. I see my Missing in a different light. I'm not the one filling the hole they leave behind. I'm the one escaping, and I feel a rush at the thought of simply fading to black. But I want one more moment with Braydon.

He's not in the other bedroom. I tiptoe down the stairs. As I reach the entryway, there's a faint knock on the door. I panic and search for a place to hide. I duck into the coat closet. I keep the door open a crack to let a little light seep in. I position myself so I can see the front door. The house is quiet. Maybe I imagined it. As I prepare to slide the door open, I hear it again. This time the taps are insistent.

Braydon appears in my limited field of vision. I should stop him. He hesitates at the front door and glances up the stairs as if he's checking to make sure Sanna and I are still tucked in his bed. What is he doing?

He opens the door halfway, his body a barrier between me and whoever is outside.

'Braydon, where have you been?' A rough male voice slices through the silence.

The door is being forced open, but Braydon stands his ground. He struggles to close the door a little further. 'I've got the situation under control.'

'I doubt that.' The door is thrust open and in strolls a man in a police uniform. I bury myself further into the musty coats behind me.

Braydon steps in front of the officer and blocks my view. 'I said I would handle it.'

'You've made a mess of things so far, Braydon.' He laughs.

I can't process what's happening. I don't understand.

'Just back off and let me do my job.' Braydon shoves the officer, pushing him into the doorframe.

The officer pokes a black-gloved finger at Braydon's chest. 'You need to watch it. We've tried it your way. Now we do it mine.'

'I can still turn them. I'm so close.' What is Braydon saying?

'We want to make an example of them—'

'And you will,' Braydon interrupts.

Time stops. I can't believe what I'm hearing. I've been dropped into a black hole, my senses muted. I hear Braydon say the word *complicated*. I listen hard for the officer's response.

'I expect them to be delivered to the Central Police Station by midnight tonight.' The officer's words rise through the rubble in my brain.

Braydon's nodding and edging the man out the door. He glances up at where I should be sleeping, then follows the officer outside and shuts the door behind them.

I want to scream. The realization shocks through me like an explosion ripping feeling and emotion and life from me. He's working for the government. I can't believe it and yet the truth resonates to my core. I've been so stupid. Has everything been a lie? All that talk of running away together. Has it all been an elaborate trap? He's engineered everything, even my heart. I should have trusted my first instinct. All the puzzle pieces fall into place. That's how he lives here. How he has new clothes and other things none of the rest of us can get. That's why he singled out Sanna. That's how the police have tracked me down. That's why he kissed me in the dark.

The only piece that doesn't fit is why he saved us. He could have left us at the Empowerment Centre. I don't understand, but I know I can't trust him any more. I befriended a snake and shouldn't be surprised when it bites. I won't let him rob me of my freedom. I won't let him destroy Sanna. I block out everything except my need to survive. I race up the stairs and, as quietly as I can, I wake Sanna. She's confused, but I tell her we have to go. Now. I think of the only lie that will get her moving. 'Braydon's in trouble.'

She's on her feet. We communicate wordlessly, the way only two people can when their lives are as intertwined as ours have always been. Sanna follows my lead and helps arrange the pillows to make it look like we're still in bed and asleep. I open the doors that lead onto the balcony, which overlooks the back garden. I see the garage and know the van is our only means of escape.

I climb over the balcony railing. Sanna follows my lead.

I bend down and grip the lower ledge as I cautiously dangle my legs over the side. My toes are about five feet from the ground. I let go and fall with a thud. I spring to my feet and raise my arms to help break Sanna's fall. A strange thought flashes through my mind: I've got to protect her because she's pregnant. But maybe they didn't do that to her. Maybe we got to her in time.

I catch Sanna, and we run towards the garage. A car engine starts. I pull her to the ground and clumsily drape myself on top of her. I try to decipher which way the car is moving. There's a crunch of gravel and then the roar of the engine fades. I hope this means that the police officer has left. I search for a back way out, but I can't risk getting trapped. I lead Sanna to the garage and open the door as soundlessly as possible. We climb into the van. I start the engine and fumble with the gear-stick. It's an automatic and I squint to see when the D for drive lights up. I've only watched my parents drive. I've never been behind the wheel. I tap the accelerator and the van lurches forwards and stops. I ease the accelerator down again and carefully steer along the dirt alley that leads to the front drive.

'What about Braydon?' Sanna says, pressing her palm against the windscreen when we both spot him staring wide-eyed at us from the front door.

'We're meeting up with him later,' I lie. 'Get down and stay out of sight.' I shove her onto the floor with my free hand so she can't see Braydon chasing after the van. I press the accelerator until it makes contact with the floor. I consider for a second if I should run him over. But I can't waste time. Grinding his body into the gravel won't make a damn bit of difference. Braydon's already dead to me.

CHAPTER THIRTY

N ight is closing in, and the chill is inside me, emanating from me. I can't believe how stupid I've been. From the first moment I met Braydon, my gut told me not to trust him. Then we kissed. That horrible, treacherous kiss. I wipe my mouth on my shirtsleeve at the thought of it. His shirtsleeve. I want to rip off his clothes and tear out the part of me that he touched.

I glance in the rear-view mirror. Sanna's asleep in the back of the van. How can I tell her about Braydon's betrayal? It would kill her. The thing I keep trying to focus on is that I'm leaving tonight. I will take Sanna with me, and we will put Homeland and all its death and corruption behind us. I will make myself forget about Braydon and the last few days. I will be reborn when I emerge from the Protectosphere. That thought gives me a little comfort.

I have one final stop to make. I park the van in the alley behind my house. I leave Sanna sleeping. I cover her with one of the blankets Senga gave us so she's partially camouflaged. If Braydon has contacted the police, then nowhere is safe. But I've got to risk it. I've got to warn my mum, tell her what the government is doing. I watch the house until I'm sure Mum is alone. I crawl under the ramshackle fence that borders our back garden. For once I'm pleased nothing gets repaired. I open the back door soundlessly. I'm startled when I hear a baby cry. I follow the noise to my bedroom. I peek inside.

'It's OK,' my mum coos as the baby's cries subside. She's pacing across the room, bouncing as she walks. Her ponytail is loose and hangs to one side. Her face has the bleached look of someone who has been crying. She cradles a baby close to her chest. 'That's my girl. It's nighty-night time.' She used to say that to me. She starts to hum a lullaby. I haven't heard that melody in years, but I recognize it instantly. She presses her cheek to the baby's. She sways and hums as if in a trance.

'Mum,' I whisper, breaking the spell between mother and baby. She doesn't hear me. 'Mum,' I say a little louder.

She screams. The baby starts crying again. Her whole body starts shaking, and I think she's going to drop the baby. I rush to her and scoop the baby into my arms. Mum throws her arms around me and sobs into my neck. 'They told me you were dead.'

I wriggle free to give the crying baby some air. She's so tiny and fragile. Her face is red and blotchy and her cheeks are damp with tears. All I want to do is stop her flood of tears and see her pouty lips smile. *Her* sadness I can remedy. I bounce, and the baby's cries turn to a whimper.

'She likes it if you walk,' Mum says, wiping the baby's tears.

I pace the floor. All my furniture is crammed into one corner. There's a crib where my bed used to be. My clothes are still scattered on the floor. When I stop moving, the baby starts to cry, so I keep moving, even though I'm weary.

'I wouldn't let anyone take anything,' she says, closing the curtains.

I tell Mum everything about the Women's Empowerment Centre, what they've done to Sanna, what Braydon has done to me, and my grandma's invitation. Mum's gaze follows me, but her body is still. Her arms hang limply at her sides.

'I've heard rumours,' she says when I've finished. 'They are taking young girls, but I never thought they would go this far.

I tried to protect you, but you're too much like your grandma.'

'I'm a lot like you too.' I wish I'd known sooner what a rebel my mum was in her own quiet way. I wish we'd trusted each other with our secrets. I want her to make it all right like she used to. She could kiss a scraped knee and make it all better. She could sing me a lullaby and chase the monsters away. But I know she can't make this OK.

'Neva, you have to leave. Go and be with your grandma.' Her eyes sparkle with tears.

'Come with me,' I say, and realize that this is why I'm here. She's the only thing keeping me here.

She doesn't hesitate. 'I can't.'

'Why not?' I ask, but I know her answer already.

'I could never leave your father ... or Jane.' She nods at the baby.

She's got to stay and fight alongside the Sengas and Carsons of Homeland. Part of me wants to stay and fight too.

Tears stream in tandem down our cheeks.

She wipes her eyes and coughs back the emotion. 'You better go.'

Jane is finally asleep. I pull her close. I smell that sweet combination of milk and baby lotion. I kiss her on the cheek and hand her back to Mum.

'She's got your nose,' Mum says, touching the top of Jane's nose.

'Everyone's got my nose.' I study Jane's tiny features.

'She's got your sparkle. She's really smart. I can already tell.' Mum lays Jane in her crib. She tucks the tattered blanket around Jane's tiny frame. She already loves her. Even though Jane's been manufactured to keep Homeland alive, Mum sees her unique beauty, just like she always saw mine.

I feel a slight sting of jealousy. Jane gets to keep my mother.

'Is it OK if I take a few things?' I ask.

'Sure.' Mum fusses around me, picking up the clothes that

233

litter the floor. She strokes my hair when I pass her. She never takes her eyes off me. We are bumping into each other as she shadows me. 'You must be hungry,' she says when we collide again. 'I'll get you some food to take with you.' I couldn't eat a thing, but I know she wants to keep busy. I can't take her sad eyes watching me. It's hard enough without seeing the hurt I'm causing. I nod and she scurries out of the room.

First I strip out of Braydon's clothes. I find scissors in my desk and cut his shirt in half and half again. I want to shred his clothes until they are only a pile of thread. Then I want to burn the thread and flush the ashes. My anger is building on itself. I stare at myself in the mirror. My body is battered and bruised, but it's nothing compared to the wounds I can't see. The wounds that will never heal. For a fleeting moment, I think maybe I could stay, but I can't. Braydon has orders to turn me in. The government wants to make an example of Sanna and me. The police are probably looking for us. If I want to survive, I have to leave Homeland forever.

I've got to make it to the Capitol Complex by midnight.

I dress quickly. I dig out my journal from the mattress. I kneel by my bed as if reciting my bedtime prayers. God bless Grandma and Mummy and Daddy and Sanna. That was my order of things. I think it bothered Dad that Grandma got top billing, but she was the one who helped me memorize that awful prayer: Now I lay me down to sleep, I pray the Lord my soul to keep. If I should die before I wake, I pray the Lord my soul to take.

One night I told Grandma I didn't want to say the prayer any more.

'Why not?' she asked; we both stared at our hands, which were clasped together in prayer.

I pressed my lips against the edge of my hands and mumbled, ''Cause I don't like the death part.'

'I don't like the death part either,' she said, looking

heavenward. 'Let's see.' Her eyes seemed to search the ceiling for something and then the edges of her lips twitched in a wicked smile.

'Now I lay me down to snore,' she started. 'Make tomorrow not a bore. Give me laughter, song and smile. And keep me safe all the while.'

I press my forehead into the journal's rough cover and repeat that prayer.

I flip through the pages, stroking each one, until I come to the end of The Missing. I flatten the next blank page. I write my name and Sanna's in bold, black capital letters. I retrace each line. I write today's date and in the final column I write: 'I love you, Mum!' I pause and try to think of something more. I want to tell her I'm sorry and that I hope I don't get her into trouble. She has been living a second life for some time, not the recycled kind like her mother did, but a fresh new path she's created for herself.

'Nev?'

I gasp at the sound of my name, even though it's barely spoken. Sanna is standing in the doorway. Her fuzzy hair creates a ragged halo around her face. She's staring at me with blank eyes. I close my journal and tuck it under my shirt.

'I woke up and you were gone.' Her tone is flat and her face registers no emotion. She blinks once, twice.

'I'm just picking up a few things.' I go to her side. 'Why don't you meet me back in the van?' I cradle her elbow and try to steer her out of the room. It's as if Sanna's body is here, but she's somewhere else.

Jane makes a soft sucking sound and stirs in her crib. The noise seems to draw Sanna back. 'What's that?' She walks over to the crib.

'That's Jane,' I say.

Sanna leans over the crib and gently strokes Jane's back. She's transfixed by the baby.

I'm almost annoyed at the interruption. 'Stay here for a second. I'll be right back.'

I slip into my parents' room. I head straight for Mum's dresser. It's solid oak, a hand-me-down from her mother. The scratches from decades of use blend with the wood's grain to make it somehow appear more solid. I open the top drawer and slip the journal underneath my mum's beige cotton knickers. At the bottom of the drawer I see a hint of colour – something red and pink that reminds me of nail varnish. As I cover the journal in a pile of beige cotton, I can't help but expose the two colourful items – lacy underwear. My mum has two pairs of lacy knickers, and not the old-lady style with lace over a cotton brief. These are see-through lace, cut high to expose the curve of the hip. I'm not sure I want to think of my mother wearing sexy underwear. How did she ever get her hands on these anyway? Another mystery about my mother I will not get to solve. I put them back where I found them. I thought she was beige cotton underwear, and now I know that underneath that frumpy-mum camouflage, she's lacy pink bikinis.

When I get back to my room, Sanna's cuddling Jane in her arms. She's swaying the same way my mother did and humming a tuneless lullaby. Her eyes are fixed on something far, far away.

'I know what they did to me,' she says, not looking at me, not looking at anything. 'They examined me. They said I was ready.' She half laughs. 'Just my luck, huh, Nev? Captured in perfect time.' She's still swaying. 'They strapped me on one of those butterfly tables.'

I know what she means. I shiver at the thought of that examination table, which held my legs open, like butterfly wings.

'I knew what they were doing and I couldn't stop them.' She kisses Jane and gently lays the sleeping baby back in her crib. 'I can feel it there, growing.' She presses her hand into her abdomen.

I take a step towards her. 'I'm going to get you out of here.' I move closer. 'We're leaving Homeland forever.'

She looks directly at me as if she's trying to take it all in. 'What about Braydon?'

'Braydon's not coming.' I swallow with the effort it takes to say his name. She's got to know the truth. 'Braydon is working for the government.'

She nods, unphased, as if she's known it all along.

'Sanna, Braydon's got orders to turn us in. The government wants to make examples of us.'

She squints and studies my face but doesn't say anything.

'We've got to leave tonight.' I reach to put my arm around her, but she moves away.

'I can't go.' She wraps her arms protectively around her stomach.

'Didn't you hear what I said? The police are looking for us. We can't stay here.'

'She's right,' Mum tells Sanna, stepping into the room and handing me a brown paper bag. 'For later.'

'Thanks, Mum.'

She hooks one arm around me and one around Sanna. 'You both need to go.'

Sanna curls into my mum. 'I'm not going.'

Mum and I glance at each other and then at Sanna.

Sanna straightens herself and steps free. 'I said I'm not going.' With her tear-stained cheeks, she looks as innocent as Jane. 'Let them make an example of me.' She tugs at the tail of her shirt. 'Let everyone see what they've done to me.'

'But ... but ...' I stammer. I can see a flicker of the old Sanna glowing in her eyes. 'Then I'm staying too.'

'No,' Sanna and Mum say almost in unison.

'But—' I try again.

Sanna stops me. 'Nev, don't end up like me. Go and find out what's out there.' She lifts her gaze skyward.

'I can't leave you. Not like this.' I shrug off Mum's embrace.

'You've got to, my precious girl,' Mum says, and strokes my hair. 'I'll take care of Sanna.'

'We'll be a team again,' Sanna adds. 'You on the outside and us on the inside.'

I wrap my arms around them both. I have no intention of going. Not now. I cling to them and sob uncontrollably in my mum's shoulder. If they can stay and fight, so can I.

'Neva.' My mum's voice is cold. 'Neva, you must listen to me.' She holds me at arm's length. 'You have to go. If Sanna is pregnant, the government won't hurt her. But if you stay you will endure much worse than Sanna has.'

My reality dissolves. I don't know what to do. I can't stay, and I can't leave.

'Nev,' Sanna says softly. 'Do this for us? You aren't leaving us. You're giving us hope.'

My vision is blurred with tears. A new plan begins to take shape. If I can make it out alive, then I can save them too. I'll find a way to come back. This isn't goodbye.

CHAPTER THIRTY-ONE

After I leave my house, I drive into the City. I'm not sure I can do this. But it's not just for me. I have to be strong for Mum and Sanna. I ditch the van on an abandoned, dead-end street and zigzag through the City on foot. My reality has shifted, and I'm amazed that life is playing out around me as usual. Even though I try to act casual and blend in, I'm surprised people can't see the change in me.

I never stop moving, not for one second. I play hide-and-seek with a few policemen, but it's approaching midnight and the capital seems empty. Thomas said most of the police and Border Patrol would be guarding the border during the renovation.

The bells of the clock tower begin their out-of-tune melody. It's midnight and I'm hidden among the wreckage of the Capitol Complex. I wander out from my hiding place and take a look around. Even though I don't see anyone, I feel as if I'm being watched. The shadows seem to move and form new shapes. The last time I was here was when Ethan was arrested. I can still see him smiling down at me from the top of the rubble. Everything has changed since then. If he hadn't been arrested. If we had never had a Dark Party. But all those events led to this moment and the truth.

I turn in a slow circle, searching for a signal or a sign. Suddenly a dark figure emerges from the wreckage. The person is wearing a baseball cap pulled down to shadow his face.

I have to look hard to see the outline of his body. It almost blends in with the surroundings. He waves me over. I walk forward, stopping a few times to look over my shoulder.

'Are you Thomas's friend?' the person asks when I am within arm's reach.

I nod.

'Identity mark?'

'It's a snowflake tattoo. Here.' I press my hand into the valley between my stomach and hip.

'I must have visual confirmation.' He looks around and draws me deeper into the rubble.

Now I wish I'd made my mark easy to see. I step in closer and pull the waistband on my jeans low. I lean back so the moonlight hits the spot on my skin.

'That's fine.' He turns towards the heart of the rubble. 'Follow me.' He's weaving his way between the twisted metal. He's heading farther into the collapsed building. This could be a trap. 'Come on,' he says when he notices I haven't moved.

I've come this far. I can't go back home, so I blindly follow this stranger. There's no way out. I don't understand where he's taking me. He slips through a gap between an old door frame and a steel beam. He raps three times on the beam and the rubble behind the door slides aside. 'Your guide will lead you through the tunnel.' The stranger in the baseball cap steps aside and then walks away.

The only light sources are well behind me. My eyes adjust to the hazy grey as panic burrows down to my bones. I hear someone coming towards me.

'Say something so I can find you.' The voice is closer and deeper, definitely male.

'I'm right here,' I say and step forward. I wave my arms in front of me and am surprised when my fingertips brush a body.

'OK. Follow me.' He finds my hand and places it on his shoulder. He takes off, accidentally kicking my shin. 'Sorry.'

We take a few steps and I tread on his heels.

'Too close,' he says.

The space is pitch black. I take a deep breath, keeping my fear at bay. I will not let the darkness rob me of my freedom and Sanna's hope.

We eventually get the hang of walking together. The walls are close. If I move an inch to the left or right, I'm scratched by stone or metal. The darkness constricts. My skin is damp with sweat. I concentrate on putting one foot in front of the other, but my breath comes faster and faster.

'Where are you taking me?' I ask, shuffling behind him.

'Out the other side.' He half laughs.

'But how—'

'Do I see?' He finishes my sentence. 'This is my domain. I know these tunnels better than I know the City streets.'

'I never knew there were tunnels in here,' I say breathlessly. My head swims as panic grabs hold.

'They've been here for years,' the guide says, his business-like tone softening.

Don't think about the dark. 'Where do they lead?' I ask, and try to steady my breath.

'They tie into the old underground train systems. You can walk out of the City underground.'

'What?' Not only is there a tunnel through the ruins of the Capitol Complex, there were once underground trains?

'I forget they don't teach you about that any more.' His hair brushes across my hand. I think he's shaking his head. 'The government erases so much of our real history.'

I know who erases it. There's so much more my dad never told me, never told anyone. He's not the Minister of Ancient History. He's the Minister of Invented History.

'How much farther?' I trip and let go of his shoulder for a minute. He grabs my hand and keeps me from falling.

'We've got a ways to go. Stay right behind me.' He places

my hand on his shoulder. 'It's probably better if we stay quiet. There are old vents and grates that open to the surface.'

My eyes keep trying to adjust to the darkness to see something, anything, but the black is intense. The darkness feels as if it has mass and weight. I'm suffocating and being crushed simultaneously. We are walking down an incline. I don't want to think about being led deeper underground. The air cools. I steal a lung-filling breath. I can tell that we've moved from our tiny tunnel to somewhere more open. The sounds of our footsteps seem to be swallowed up in this new, vast space. A breeze flicks the ends of my hair. The ground is smoother, not dirt and debris any more. Walking is easier, but I am unnerved, not knowing what surrounds me. The darkness closes in. If we lost touch, I would be stranded. I would never find my way back in this maze.

'Relax,' the man says. 'Not much farther.'

I try to imagine the space. I give it a high, rounded ceiling and square tiles on the floor. I paint the tunnel white and illuminate every nook and cranny. I concentrate on following him.

I think I see a speck of light ahead. Light. I focus there. My eyes start to adjust. Shapes start to form. I step next to my guide and we walk for a while. 'You can go on alone from here,' he says when the exit is clearly visible. I must look scared because he reassuringly pats me on the back. 'The worst part is over. There's a van outside.'

I think of the government vans that transported Sanna and the others to the Women's Empowerment Centre. A new fear flashes through me from head to toe.

'You've got to go now.' He prods me forwards.

'And then what?'

'I only know my part of the journey. I've brought you this far. I've done my part.'

'OK.' The warmth drains from my body.

'I can take you back if you've changed your mind,' he says, sensing my uncertainty.

'No.' I clear my throat and speak more firmly. 'No, I'm ready to go.' My voice wobbles a bit. 'Thank you.'

'Good luck.' He shakes my hand and walks back into the tunnel.

Once outside, I drink in the cool night air. A woman is standing between me and the van. She doesn't really look at me as she opens the doors to the back of the van.

I hesitate. 'What happens now?'

'I take you to the border.' She jerks her head towards the van, encouraging me to get in.

I don't budge. I can't aimlessly follow any more. 'And then what?'

'When you arrive at the border, you will wait for a signal. The Protectosphere is under renovation. Each section of the Protectosphere is turned off while the panels are upgraded. You will have a few hours – I don't know how many exactly – to make it through the tunnels before the Protectosphere is electrified.' It's obvious that she's given this speech before. 'We take back roads to the border and we've found a way to avoid the Border Check Points, but the government has increased security. I can't guarantee your safety.'

I nod.

'We need to go now,' she says in a way that discourages any more questions.

I climb into the van and am relieved to discover that I'm not alone. It's hard to see clearly, but I think there are seven other people sitting in a circle with their backs pressed against the sides of the van. The seats have been removed. A wooden partition separates us from the driver. The two square windows on the back doors have been blacked out with paint. The driver closes us in.

This is it. I'm leaving. I will soon know what's outside the

Protectosphere. It's almost like finding out what's after death. I hope I don't find that out too. I try to focus on a new beginning, not the end of so much.

The van subtly vibrates. With every bump and turn I feel more claustrophobic. I can hear my fellow passengers breathing. They are sucking the oxygen out of the space and leaving none for me. I try to picture my future, but I can't conjure up my grandma's face. I can't seem to remember what she looked like. I try to imagine a vast ocean with a ceiling-less sky, but I don't know how to picture that kind of freedom.

There are a few spots of light where the paint on the windows has chipped. I let my eyes adjust and trace the outlines of the figures in the van. And suddenly the loss is overwhelming, not just leaving my family and country behind but the loss of innocence and trust – the things Braydon has stolen from me. I reach out and find the hand of the person sitting next to me. It's a small hand, a child's. I smile down at her even though I know she can't see my face. I feel her move, then hear the shuffle of hands around the van. I can hear the soft clap when hands meet.

After a period of time that is immeasurable, the van skids and swerves. We free our hands and brace ourselves, but we are tossed into one another and bang into the side of the van. The vehicle jolts to a stop and we slide forwards and pile into the partition separating us from the driver, then spring back now the van is at rest.

Before we can untangle ourselves, the two back doors are wrenched open and we squint up at a bright light. The light doesn't have any warmth. It's white and artificial. Its source is slowly revealed. Two figures are holding powerful flashlights. They move the beams and I can see more dark figures behind them. One of them grabs a leg from our pile of bodies and pulls the person out of the van. The body is lifted and practically thrown to another dark figure. Border Patrol. My insides feel as if they are perpetually falling.

I search for the child who was sitting next to me and reach for her. Her round, wide eyes plead with me to save her. I pull her closer, but I am being dragged from the van. Gloved hands pry my fingers from the hand that I've been holding. A needle-sharp pain stabs my left thigh, and then everything fades to black.

CHAPTER THIRTY-TWO

M y name is whispered in my ear. At least I think the sounds form my name. I try to speak. I want to tell them to leave me alone. I'm floating, my body feels like liquid, and my brain is peacefully static. I don't want to lose this feeling.

I close my eyes tighter. I'm beginning to feel my body, to reconnect, but I don't want to, not yet. Someone is speaking, shaking and ripping me from this in-between place.

'Neva Adams, wake up.' The voice isn't whispering any more.

I try to open my eyes, but it's as if I don't remember what muscles to use. I raise my eyebrows and try to pull my eyelids open. The images come back to me. My trip through the secret tunnels under the City. Escaping in the van. Getting caught by the Border Patrol.

I open my eyes a crack. A dark figure looms over me and I scramble as far away from him as I can. The room is completely white. It almost glows. I'm huddled on a grey-and-white-striped mattress. If I lie or stand and stretch my arms up above me, I could touch the room's walls or ceiling. I want to close my eyes again.

'Where am I?' I ask, and I cough to clear what feels like a dry wad of cotton from my throat.

'We are at the Border Patrol Detention Centre,' the figure says.

I once again inhabit my body. I have an orange bracelet with my name printed on it. How did they know my name? My hand presses my tattoo through my jeans, which are unbuttoned. I feel violated. I clutch my throat, searching for my necklace, and exhale when my fingers find the snowflake pendant.

'Come with me.' The figure extends a black-gloved hand to me, but I ignore it and roll to my feet.

He leads me down a long corridor. Tiny spotlights high on the walls create crisscrossing beams of light on the ceiling. The walls are black. The floor is white. There are no door numbers or markers of any kind. They have created an escape-proof maze. There's nowhere to run, only endless halls.

The guard stops. He pushes on the wall and a door swings open. He shoves me inside. 'Sit,' he barks. I sit. He handcuffs me to a silver bar that runs the length of a plain wooden table then leaves.

The room is dark except for a desk light illuminating a circle on the table with two matching chairs. No one knows where I am. In this soundless, soulless place, they could do anything to me. Anything.

I realize I'm not alone. There's someone hiding in the shadows. I look at the shoes first, expecting to see pointy-toed red boots. Instead I see plain, dingy tennis shoes. For some reason I'm relieved and disappointed it's not Braydon. But I recognize the shape of this body. Those dark eyes. I gasp when Ethan steps into the light.

'I'm sorry, Neva,' he says without looking at me. 'But I had to do something. I couldn't lose you. It's for your own good.'

It takes my brain a minute to register what he's saying. 'My own good?'

'We can go home now and start over. We can have a family.' His voice dips and cracks.

'What have you done, Ethan?' My voice is flat.

He walks over to the empty chair and sits across from me. 'I'm saving you.' He reaches across the table.

I ball my hands into fists. 'I don't need saving.'

'You were going to leave me.' He recoils. 'You were going to leave and not even say goodbye.'

Betrayed by Ethan. It doesn't seem possible. 'How did you know?' I clench and unclench my fists.

'After your Dark Party, I started following you whenever I could. I was watching over you, making sure you were safe. After your meeting with Thomas, they contacted me.'

'They?'

'Them.' He gestures to indicate the entire room. I know who he means: the ones watching me, always watching.

'Why didn't they just arrest me?' I slump back into the chair. I thought I was so clever, so careful, but they knew. I thought I had a choice but I was only a rat in a maze. I was always going to end up here.

He stares at the space between us. 'Your family. Your heritage. They couldn't just arrest you.' He scratches his head and I can see his hands are shaking. 'They had to be sure. They hoped you'd lead them to other traitors.'

I wasn't even the rat. I was the cheese, the bait.

Ethan keeps mumbling on, desperate to explain how his betrayal was for my own good. 'They said if we cooperated you could come back to live with me.'

I can't hear any more. I pound my fist on the table. 'Just shut up! Shut up!'

'You went off with Braydon.' He rocks back and forth. 'How could you?'

'How could I? How could *you*?' I ask, glaring at him. 'How could you turn me in? You said you loved me.'

'I do love you,' he whispers. 'They told me you were dead. I knew that couldn't be true. I watched your house. I knew you'd go back. But I never thought you'd try to leave again.'

My face hardens; my teeth grind together.

He gently strokes my fingers. 'All you have to do is sign the pledge, Neva. It's easy. We can put this behind us and get on with our lives.'

He's touching me as if he knows me. He has already mapped out our lives together. He's had me chained to this table and now he wants me chained to him, tethered to this place for the rest of my life.

'Go to hell, Ethan!' I lunge for him, not knowing what I would do if the handcuffs didn't restrain me.

He leaps from his chair. 'Don't be like that.' He's back where he started, in the shadows.

'Leave me alone. Just leave me alone.' I can't see him any more.

'But I can't lose you.'

'Ethan, I'm already gone.' I bow forward and rest my head on the table.

He waits in the shadows for a while. I can hear him breathing. His breath halts as if he might say something, but then his deep and steady breaths return. Ethan walks over. He leans down an inch from my face as if he might kiss me. I don't move. 'No one can save you now,' he whispers, and then shuffles to the door and knocks.

The door clicks open, but I don't hear it close behind him. Voices are buzzing outside. I concentrate, trying to understand what is being said. I can make out three or four separate voices. Ethan is mumbling. One guard says something like 'you did your best'. I hear the squeak of his tennis shoes as he walks away.

'Apparently this type of impudence runs in the family,' a deep male voice rings above the others.

'Her father is demanding we release her to his custody,' another voice adds. 'Adams is a good patriot. If she doesn't sign, he will probably have to commit her to the Reproductive

Centre for nonconformists. Wouldn't wish that on anyone ...'
The voice fades as the click and tap of shoes echo down the hall.

Pure, raw horror engulfs me. If I don't sign the pledge, this is only the beginning of my torture. Maybe I should sign. Maybe they'll let me go home if I promise to get a job and start a family. I'm not strong enough to endure what's next.

'OK, I'll sign,' I shout. It's got to be better than whatever Dad has in store for me. I try not to think of my life beyond the next moment.

A guard brings in a sheet of paper and a plastic pen and lays them both in front of me. I expected a quill dipped in my own blood or something more dramatic. I'm going to sign away my life with a disposable pen – how poetic. I roll the pen between my fingers. Through the clear plastic I can see that the ink cartridge is nearly empty. So many people have been broken and resigned themselves to this domed prison. I expected pages of copy with detailed dos and don'ts, but it's only a few simple sentences:

I hereby solemnly swear to rededicate myself to Homeland. I am a citizen and a patriot. My life will be in service to the government and to our way of life. I admit that I was wrong to jeopardise my civilization. There is nothing outside the Protectosphere. I denounce my past resistance and will follow the order established by generations. I pledge my allegiance to Homeland.

I pick up the pen. It's only my name. Two words that represent me but don't mean anything. Scribbled black lines that form the mortar, the very foundation of the Protectosphere. One more name added to the thousands before me. I touch the pen to the paper. The black ink begins to bleed onto the white. The dot grows. I don't have the strength to move my fingers in the tiny precise movements necessary to transfer my name to the page. I can visualise my name sitting on the line. The name that my grandma gave me.

My grandma wouldn't sign. Signing my name means they've won. If I sign, I'm no better than Ethan or Braydon or my father. I can't change the government or get them to open the Protectosphere all by myself, but every tiny act of defiance adds up. Maybe this one snowflake can start an avalanche. I drop the pen and it clatters on the table top.

Maybe all that will remain of me is that small black ink spot on our crisp white history. But maybe that's enough.

'I can't,' I say, and place my palms flat on the table. I won't give in.

The paper and pen are snatched from me. The lights go out. But I am not afraid any more.

CHAPTER THIRTY-THREE

M y dad won't look at me. And I'm glad. After everything
I've been through, I can't bear to see the disappointment
that's always there. I sit up straight and don't flinch when they
remove my handcuffs and the orange identity bracelet. I shake
free of the guards who are hauling me to my feet. Dad's hair is
slicked back. He's clean shaven. He seems polished in a way
I haven't seen since Grandma disappeared.

My dad's making no effort to hide his conversation. He
is addressing a man in a dark blue suit and a burgundy
shirt and tie. The guards nod at everything the man says.
He is a few inches taller than my dad. The men converse
like they are old friends, talking about the weather, as if I'm
not standing there waiting for my last rites. The man in the
blue suit dismisses the guards. Now the two men step closer
to each other. I inch forward so I can hear their hushed
voices.

'I was sorry I had to make the call, George,' the man in the
blue suit says. 'I thought you should know.'

'Thanks, Harold. I know I'm asking for a lot, but it's not the
girl's fault.' Dad's voice is deep and friendly.

'I'm not sure I can make an exception.' The man clamps
a hand on my dad's shoulder. 'You understand, don't
you?'

My dad draws his shoulders back, freeing himself of the
man's grip. 'Harold, I understand a lot of things. We all make

mistakes that we wish we could erase.' He pauses. 'Some people have family who voted against the Protectosphere. Not a fact I'd want to get around, if I hoped to be elected as a representative in the next elections.'

The man's face reddens. 'No, certainly not.'

'The girl has mental difficulties' – Dad's voice lowers to a whisper – 'like her grandmother.'

I stiffen.

'I couldn't save my mum, but I have a chance to save my only daughter. Harold, I'm asking you to let me.' Dad is almost pleading. Harold's face remains unchanged. Dad continues, 'My mum was one of those crazies that thought life existed outside.'

'What happened to her?' Harold asks.

'I had reports that she was electrocuted by the Protectosphere as she tried to escape.' His voice is even, no emotion.

My knees buckle, and I have to steady myself on the nearby chair. It can't be true. It just can't. She is waiting for me. I know she is. But his words create a fist of doubt.

'It's not the girl's fault that her grandma filled her head with delusions. Let me get her some help. She's sick.'

The man shakes his head. 'I don't know, George. What will you do with her?'

'If you must know, I have found a psychiatric institution that has had some success with chemical reprogramming. You have my word she'll procreate then.'

I can no longer hold my own weight. I slide down into the chair. I'd rather stay here and take my chances.

Harold swallows. 'But how can I—'

Dad interrupts, 'She was never here. Do you understand? No one is better than you at making people disappear.'

'George, what you are asking me is—'

Now Dad grips Harold's shoulder. 'History has a way of

shaping the present. Men can be portrayed as visionaries or fools,' Dad says. 'I'm a good friend to have, and I never forget a favour.'

Harold pops open a panel in the wall. He punches a number of buttons. 'I'll take care of the rest from the main control room.' He nods in my direction. 'Get her out of here.'

The men shake hands. Dad grabs me by the arm and leads me down endless corridors. He's been here before. At least he came for me. But I don't feel lucky to have a dad who knows the way around this maze. My grandma is dead and my dad is sending me to some institution to have my brains scrambled.

'Don't say a word. They're watching,' he says when we are alone in the car. We drive. I watch the scenery pass and wonder if it's the last time I will see the outdoors.

'Does Mum know what you're doing?'

'She thinks I'm working late.'

'Don't tell her, OK? Tell her anything, but don't tell her where you're taking me. Don't tell her what you did. Tell her I escaped.'

He looks at me and then turns back to watch the road. He drives faster. I want to hold on to something. I force myself deeper into my seat. 'Dad, please.'

'Neva, keep quiet. No matter what. Don't say a word.'

We are heading to the border. The caution signs fly by. Dad flashes a badge when we are stopped by the Border Patrol at the first checkpoint. The institution must be near the border; where else would Homeland keep its misfits?

At the second checkpoint, an armed guard looks in the car. 'Does she have a pass?' he asks, shining a flashlight in my eyes.

'She's my assistant. We have emergency work on the Protectosphere.' He flashes his badge again. The guard looks at his clipboard and flips through the pages.

'Dr Adams, you aren't on the list,' the man says, almost apologetically.

'I said it's an emergency. Didn't my office call you? I'm tired of this incompetence,' he shouts, and pushes open the car door. He stands. 'Where is your boss? I need to speak to the person in charge.'

'It's the middle of the night, sir,' the guard says by way of excuse.

'So he's sleeping on the job. Is that it?' He glances at the guard's name badge. 'Is that it, Mr Leighton?'

'No, sir, I mean he's not sleeping, sir, it's just . . .' The guard is flustered.

'Listen, it's been a busy night. I'll forget this ever happened. You'd be smart to do the same.' Dad gets back in the car.

'Yes, sir. Thank you, sir,' the guard says, and punches the button to raise the security gate.

Dad grips the steering wheel, but not before I notice his hands are shaking.

'We're almost there,' Dad says a few miles later. The landscape is getting more and more barren. Up ahead red flashing lights illuminate a billboard: TURN BACK. ROAD ENDS. As I get closer, I can read the smaller print: DANGER. PROTECTOSPHERE ENGAGED. DO NOT CROSS. I try not to imagine my grandma being electrocuted.

Dad stops the car. 'Get out,' he says, and I jump. He's not taking me to an institution. I can't breathe. 'There's not much time.' He reaches across me and opens my door. I recoil from him.

'Dad, please don't. Please.' My eyes are flooded with tears. He's taking me out here to die. My own father. I'm going to be electrocuted by the Protectosphere, just like my grandma was.

He unbuckles my seat belt. I should run, but my legs are like jelly. I hit him, but I have no strength left. He wraps his arms around me. He's pulling me to him. My face is buried in his chest and I'm hugging him. He is talking, but I can't hear him over my sobs.

'Neva. Neva,' he shushes me. 'Neva, I'm so sorry.'

'I'm sorry too. Don't do this. Please.'

'Neva, calm down and listen to me. In less than an hour, the Protectosphere's force field will re-engage. You must be through the tunnel by then.'

I pull away and stare at him.

'Pass the sign. You'll see a wall with a door. The electric lock is disengaged as is the Protectosphere in this area right now. You'll climb down a set of stairs. The tunnel will be directly ahead of you. You will need to run. In about a mile, this tunnel will spill into a large chamber that merges with a number of other tunnels. I don't know what it will look like. But the force field is deadly. That's no lie. Anyone caught in, or attempting to pass through, the force field will be electrocuted.'

'Like Grandma,' I say, and hot tears sting my cheeks.

'I hope your grandma will be waiting for you.' He smiles and reaches out to cradle my face.

I can't believe it.

'What's out there, Dad?' I ask, feeling closer to him than I ever have.

'I have no idea. I hope it's what you want, Neva. It must be a better future than the one you'd have here.' Now he's crying. 'Neva, I didn't know. I didn't know what they were doing. They said they were re-educating – brainwashing – young girls. That's all. Then after Effie ... I went up there ...' He pushes me out the door. 'Please, Neva, you can't stay here.'

'What will happen to you and Mum?'

'Don't worry about us.' His tone changes. His words become clipped. 'Now, go. I mean it.' He rakes his hands through his hair. 'I'm so proud of you.'

It takes every ounce of strength to haul myself out of the car and walk away. I pass the warning signs. I turn around. He's still standing there, glowing red in the flashing lights. He waves, and I run.

CHAPTER THIRTY-FOUR

The tunnel is pitch black. I let the darkness pass through me. I'm no longer afraid of this nothingness, of the unknown. I take one step and then another. I am running. I trail my hand against the cool tunnel wall. Each fingernail has a crescent of dirt embedded underneath, pressing at the soft, sensitive skin. I stumble and fall. I pick myself up. The acidic smell of damp earth is overwhelming. I feel as if I've been running forever. I wipe my arm across my upper lip and feel the transfer of dirt and snot.

The only sound I hear as I fumble forwards is my own panting breath. I am coated in sweat, which attracts the dirt. My skin stiffens. Have I taken too long? I expect to be zapped by a thousand volts any second. With every step, I wonder if I am one step closer to freedom or death. I keep pushing forwards. Up ahead, I see a flicker of light. Was that the Protectosphere being electrified? My pace slows. Another flash. I am paralyzed with fear but only for a moment.

I run faster. My tunnel spills into a huge chamber with several smaller tunnels surrounding it but only one tunnel ahead, three times the size of any of the others. It's not as dark as before. I walk slowly forwards, conscious of the time but also conscious of the sadness growing inside me. This is really it.

As I approach the big tunnel, someone grasps my shoulder and spins me around. Before I can react, a hand cups the back of my neck and draws me close. His lips find mine.

Braydon.

My lips respond with a familiar fire. He wraps his strong arms around me and we are once again one with the dark.

Then my brain kicks in.

Braydon.

The betrayal.

The lies.

Even after everything I've been through, it's his deception that cuts the deepest.

Anger consumes me and I struggle against him. My fists are flying and I'm making contact again and again.

He raises his arms to protect himself. 'Neva, stop it.'

But I don't stop. My punches become less frantic and I strike with more precision and force.

'Neva!' He pins my arms to my sides.

I try to catch my breath and collect myself for another attack.

'Neva.' He shakes me.

'Let me go,' I growl. I flex my arms and break his grip. 'How did you find me?'

His hand traces the line of my necklace and rests on the snowflake pendant. 'I attached a tracking device to your snowflake.'

I brush his hand away. 'At our first kiss?'

He nods.

I choke back a sob. He's so close. He's staring at me with those eyes that made me surrender. I don't know who he is, but something inside of me still longs for the boy I kissed in the dark. But that person wasn't real. I blink back tears.

This is it. This is how it all ends.

I stand up straight. 'If you are going to arrest me, just do it. No more games. I heard what you said to the policeman. I know you're working for the government.'

He deflates in front of me. Everything that is so strong and confident seems to melt. 'I was sent to watch Sanna, to keep tabs on her.' His voice is barely audible. 'But from the moment I met you, I knew you were the one to watch.'

'Me?' It's too painful to look at him.

He closes the distance between us. There's nowhere for me to run. 'You are the dangerous one.' He brushes the hair off my face. 'You changed everything.'

'How can you work for the government?' I whisper, hoping that his answer will redeem him and save me.

'They have my parents and my little brother,' he says. 'They told me that if I worked for them I could get my family back.'

And I understand. I never gave up on my grandma. I risked everything to save Sanna. My dad and mum have risked everything to save me. I know I'd do the same for them.

A glow starts in one of the tunnels, and I can finally see Braydon clearly, every unique detail.

He holds my face in his hands. 'I love you, Neva. You have to know that. No matter what happens, never doubt that.'

My anger fades, but my body still twitches with each passing second. Time is running out. I feel a powerful urge to run and an equal desire to stay with Braydon forever. He kisses me. Tears mix on our lips. Maybe I can stay. Maybe we can be together. I try to hold on to him, but he wrenches free from my embrace.

'I've found her,' he shouts. 'She's over here.' He shoves me away. I stumble but manage to stay on my feet.

Rage. Panic. Fear. Ignite in one hot burst.

The tunnels pulse with the sound of angry feet stomping towards us.

'Go,' he pleads. 'Get out of here.'

I run. Somehow. I run.

I glance back. Braydon is running in the opposite direction, into one of the smaller tunnels.

'She's right here,' he calls as he disappears into the darkness.

He has saved me.

I move as fast as my legs will take me.

The tunnel isn't straight, and I am bounced from wall to wall. I am going to die in this tunnel. No one will ever know what happened to me. I will never know what's out there.

The air around me sizzles. Every hair on my body stands to attention. This can't be the end. I am too close.

There is a loud pop, and an electric shock passes through me. My back arches. I feel myself thrust forwards and slammed to the ground – and into darkness once more.

CHAPTER THIRTY-FIVE

I am erased.

    That's what it feels like. I am nothing but a thought of nothing. I have no edges or shape. I am the darkness.

I try to hover here, to not think or feel, but thoughts and memories start to spark. Then everything comes flooding back. My life plays in fast-forward and crashes to a halt at this moment.

My eyelids spring open, and I take a huge gulp of air. My skin starts to tingle as feeling returns. The tingle deepens into a throb, every muscle, every bone hurts.

I am still in the tunnel, but up ahead I can see an archway, glowing with a brilliant white light. Behind me is only darkness. My parents, Sanna and Braydon are trapped beyond that black. I am painfully aware of what they've sacrificed to help me escape. Grief casts a long shadow, but I head towards the light.

At first my body resists my brain's impulse to move, but slowly I'm able to draw myself to all fours. I crawl and then evolve to standing.

As I stagger forwards, I am dazzled by the light. I shield my eyes. As I emerge from the tunnel, I blink and the world comes into focus. A colourful blanket stretches out in front of me. I squint and the details become clear. These individual dots are people. People of all shapes and sizes and colours.

There is life outside the Protectosphere. Nothing stands

between me and the endless horizon. My eyes sting with tears.

I look out over a sea of humanity, searching for a familiar face. I soon realize there are a lot of familiar faces. Some of the people in the crowd could be my sister, brother, father or mother. Reunions are taking place around me. I am not the only one who escaped.

I glance back at the Protectosphere. From the outside, its surface isn't transparent but silvery, sparkling in the sunshine and reflecting the bright blue sky above.

A beautiful brown woman at the edge of the crowd notices me. She has long curly black hair, not frizzy like mine, but smooth. She smiles the most stunning white smile. Is she human or something else, something new from this vast place that seems to have no beginning or end?

'Oh, my Lord, are you OK?' the woman says to me in a deep voice that dips and springs in a way I've never heard before. 'We saw the flash as the force field was electrified again. We didn't think anyone else made it out.'

I take one step towards her and stumble. She rushes over to help me to my feet.

'What ... ? How ...?' is all I can manage to utter.

'They've been coming for hours, emerging from the tunnel in twos and threes,' she explains. 'The word spread and people from all over started to gather, wondering if their loved ones would make it out. Do you have someone here?'

Oh, I hope so. 'My grandma,' I say, finding my voice. 'Ruth Adams.'

'Ruth Adams,' the woman calls, and my grandma's name multiplies in hundreds of voices.

It may be my imagination, but a hush seems to fall over the crowd. What if she's not here? I couldn't bear it. Then a murmur starts near the back of the crowd and rolls forwards.

I move towards the sound. People are welcoming me. I want to study every face; each one is unique. People of different colours are clinging to each other. I notice some are speaking words I don't know, a whole language I have never heard before. I walk more quickly, and the crowd shifts to let me through. I'm bumping and spinning and racing forwards now. The crowd parts like a curtain. I hold my breath as a figure steps into the cleared space.

'Grandma,' I say.

What was lost is found.

She opens her arms wide and breathes more than says my name. 'Neva, my snowflake.'

Hope gives my heart wings.

ACKNOWLEDGEMENTS

Any book is a collaboration. I should probably simply thank everyone I've ever met who has inspired me in one way or another, be it consciously with a word of encouragement or accidentally by sitting next to me in my high school English class, uttering something intriguing while I was in earshot, or bumping into me on the London Underground.

But a few people deserve special thanks:

My family. They endured my prose and poetry (not to mention my attempts at singing, visual art, and drama) since I was a little kid and encouraged me every step of the way. In elementary school, I was asked to write an essay about who I most admire. I picked my parents – and if asked the same question today, I'd give the same answer. They demonstrate how to live a life with honour, compassion, and a great sense of humour.

Sara O'Connor and Megan Thie. There would be no *Dark Parties* without Sara and Megan. They were the first people to read the short story that served as the spark for this novel and demanded to know what happened next. Sara offered endless editorial feedback and words of encouragement. She's not the 'other' Sara, she's the original.

Jenny Savill. My heartfelt gratitude to Jenny for plucking me from the slush pile and being a true partner in this process. Her editorial guidance, patience, and friendship are invaluable. Also thanks to the team at Andrew Nurnberg

Associates for supporting Jenny and me on the roller-coaster ride of publishing.

Amber Caraveo and Jenny Glencross and the Orion team for believing in *Dark Parties*. Amber matches a careful editorial eye with contagious enthusiasm. A huge thanks to her for her support and encouragement, both personally and professionally.

My tutors at Goldsmiths College Creative Writing MA – Maura Dooley, Pamela Johnson, Blake Morrison, and Susan Elderkin – for their insights and inspiration.

My SCBWI friends on both sides of the Atlantic and all the wonderful writers in my life who continue to inspire, encourage, and instruct me: Karen Ball, Trish Batey, Ashley Dartnell, Emily Jeremiah, Vinita Joseph, Carol Katterjohn, Bronia Kita, Elizabeth Mercereau, Jasmine Richards, Kate Scott, Pete Welling, and Sandra White – with an extra special thanks to Margaret Carey for critiquing the novel at multiple stages and still asking to read it again.

My grandma. Eternal thanks for her bedtime stories and for always making me feel special.

And, finally, to my husband, Paul. Thanks doesn't begin to describe the gratitude and love I feel for him. He's my muse, cheerleader, and safety net, as well as my editor, psychologist, hero, and best friend.